THE CENTURION

THE CENTURION

KEN GIRE

MOODY PUBLISHERS

CHICAGO

© 2016 by
KEN GIRE

Published in association with the literary agency of WordServe Literary Group, Ltd.

Edited by Pam Pugh   Interior Design: Erik M. Peterson
Cover Design: Faceout
Cover photo of centurion copyright © by Nejron Photo/Shutterstock (54640735).
    cape copyright © by Nejron Photo/Shutterstock (155397845).
    armor (arm) copyright © by Tereshchenko Dmitry/Shutterstock
    (65532562).
    armor (chest plate) copyright © by Kiselev Andrey Valerevich/
    Shutterstock (176536778).
    sky/clouds copyright © by Krivosheev Vitaly/Shutterstock
    (73570444).
    pathway copyright © by Dudarev Mikhail/Shutterstock
    (99605942).
    texture copyright © by Miro Novak/Shutterstock (131820056).
    author bar 1 copyright © by caesart/Shutterstock (36943303).
    author bar 2 copyright © by caesart/Shutterstock (59546662).
    3 crosses copyright © by Olga Galushko/Veer (3956521).
All rights reserved for all of the above items.

Library of Congress Cataloging-in-Publication Data

Gire, Ken.
The centurion / Ken Gire.
  pages ; cm
ISBN 978-0-8024-0894-5 (softcover)
1. Soldiers—Rome—Fiction. 2. Mary Magdalene, Saint—Fiction. 3. Rome—Army—Officers—Fiction. 4. Man-woman relationships—Fiction. I. Title.
PS3607.I4696C46 2016
813'.6—dc23

                      2015023278

We hope you enjoy this book from River North Fiction by Moody Publishers. Our goal is to provide high-quality, thought-provoking books and products that connect truth to your real needs and challenges. For more information on other books and products written and produced from a biblical perspective, go to www.moodypublishers.com or write to:

River North Fiction
Imprint of Moody Publishers
820 N. LaSalle Boulevard
Chicago, IL 60610

1 3 5 7 9 10 8 6 4 2

Printed in the United States of America

DEDICATED
To

my big sister
Loma Linda Kiehn

As a young boy, learning cursive,
slowly and with great care
I tried to emulate her handwriting,
which was beautifully and effortlessly graceful.
As an older man, still learning,
I am now trying to emulate her heart,
which is still effortlessly graceful but even more beautiful.

CONTENTS

"Eli, Eli, lama sabachthani?"

From *Metamorphoses*
OVID
(43 BC–AD 18)

When Halcyon, daughter of Aeolus, guardian of the winds, came of age, she married Ceyx, king of Trachis. Their love and devotion for each other was so great, it was known throughout the kingdom.

One day when Ceyx sailed from the land of Trachis to consult the oracle at Delphi, he was shipwrecked. Wakened from a frightful dream about the wreck, Halcyon ran to the seashore, looking for her beloved. As she searched for the wreckage, the tide washed her husband to her feet. He had drowned. Distraught, she threw herself into the sea to join him.

When the gods looked down, they could not bear the death of two people so passionately in love, and they transformed the couple into sea birds. During the winter, the gods ordained a week of calm so they could brood their young in a nest that floated undisturbed in the safety of a windless sea.

Ever after, that week in winter has been known as halcyon days.

PART I

AD 33

JERUSALEM

1

Dawn came as a pale brush of pink across the eastern sky. It came without flourish, giving dimension to the featureless landscape and color to the somber collection of grays left over from the night. Jerusalem caught something of that pink in the stone walls that surrounded the city, in the walls of the Temple, and in the walls of the Fortress of Antonia that adjoined it.

In a room of that fortress, a centurion dressed for the day's duties, his statuesque features looking as if they had been chiseled from the quarries of Cararra. His skin was smooth, as if polished by finely gritted abrasives. It bore no pits, no scars, no imperfections at all. Over his red woolen tunic he pulled a fitted leather jacket with short shoulder pieces and long overlapping straps extending mid-thigh.

He buckled his belt on which hung two scabbards: one sheathing a two-foot sword; the other, a dagger.

He sat on a chair and put on a pair of sandals, their soles layered with leather and inset with short, metal studs.

He stood to put on a bronze helmet, fitted inside with an iron casing and lined with heavy cloth. A crest of crimson plumage ran across the helmet, the color matching the cape he draped over his shoulders and fastened with a clasp.

Finally, he picked up a rod made from a sapling, the characteristic emblem of authority for centurions.

Wood, metal, leather, muscle—together they represented the strength of the military, which, over the centuries, had turned a mere village into the mightiest empire the world had ever seen.

His first name was followed by those of his clan and of his family: Lucius Alexander Titus.

Lucius had grown up in Alexandria, Egypt, his father a librarian there. His mother had died when he was too young to remember, and his father, in a compensatory gesture, took him to work and let the boy have free rein. At his fingertips in that library lay the greatness of three cultures: Egyptian, Greek, and Roman. The Egyptians were better farmers, better breeders of animals, and more awe-inspiring builders. The Greeks were better thinkers, better writers, better at almost everything. But the Romans, they were better soldiers. The Romans were, in fact, the best warriors the world had ever seen. As a young boy, Lucius stood in awe of the soldiers he had read about in Caesar's *Gallic Wars,* aspiring one day to stand in their ranks.

Though not more original builders than the Greeks, the Romans were more prolific, especially with aqueducts and roads, both essential if they were to realize their destiny to rule the world.

Under the weight of Augustus' leadership, the Republic had crumbled. Out of its rubble, he had built an empire. "I found Rome a city of bricks," he once said, "and left it a city of marble." The reign of Augustus had ushered in a period of rest from the civil wars that had plagued the Republic since its inception. Though skirmishes flared up on the Frontier, like sudden but containable wildfires, most of the Empire enjoyed an unprecedented era of peace and prosperity.

A web-work of roads connected the Empire, facilitating trade and the exchange of ideas. For the first time in history, Syrians and Italians were using the same weights and measures. Britons and Africans spoke the same language. And all followed the same laws, swearing allegiance to the same emperor. Under the shelter of this peace, the *Pax Romana*, Lucius was born, raised, and educated.

Few soldiers could read or write. Only those born to patricians, the elite class in Roman society, could usually claim such learning. But Lucius could do both, and he read voraciously. The stories about soldiers fighting on the Frontier led to his curiosity in maps. The very sight of a map would send the boy he once was to dreaming of distant lands and uncharted seas crashing against their misty coastlines, of daring adventures awaiting him, of decisive victories, all of which would bring honor to him and glory to Rome.

Because of his physical prowess, intelligence, and natural leadership qualities, Lucius had risen through the ranks from infantryman to centurion. The major unit within the Roman army was the legion, comprising forty to sixty centuries of eighty to a hundred men each. Because the chief centurion oversaw all the centuries within the legion, he had a place of prominence at the war council, a position of honor where distinguished service was richly rewarded.

It was to such a position that Lucius aspired. If promoted, he would be sent to Caesarea for training; from Caesarea to the Frontier; and from the Frontier to Rome, where he hoped to finish his career.

For now, he served in Jerusalem, neither a place of adventure like the Frontier, nor a place of appetite like Caesarea, but rather merely a place where a Roman soldier was stationed while waiting to be stationed somewhere else.

As the sun rose, it turned Jerusalem's weathered limestone white and chased away the morning chill from the city streets. Visitors from Judea, Samaria, and beyond had made pilgrimages to celebrate Passover, the second holiest day in the Jewish nation's calendar. The city was abrim with people from far-off lands, a confluence of foreign tongues and regional accents. The distinctive scent of wool and the incessant bleating of sheep filled the air, along with the smell of foreign sweat and unwashed clothes.

The Fortress of Antonia adjoined the Temple on the northwest wall, strategically placed to cast its imperial shadow over all who assembled there. During holy days, especially a holy day like this one, soldiers stood sentry on those walls, overlooking the Temple courtyard to quell any stir of hostilities before these could froth to insurrection.

The centrality of the Fortress to the religious life of the city was strategic. Pilate's alliance with the religious authorities was one he needed. But it was one they needed, too. Pilate had arranged for the ceremonial vestments used at Passover to be kept under armed guard in a locked room in the Fortress so that the High Priest had to come to *him* for permission to get them. It was an uneasy but an expedient alliance. Both parties knew it and accepted it for what it was. Both had gone out of their way to cultivate it.

In his palatial quarters within the Fortress, Pilate was going over his schedule for the day as his dresser fussed over a new toga. The fabric was a large circle of white wool, finely combed and woven, luxurious to the touch. But it was heavy and cumbersome, and the dresser was struggling to drape it just right so it would cascade from Pilate's shoulders in elegant folds.

It had been a restless night for Pilate, a lot on his mind, a lot on his schedule, and his wife's tossing and turning had not helped. Receiving a note requesting an earlier-than-normal appointment, Pilate pushed aside his dresser who was trying to position a laurelled wreath on his head.

"Forget the laurel; get the sandals!"

The dresser dropped to his knees, fitted the sandals onto Pilate's feet, and twined the leather straps around his calves. The ruler gathered his toga to keep it from sweeping the marble stairway and walked with his entourage of legal counselors and administrative attendants who briefed him on the urgency of the case before him.

Lucius, meanwhile, left his quarters, descending the stairs where his first stop was the carpentry shop on the lower floor. Two criminals were scheduled for execution, the paraphernalia for the ordeal already loaded on a small wagon—mallets, nails, ropes, and a ladder, along with supplies for the day. He knelt, picked up a handful of sawdust, and brought it to his nose. He loved the smell of freshly milled wood, its sweetness reminding him of home.

Lucius turned his attention to his steed, still in its stall. A beautiful animal. Regal in every way, especially how he held his head, as if he knew it were in service of the greatest empire in history. Lucius patted his neck. The horse turned to nuzzle him and snorted.

At the Temple, priests prepared for their day's work with their ceremonial washings. Dressers covered the priests with sacred vestments, one layer after another, slowly and methodically, brushing off any foreign matter, smoothing out wrinkles. Some of the priests started sharpening knives. Others stoked the fire in the altar. All readied themselves for a long and arduous day.

At the Fortress, a chorus of chants came from the Praetorium. Lucius stopped to listen.

"Crucify! Crucify!"

He dipped a ladle into a nearby bucket and drew water, filled his mouth but did not swallow.

"Crucify! Crucify! Crucify!"

Lucius gave the helper in the shop an inquisitive look. The man shrugged his shoulders. Lucius swallowed his water and replaced the ladle on its hook.

At the Temple, long before the priests were ready to receive them, men stood in line to offer their sacrifices. Soon smoke ascended from the altar, curled into the early morning sky, sweetened with the aroma of cypress and carried away to the Fortress, where a scribe rushed into the stables with a scrolled page of papyrus, an addendum to the centurion's orders. Lucius was used to this. He often had his orders altered, even rescinded, especially when visiting dignitaries were in town, and most especially when that dignitary was Pilate. He read the scroll and called to the carpenter.

"Wood for one more." He pointed to the wording on the scroll. "Write his name, his crime."

By midmorning the smell of charred fat and gristle hung over the city like a thick, low cloud.

Priests stood at various stations around the altar, each with his assigned duty to perform in the ritual of sacrifice. The line of men with lambs on their shoulders threaded through the Temple, tangled itself in the courtyard, and unraveled out the main gate.

Teams of priests worked in shifts to keep up the pace. Each took his respective post, executing his assigned duty with precision. The killing was routine. A simple ritual, one lamb after another after another. By midafternoon the work would mostly be done, time enough for the animals to be roasted and brought home.

The killing was swift. The lamb was held down by a layman. A priest pulled the blade of his knife across the exposed throat. Another priest caught the blood in a golden cup. He then handed the cup to the next priest, who gave him an empty one in return. The cup was passed through a line of priests until it reached the one closest to the altar. That priest splashed the blood on the side of the altar, where it dripped down the base and was caught by a gutter with two holes in it that channeled the blood to underground viaducts.

Another priest took the slain lamb and put it on tenterhooks, where, with a few quick cuts and hard yanks on the wool, he skinned it. He then made a vertical stab that released a slippery mass of entrails, which were caught and washed. The fat, according to Levitical law, was carved from the body, placed in a ceremonial vessel, salted, then poured onto the altar, where it sizzled on a grate, relinquishing its savory aroma as its smoke curled heavenward.

On a hill outside the city walls, another ritual was being performed—the ritual of executions for crimes against the Empire.

19

2

Lucius was the centurion who oversaw executions. Once the crosses were erected, the rest of the day was spent guarding them, which mostly meant watching and waiting for death to come, sometimes taking days.

Death came from any number of causes—dehydration, fever, infection. But mostly it came from asphyxiation. The victim was positioned in such a way that the weight of his upper body slumped into his chest, folding the lungs. To get a full breath of air he had to push himself up from a small block of wood where his feet rested. When his legs were too weak, he would eventually pass out, then die. To hasten death, when necessary, the executioners would break their legs, making it too painful for the condemned to make the push.

Overhead, the midday sky held a few vultures that made patient circles above the skull-shaped rock, known as Golgotha. An unusually large number of people had gathered to witness today's executions. It was not the typical group of mourners. Mingled among them were religious leaders of one station or another—scribes, Pharisees, rabbis. Their attention was focused on the one hanging from the central cross, whom they mocked mercilessly.

"Let this *Messiah*, this *king* of Israel," one of them shouted, "come down from his cross that we may see and believe!" Others joined in the taunting.

Lucius removed his helmet and wiped sweat from his forehead. He ladled water from a bucket, swished it around in his mouth, spit it out. As he did, he caught a glimpse of a woman. He was drawn to her as to a dream upon waking. *I know her from somewhere,* he thought. *But where?* A veil covered the lower half of the woman's face. Her olive skin glistened, and although her black hair hung in wet strands framing her lowered eyes, there was something about her, even in her despondent state, that drew him.

He did not know her from Jerusalem, he was sure of that. *Galilee, maybe?* Four years earlier he had sought leisure there with some men. *Or was she from Alexandria?* Perhaps a childhood friend, long forgotten.

A moment of recognition came over her—another time, another place, another life. Her face flushed, and she looked away. At that moment a gust of wind blew the covering from her head, and her long black hair came undone.

A memory flashed, the way that scales of a fish catch the sun as they approach the sea's surface. But as quickly as the memory came to him, it slipped away. Try as he could, he could not summon it.

Lucius walked toward her and overheard her speaking. Her accent lifted the veil on the mystery of her identity, or at least part of it. She was Galilean. He had spent time in several towns along the Sea of Galilee—Capernaum, Korazin, Magdala.

Throughout Galilee were terraced villas and wealthy estates of those who had profited simply by the fortune of good geography. Because it was a large body of fresh water, the Sea of Galilee was not only lucrative for fishing but for trade. It was also a haven for leisure. And many went there to find theirs, soldiers as well as foreigners.

Could she be one of the local prostitutes? he wondered. *No, she looks nothing like any of them, no hardness in her eyes, no cunning in her expression, nothing of their seductions in her clothes.* He tried dredging up a memory. *One of the many who were on the streets, begging alms?* But he dismissed that, too.

Lucius approached one of the soldiers, whose name was accented on the third syllable, giving it a lilt of authority.

"Antonius."

"Sir."

Lucius pointed to the woman. "She look familiar?"

Antonius studied her a moment, then nodded. "From Magdala, I think. When we were on leave there, a few years ago. A wild mare of a woman, as I recall. Troubled soul. Strange. Possessed by demons, or so the villagers said."

"Looks like her," said Lucius, "and yet . . ."

That is when Lucius noticed the sky behind her, a clotted darkness that tumbled toward the hill. It came not as the darkness of night, a welcomed end to the day's work, but rather as a bruise inflicted by a sudden blow, first mottling the skin, then purpling it, finally blackening it.

Everyone on the hill saw it. The heckling stopped as eyes widened and fears gave way to sudden bursts of repentance. The moisture in the air began condensing on their skin, and it seemed as if an ominous presence were breathing over them with its clammy breath.

"What do you think?" asked Massina, a Syrian conscript. He nodded toward the sky.

Valassio shook his head, his eyes peering into the darkness as if to pierce its mystery. "I don't like it."

As the darkness crept toward the hill, the crowd filled the

eerie silence with nervous chatter. "What is happening?" "What could it mean?"

"What if we angered the gods?" Valassio asked. "You believe in the gods, don't you?"

"Roman ones."

"What if there's others?" mused Massina, and you Romans, by giving homage to your own, make them jealous? Ever think of that?"

Antonius walked by himself to the brow of the hill, the foreboding sky luring him. Lucius was lured there, too.

"Does it not say somewhere: 'the sun shall give you signs'?" the soldier asked.

Lucius searched his memory. "'After the Caesar sank from sight . . . the sun wrapped his countenance in darkened gloom.'" The two looked at each other. "The blotting of the sun," Lucius said. "It is said to happen at the death of a divine ruler. According to Virgil."

They turned to look at the man impaled on the middle cross.

The rest of the city stopped its business, people pointing, commenting, lamenting.

For three hours darkness shrouded the city.

After a while, though, the city returned to work, for much needed to be done before the first star in the evening sky heralded the Sabbath. The centurion's household slave, Ashuk, who seemed carved from a block of obsidian, watched the sky as a street vendor pulled a roasted lamb, stretched across a pomegranate spit, from his earthen oven. Money changed hands, and the vendor passed him the lamb.

Those hours were a much-needed reprieve from the normally unrelenting glare of the sun, at least for the two criminals on either side of the man in the center. Lucius eyed him curiously. Over his head a wooden placard had been nailed, inscribed in Hebrew, Greek, and Latin. His eyes rested on the Latin, giving the name of the accused, along with the crime of which he had been convicted:

IESUS NAZARENUS
REX IUDAEORUM

King of the Jews, thought Lucius. *He looks anything but a king.*

Below this unlikely king stood a few of his followers, women mostly, along with the condemned's mother, steadied by the only man among them. The soldiers were distracted with other things, except for Massina, who watched as one of the thieves turned his head to Jesus and proffered a plea.

"Remember me, when you come into your kingdom."

His words drew Lucius's attention.

Jesus turned his head, slowly, wearily, and something in the pools of the thief's eyes seemed to refresh him.

"Truly I say to you, today you will be with me in Paradise."

The thief started to speak, but a sudden spear of pain pierced Jesus from somewhere deep inside him, and he writhed in agony. His head jerked to one side as if struck by a fist. His stomach convulsed, spilling bile out his mouth and down his chest.

Lucius and Massina winced.

At the sound of a man sobbing at the edge of the crowd, Lucius turned. The man's head was cloaked, and he could not see his face, but he buckled to his knees and knelt there.

Hearing a painful cough from the cross, Lucius turned back to Jesus.

What little strength the man had left he summoned to his thighs, their muscles flexing, pushing down against the nail in his feet. Clenching his teeth, he pulled himself up, straining against the nails in his hands. Seeing the sudden movement, those gathered looked up. They watched as he sucked in a great gulp of air. And everyone listened as he cried out.

"Eli . . . Eli . . . lama sabachthani?"

After saying it, he collapsed against the wood.

"He is calling to Elijah," one onlooker said.

"No," said another. "He is calling to his god."

Jesus pushed his weight against the wooden footrest. "It is finished," he called out, almost triumphantly.

His body slumped, his head bowed, and a prayer escaped his lips. "Father, into your hands I commit my spirit."

For a moment everything stilled. There was no sound, no movement. No one spoke, no one moved.

Lucius stared at the contours of the man's body. It seemed to him a war-torn landscape in the aftermath of battle. The sunken muscles seemed like sloping hills, trodden under an enemy's brutal heel, their soil stained with the blood of the fallen.

But a jolt shook free Lucius's thoughts, followed by a groan within the earth, deep and low. A tremor shook his feet, then a violent quake. People all around him fell to the ground or ran away, screaming.

The quake struck the market. Merchandise fell from vendors' wagons. Ashuk's legs unsteadied him.

The quake sent fissures through the Temple. A few capstones on the walls fell to the courtyard below. The shaking ran through the foundation. Marble columns swayed back and forth. Inside, carved woodwork strained and cracked. In the Holy of Holies the gilded masonry shook violently. Then suddenly, as if two hands had grabbed the top of the expansive curtain, it was torn in two.

The quake traveled through the Fortress of Antonia, shaking it and everyone in it. Horses in the stables whinnied and broke their tethers. Soldiers were in disarray. Pilate's wife screamed into the silk-covered pillows on her bed, her husband beside her, holding her.

Back at Golgotha, the crosses swayed to one side. Screams slashed the silence. A jolt, and several people stumbled into one another. Terror filled their eyes, their voices. A great lurching threw everyone to the ground. Flat on their faces, people clutched the earth, confessing their sins, crying out for mercy. The crosses pitched back and forth, tearing muscles, rasping bone, snapping tendons. Screams from the crosses intensified the terror.

Then, as suddenly as the earthquake started, it stopped.

Having been thrown to the ground, Lucius was on his knees before the cross of the young Jewish revolutionary. He looked up, his mind aswirl with questions. He wondered that if there were such a place as Paradise, might the ragged borders of this body be the terrain that led there?

Then these words, these very seditious words, stole past his lips.

"Surely this was the son of God."

Whatever battle had been fought on that hill, it was now over. In that abrupt armistice, Lucius stood dumbstruck, as soldiers sometimes are struck in the aftermath of combat. All was silent, hushed and still. Any movement was imperceptible, slow and uncertain. The only sound he heard was the pounding of his heart; the only movement, the coursing of his blood.

As a shaft of western light pierced the darkness, moans from the crosses shattered the silence.

Lucius jumped to his feet, gathered himself, and took charge. "To your tasks. Be quick."

The soldiers collected themselves and went about the routine of clearing the hill. Valassio was first to his task. Picking up a club, he approached the more hardened of the thieves. He took pleasure in ending the constant barrage of curses the thief had hurled at him throughout the day.

A crack of wood against shins. The splintering of his legs caused a scream . . . more curses . . . a watery cough . . . a low moan.

Then silence.

Massina approached the other thief. Pity was a contraband emotion for Roman soldiers. Yet, as though some pulled ligament of remorse were holding him back, he hesitated.

"I begrudge you not your duty," said the thief.

The soldier looked up at the lifeless body of Jesus, then back at the thief, and offered a benediction.

"God have mercy."

"His mercy is in your hand," the thief replied. "I am ready to receive it."

The soldier clutched the handle with uneasy hands and swung blindly, breaking both legs with a single blow. The thief took the pain into his lungs and held it, grimacing, then releasing it. When the soldiers came to Jesus, it was clear he was already dead. To make sure, though, Antonius took a spear and placed it on Jesus' chest, feeling for a fleshy spot between the ribs. Finding it, he thrust the spear into the heart.

At the Temple, the high priest signaled the other priests, and they lifted several amphorae of water to wash down the altar. Drains at the altar's base led to an underground pipe that shunted blood out the side of the city wall into the Kidron Valley. The water mingled with the blood as it flowed out the shunt until it became mostly water with only a trace of blood. With the cleansing of the altar, the work within the walls of the Temple was finished.

So was the work outside the walls of the city. The soldiers began removing the bodies so they could dispose of them before sundown, in deference to Jewish law. As they went about the grim work, Lucius searched among the mourners for the woman he saw earlier. The once frayed crowd now looked like knots on a prayer shawl, strands of humanity drawn together by the quake.

The woman Lucius had recognized earlier wrapped an arm around the mother of Jesus, drew her close, and led her away.

Fearing the woman would disappear in the crowd, Lucius called to her. "You, there. I know you, from Magdala."

The woman looked over her shoulder. "I have known a lot of men."

"And *him?*" he asked, nodding to the cross in the middle. "How did you know *him?*"

"You would not understand." And she resumed walking.

"I understand the difference in who you were then and who you are now."

The woman whipped around, her eyes lit with anger, and stepped toward him. She stopped a sword's thrust away. "Have you no shame! Do you know what you have done here today? Do you have any idea what you have done?"

"I have done my duty."

"You say it as if you thought it noble."

He stood in the presence of her disgust, disarmed. It was as if she had unsheathed his sword and was pressing its tip to his throat, threatening to slash it if he uttered another word. He stood silent, at the mercy of her indignation.

But it was she who dropped the sword of words, she who

turned, she who walked away. He was left standing there, the place where the edge of her anger touched him, standing there, stinging from the encounter.

3

Pilate, meanwhile, had given audience to Nicodemus and Joseph of Arimathea, two respected men in the city's religious hierarchy. They were good men and just, waiting for the kingdom of God, disciples of Jesus, but keeping their relationship with him in the shadows for reasons that were professionally expedient. But now, in a bold move, they stepped out of the shadows.

"You want the body?" Pilate asked, incredulous.

"Our people have a law," said Nicodemus. "A man who dies on Shabbat must be buried before evening's first star."

"I have a tomb," said Joseph, "just below the hill."

Pilate called a soldier on guard. "Has the centurion returned?"

"Not yet, your Excellency."

The late afternoon sun bronzed the hill outside the city where the bodies were being removed. Lucius watched as his soldiers lowered one of the thieves, tossing the body in the wagon, where it landed next to the contorted body of the other thief.

"Valley?" asked Antonius.

Lucius nodded.

"And *him?*" asked Valassio, nodding in the direction of Jesus' cross.

"They have asked to bury him," Lucius said, gesturing to a few of his followers, knotted in conversation. "But I will need permission."

Lucius mounted his horse as the soldiers dismantled the two vacant crosses and pushed them into the wagon next to the bodies. Antonius and Massina got into the cart. Massina shook the reins, and the horses strained against the dead weight. The road was rocky, and the cart jostled from one side to another on its way to the Valley of Hinnom.

Lucius stared a moment at the mourners who were huddled around the remaining cross. He nodded to Valassio. "Guard the body."

He kicked the flanks of his horse, and it trotted across the uneven surface of the hill. As the horse passed through the gate in the city's wall, it parted a sea of people making last-minute preparations for the feast. He picked his way through the crush of people, the hooves of his horse clopping against the stone paving. Along the way, he looked at no one, spoke to no one.

Coming to the Fortress, he nodded to the guards at the gate but did not greet them. He simply stepped off his horse, handed the reins to a stable boy, and proceeded to the Praetorium.

"Ah, there you are," Pilate said. "Is he dead, this Jesus?"

"Yes."

"You're sure? You saw him die?"

Lucius nodded.

Pilate sighed. "Let's hope it's finished then, and the whole unfortunate turn of events behind us." He turned to Joseph and Nicodemus. "He deserves better. Take him."

The two followers hurried down the narrow streets, both of them loaded down with a length of linen, along with a mixture of myrrh, aromatic resin, aloes, and shavings of scented wood to place between the layers of cloth, as was the custom of their people.

Huffing up the hill, they dropped the linen and the bags of spices. John was still there, along with the women, among them Mary of Magdala and Mary, the mother of Jesus. Several others had stayed, too, to keep the dogs away, and the vultures, and any enemies that might want to further desecrate the body.

"We will have to hurry," Joseph said, looking at the descending sun.

Valassio looked on as the others went to work. Two men planted a ladder at the base of the lone cross, resting it against the back of the crossbeam. Nicodemus steadied it as Joseph stepped onto the first rung. With each rung he climbed, his legs grew heavier.

Once on top, he bent over the beam. The hole in Jesus' wrist was much larger than the nail, and he could see the bloody whiteness of his bones, the fraying pink of his muscles. He lifted his right arm gingerly from the grip of the nail, and it fell, the weight of the body shifting to one side. Joseph lifted the other arm and waited until those below were in position to keep the body from falling to the ground. As Joseph lifted an arm from the nail that held it, he eased the body into the waiting arms of Nicodemus, John, and the women.

Valassio lay down his spear and drew closer, helping with the body.

It was slick with blood and hard to steady. They pried the feet from the remaining nail that held him.

Slowly, reverently, they laid his body on the ground. Both shoulders were dislocated. On one, a flap of skin was folded to one side, exposing cartilage and ligaments at the end of a ragged weave of muscle. His face was swollen from Roman fists; his flesh, torn by Roman whips; his blood, clotted in jagged trails down his face.

A woman came with a bucket of water and knelt beside him. Taking out a cloth soaking inside it, Mary Magdalene washed away the cruelty wrought by Roman hands. Others took the corners of their garments and dipped them into the bucket, touching them to Jesus' skin, dabbing up the blood.

With his arm around Jesus' mother, John looked on. No one spoke. As Jesus' mother knelt, the others made room for her. She moved her hand over her son's chest, touching the wound in his side. She stroked his face, delicately, as if it were that of a sleeping child. She cradled his head with her hand, pulling him to her with the aid of John and Mary Magdalene. She folded herself over him, drawing his limp body to her chest. As she rocked him, she sobbed.

The others touched her arms, her shoulders, leaned their heads against hers and wept. Then slowly, she relinquished her son, returning him to the earth.

John offered his hand. She looked at it blankly, looked at her son, then back at John, whose hand trembled. She took it in hers, placing her other hand on top of it, imparting a measure of strength. And with her strength, he pulled her to her feet.

Joseph and Nicodemus carried the body of their teacher to a garden below the hill. The garden was enclosed by a wall of low stones. Inside, the shrubbery had been well tended. The sun was losing its fullness on the horizon, the way of an egg as it fries. They laid him down and paused to catch their breath. The sun had broken against the horizon, spilling its yolk into the landscape, into the garden, onto the body. A breeze rustled the low leafy branches on the trees, as if servants fanning the small group of mourners.

They picked up the body and carried it to the front of a tomb that had been carved out of a slope of limestone, its whiteness in contrast to the weathered stone around it, giving evidence that it had been recently hewn. A trough had been chiseled into the ground before it. A circular millstone, half-again the height of a man, rested in the trough, ready to be rolled to seal the entrance.

The women wrapped the body in linen cloths, but Passover was drawing near, and the work was cut short. Several picked up the body on a sheet of linen and carried it to the tomb. They placed it on a stone slab. A dusty shaft of light from the dying sun angled through the small high window to frame his form.

"We must go," John said.

Valassio and John put their shoulders to the stone but could not budge it. The others joined in, but it took all their strength to roll it until it lodged in place with a heavy thud. Jesus' mother winced, bringing her hands to her mouth. The thud came with bracing finality. It was over. And this, the one final memory they would have of Jesus. The sight of linen. The smell of spices. The sound of stone abrading stone as the tomb sealed his fate, sealed theirs, sealed hers.

Mary wrapped her arm around Jesus' mother, steadying her. Reluctantly they followed the others up the path from the garden. Mary stopped to look back, the descending sun silhouetting her as she did.

4

After Lucius signed the death certificate, he trudged up the stairway to his quarters. Fluted columns lined the main room like dutiful servants. Tapestries draped the walls, each telling a story of Roman triumph. Urns plump as senators sat in corners, circumscribed with stories of their own. The floor was inlaid with small squares of variegated tile, which together also told a story. The seating area was an intimate grouping of couches, strewn with cushions.

He pulled off his helmet, letting it fall to the couch, unclasped his cape, draping it over the armrest of one of the chairs. On a table next to the chair were worn leather copies of works written in Latin and Greek. The centurion enjoyed the mental exercise of philosophical enquiry, the thrill of reading history, and the magical spells that Roman mythology cast. He especially loved the mythological stories of Ovid. He did not believe a jot of them, but they brought back the boy who once dreamed with such wild and extravagant abandon, the boy who had long since surrendered to the realities of adult life.

Ashuk put a platter of carved lamb on the table.

"I have no appetite," Lucius said. "Tonight I should like strong drink and someone to share it with."

The only sound was wood scraping tile as he moved his

chair. He sat, resting his head in his hands. Ashuk took a bottle and tilted it to fill two goblets. The centurion wrapped a hand around his goblet, gripping it. He took a gulp of the heady swill. Wiped his mouth. Stared, vacantly.

"I saw something today." He stopped, as if dazed. He took another drink. "Something beyond words. For a long time, I stood, watched. Then came the darkness. You saw it, did you not?"

Ashuk nodded.

"The quake. You felt it?"

The slave nodded.

"It threw me to the ground. And everything around me, within me, dear to me, all of it, in one unsettling moment, fell away."

Outside his window, the sun slipped beneath the horizon. A lonely star shivered in the twilight. From the Temple came the sound of a priest blowing a ram's horn. From there, other horns in other parts of the city announced the arrival of the Sabbath. With the exception of a few tardy feet hurrying to their homes, the city had hushed itself.

Ashuk poured another drink.

"I have seen men die. Many," Lucius said, half to himself. "But never like this. He called to his god—not an uncommon thing for a dying man. But he addressed him as 'Father.' A very *un*common thing. What god would that be, Ashuk?"

"Not Egyptian. Its royal courts crawl with alligators and cats and dung beetles."

"Nor Roman," said Lucius. "Our gods are off cavorting with one another like beings filled with lust and envy, paranoia even. Petty deities, the whole capricious lot, unworthy to father such a son as I saw today." He took another swig from his goblet.

In shadowy parts of the city, Jesus' disciples hid in clumps of threes and fours, tired, despondent, afraid.

Several of the disciples sought refuge in the city's underground aqueduct, built to catch run-off rainwater and channel it to a pool in the southern part of the city. It had low vaulted ceilings, and it was lined with slabs of rough-cut stone. The aqueduct was dry now, except for shallow poolings of water on the uneven floor. Every so often uncertain sounds echoed through the hollow darkness, startling them.

Others hid outside the city in the Kidron Valley. The ravine was steep, and the ancient overgrowth near the wall offered safe haven, for the night anyway. They sat in a close circle, whispering among themselves. They were covered by a canopy of branches, but still they were fearful the ascending moon might betray them.

One of the disciples, Peter, was off by himself in another part of the city, slumped against a wall, his arms wrapped around his knees, hugging them to keep from shaking. Not thirty yards away stood the palace of High Priest Caiaphas. Peter had been outside the palace gate, waiting while Jesus stood before a gathering of the Sanhedrin. He was among the throngs milling about the courtyard, listening to the proceedings.

There, in that courtyard, he denied any association with Jesus, denied even knowing him. In the blur of bitter tears that followed, Peter ran and hid. He hid until the sky darkened, concealing his movement as he circled back to the execution site, cloaked himself, and watched from a safe distance. The dusk had deepened as Peter ascended the steps that led to the city wall. He stopped, gazed across other countryside, his fugitive thoughts cowering within.

The rising moon stretched shadows across the valleys that bordered the holy city: the Kidron Valley on the eastern side and the Valley of Hinnom to the south and west. The valleys cupped the city the way the hands of a stonecutter might hold a finished piece of work, lifting it to the light and admiring it.

The Kidron was deep and cool with a slender necklace of water, silvered by the moon, dangling atop its velvet moss. Looking across the city beyond the eastern wall, toward the far side of the valley, Peter could see the twisted trunks of trees that formed the Garden of Gethsemane. Opposite the Mount of Olives sat the Temple, surrounded by high stone walls.

Peter looked into the Valley of Hinnom, which cut through the side of the city like a gaping wound. Ever since the reigns of Ahaz and Manasseh, when child sacrifices were made there, the valley had been cursed and became the city's garbage dump. Scattered fires burned there continuously, stoked with the bones from family meals, the sweepings from stable floors, and any unclean thing in need of disposal. Bodies of criminals were sometimes left to rot there, but the bodies of those crucified always ended up there. Being denied burial was part of the sentence, for the arm of Roman justice was as long as it was strong, stretching to the gate of hell itself.

Within the valley, wild dogs bared their teeth, each one claiming rights over the bodies. The dogs faced off, growling, lunging, nipping at one another's paws, biting each other's necks to win those few square feet of human flesh. The moon sent tall shadows into the ravine, gathering around the contested area.

That same moon sent shadows into the Fortress of Antonia, where they found the contest within the centurion's soul intensifying. Ashuk filled his master's goblet, slowly, carefully, but the centurion kept signaling for more until the brew brimmed the cup. Only then did Lucius signal "enough."

Lucius stood and walked the room on tentative legs. He steadied himself at a table of imported teak, inlaid with mosaic tiles depicting Romulus and his twin brother, Remus, being suckled by a she-wolf. Spread across the table was a parchment map, its corners held down by weighty images of four of Rome's lesser deities.

The Great Sea was at the center of the map and at the center of the centurion's boyhood dreams. The sea had fascinated him since childhood when he played in its surf, the mystery of other lands afoam around his feet, faraway adventures calling to him from the seashells he put to his ear, the driftwood bobbing in the waves like mermaids. On the map unfurled on the table, the Mediterranean was labeled in Latin, *Mare Nostrum,* "Our Sea." And indeed it was. It belonged entirely to the Romans, as did every country whose shores encircled it.

He traced his hand over the shoreline of the map, then rested it on a sculpture of Neptune. Of all the Roman deities, Neptune was the centurion's favorite. The brother of Jupiter, Neptune ruled the sea. A sculpture of him stood on a pedestal, one foot resting on part of a ship, a trident in his right hand, a dolphin in his left. He was an imposing figure the way the sculptor had portrayed him, caught in a tension between great fury and great calm. Over the centuries, Neptune had not shown Rome the same fortune that Mars had. Mars, the god of war, was the father of Romulus, Rome's founder, and so war was viewed as Rome's essential nature, not only its heritage but its destiny.

As a boy, Lucius had been schooled in the classics of Greek and Roman literature, aspiring to serve in one of Caesar's legions. Perhaps someday to go to Britain and follow in Julius Caesar's footsteps.

"You think much of home?" he asked Ashuk.

"Always."

A look came over Lucius's face, like a breeze over a pond, rippling a deep stillness within him. "Later we shall barter stories. But first, a question," said the bleary-eyed soldier. "What is better: to live, a soldier . . . or die, a king?"

"If the king dies, what good is he to his people?"

Lucius pondered the question. "Perhaps the good is in the story he leaves behind."

"What is the king's story?"

"I don't know." A sudden sobriety came over him. "I don't know."

"Do you know someone who does?"

He nodded. "A woman."

In another part of the city, those who loved Jesus hid in the shadows of the second-story room where his closest companions had shared his last supper. Patches of moonlight matted the floor.

A knock at the door startled everyone. Another knock, and with it, a whisper. John jumped to his feet and put his ear to the door.

"James?" he asked.

"It's me."

John opened the door, pulled his brother out of the moonlight into the darkness.

James whispered as his eyes strained to adjust to the dark. "Anyone with you?"

"The women. The others?"

"Judas is dead. Peter, Matthew, all of them, scattered."

The conversation stopped at the sound of soldiers marching. Everyone scooted to the wall, wedging themselves into corners, crouching underneath windows. They heard the formation turn the corner and move up the street toward them.

The sound of a creaking hinge, and everyone jerked to see light angling from the door that John had forgotten to secure. A gust of wind slammed it. He rushed to hold it shut and latched it.

Soldiers were below them.

"Halt!" At the order, the marching stopped.

The breathing of some in the upper room nearly stopped, too. In the silence, their hearts beat so loudly they feared the soldiers would hear it.

"Turn about!" At the command, the soldiers turned as one man. "March!" As they did, the sound of their boots grew fainter and fainter, finally fading to silence.

Those in the upper room breathed a collective sigh.

"We must go," urged James. "Tonight."

"Where?" his brother asked.

"I don't know. Bethany maybe. Jericho."

"And from there?"

"They will ferret us out, John. All of us. The women, too."

From the shadows came a voice. "What has become of us?" Mary Magdalene stepped into a shunt of moonlight. "If we are to die, let us die here, together. And together we shall go to him. But hiding out, cringing in the darkness. He deser—" The words caught in her throat. "He deserves better."

Back at the Fortress, Lucius walked to the window, looking at the glow of oil lamps dotting the city.

"Question: Is it better to be dutiful . . . or noble?"

"The two should embrace, as friends," answered Ashuk, "not oppose each other as enemies."

"Ah, that we lived in a world ruled by shoulds."

"Yet there are places so ruled. The place of a slave, for one. A slave should *always* be dutiful."

"And a soldier? What about *him*? Should he be dutiful or noble?"

"There is nobility in duty."

"But not in *all* duty."

"No, not in all."

"I ask you again, and this time answer not as a slave but as a man."

"A *free* man?"

Lucius nodded.

"The duty of a free man is to live nobly."

The centurion lifted his goblet to toast the wisdom of his slave. "More to drink," he said, "and tonight we shall both be free."

"More to drink," said Ashuk, smiling, "and tomorrow we shall both be slaves."

Ashuk went around the room picking up clothes that Lucius had dropped on the floor and draped over the furniture when a sudden thought took wing, giving him pause.

"What say your philosophers, about a noble life? Surely somewhere they speak of it."

Lucius walked to his shelf, searching for a scroll. Finding it, he pulled it out, unrolled it a ways, and stopped. "'Men do not care how nobly they live, but only how long . . . although it is within the reach of every man to live nobly, but within no man's reach to live long.'"

"He speaks truth, whoever wrote it."

"Seneca."

"But tonight, tonight you do not consult Seneca. You consult a slave."

"Tonight there is no light in Jerusalem to read by," Lucius

said as he reshelved the scroll, "and nothing Roman I care to read."

The two stood facing each other. In his stupor, Lucius weaved, spilling some of his drink. Ashuk put down the laundry, took a rag, and wiped up the spill.

"It is late," Ashuk said at last, "and the rooster shows no mercy to the owl."

"Yes, yes, you may take your leave. Good dreams to you, Ashuk."

"And to you, Master."

As Ashuk bowed and left, Lucius called to him. "And your pardon, if I may."

The slave turned with a puzzled look. "My pardon?"

"We never spoke of your home."

"Another day. But tomorrow, find the woman."

"What woman?"

"The woman who knows the king's story."

5

The fullness of the Passover moon ladled its whiteness onto the quarried limestone of Jerusalem, spilling over the straightness of its gap-toothed walls ... over the unevenness of the structures within them ... over the narrowness of its streets that connected the sprawl of shops and homes, along with the secular encroachments of Roman occupation of which the Fortress of Antonia stood as the most egregious.

Within that fortress, the centurion lay sleeping on his bed, where a haunt of images came back to him—images that Pilate may have washed his hands of, but images that he could not. He woke with a start, his heart pounding, his chest heaving, his hair a mop of sweat. As he pushed himself up, his feet slapped the cool tile, and he steadied a head that suddenly seemed a weight too heavy to lift.

The moon was low and almost transparent against the pale gray sky.

He made his way to a wooden table against the wall, where Ashuk had set out a basin of fresh water and a clean towel. He stood at the table, cupping his hands and wetting his face, toweling it gingerly.

He took a bite of flatbread, then part of a boiled egg, but a wave of nausea came over him, and he threw up in a nearby basin.

Once dressed, Lucius went to the stables and mounted a horse. From there he crossed along the front of the Temple, its walls towering above him, along the still silent street, his horse's hooves clopping on the stone pavement. He passed through the second of the two enormous arches that flanked the street and emerged into the lower city.

He carefully guided his horse through the narrow streets. He passed small, tumbledown houses, cobbled together into neighborhoods that housed Jerusalem's poor.

As he threaded his way through the streets, the first light of dawn scudded across the sky, tinting the underbellies of clouds. A rim of sun crowned the new day, glinting off the gold of the Temple. The sun was low in the east, sending slats of light that moved down the tops of buildings, warming the limestone masonry.

The smell of roasted lamb lingered in the air, having seeped from homes to fill the streets, which made Lucius even more nauseated. The silence of the Sabbath was broken by the crow of a rooster, the bray of a donkey, the bark of a dog. Aside from that, the part of the city where Lucius cantered his horse was quiet and still.

A chill streamed low through the streets, and a mist rose from the rivulets of sewage. Here and there were the sounds of women waking, shuffling about in their houses. One of them leaned out her window for a look at who was out on this Sabbath morning, clopping through the neighborhood.

"I'm looking for a woman," Lucius said. "A Galilean. Her name is Mary."

The woman shook her head, careful not to speak and wake her family. She withdrew from the window, and he rode on down the street.

He stopped to water his horse at a fountain where a boy

had floated a small wooden boat with a sail. The boy carried a handful of rocks and threw one of them into the water, trying to capsize the boat.

"Sinking ships, on Shabbat?"

The boy swept the rocks behind his back, dropping some as he did. But then, with fisted resolve, he showed his strength by striking a stance, and proclaimed, "Defending our shores."

"By yourself?"

"The others have died, valiantly. I alone am left to save our people."

"You are very brave."

The boy smiled. As Lucius turned to leave, the boy called out to him.

"Are you a good man . . . or a bad man?" The boy's smile turned to mistrust, and he cocked his arm.

Lucius glowered at him, drawing his sword to enter into the boy's fantasy. But the gesture spooked the child and he ran, dropping his rocks along the way.

"Your boat!" Lucius called. But the boy had rounded the corner and disappeared.

Lucius dismounted to retrieve the boat, bobbing in the fountain. A breeze rippled the water. As it died, the water stilled, and his image rested upon the surface. He paused a moment to study it, put the boat on the low stone wall, stepped away from his reflection.

By this time men and women had filled their windows and doorways, looking out suspiciously, protectively.

"I'm looking for a woman from Magdala, a pilgrim." One by one the doors and shutters closed.

"It is Passover," chided one of the men. "Have you no respect?" His wife shushed him and yanked him back inside the window, closing the shutters behind him.

Lucius did not exercise the authority he could have; he simply mounted his horse and trotted off. He passed a marching guard, the cadence of their steps echoing off the walls. It was a routine patrol of the city to make their presence known, and with their presence, their jurisdiction, lest a surge of patriotism overcome the good sense of its citizenry, recruiting them to zealotry.

Arriving at the Fortress, Lucius returned his horse to the stable boy. Once inside his quarters, he stretched out on his couch, alone with his thoughts, staring at the ceiling.

Mary, meanwhile, was still in bed, curled against the cold realities of the preceding day. Her eyes were bloodshot, and she closed them to ease the burning. She took a breath, held it as if it were a great weight, and released it with a sigh.

Normally she would be up by now. But not today. Today she was slow to move. A throbbing headache. No reason to move, though, even without the headache. No desire to move. Her throat was swollen and ached. Her nose, raw and sore. The rest of her, numb.

Getting up to check on Jesus' mother, Mary crossed the courtyard and climbed the narrow staircase to the rooftop. There she found the woman, sitting against a wall with the morning sun bright upon her face. Mary touched her shoulder and knelt beside her. She rested her head against the woman's legs, her hand shading her eyes from the sun. Instinctively, the woman began to stroke Mary's hair, running her hand down her head, her shoulders, and finally leaving it there.

Neither said anything. Neither moved. They just sat together, resting, their eyes closed against the inconsolable brightness.

6

That night, Lucius could not sleep. He rose from his bed, dressed, tried walking off his thoughts. Caping himself against the chill, he retraced the way he had traveled to the site of the executions.

It was a long, slow walk. The street blotted an inky shadow that the moon had spilled before him, his only company. Once outside the city, he stopped on the brow of the hill where the crucifixion had taken place. Passing clouds streaked the stone. His eyes lingered on the dried blood around the hole that had held Jesus' cross. As he stood there, the clouds mottled the moon on his face; a pale wash of light one moment, of darkness the next.

The next morning, Lucius and Ashuk were both abruptly awakened by an insistent pounding at their door.

Ashuk was first to the door, opening it to find a soldier with anxious eyes, panting. "Your master," he said, trying to catch his breath. "Pilate wants him!"

"This moment?" asked Lucius who had stumbled from the bedroom.

"This moment."

By the time Lucius reached Pilate, the soldiers that had

guarded Jesus' tomb were standing before him.

"Take them away!" Pilate shouted to the soldiers who had rounded them up. One of Pilate's advisors spoke, but he cut him off. "Don't you think I know that?!" Pilate called to the soldiers: "Put them in separate cells. And don't let them talk to each other."

Lucius stepped into his presence and bowed, saying nothing.

"Have you heard?!"

"No, sir."

"Secured with a stone, sealed by my orders, guarded by half a dozen men—*your* men, Centurion!—and *still* they stole it."

"Stole what?"

"The body! His followers stole the body. And those guarding it, I will have their heads. I will have *each* of their heads for this dereliction of duty!"

"I know the men, your Excellency. They are the most dutiful in my charge. There must be some explan—"

Then, almost as if Pilate were talking to himself. "The stories about this man, the rumors, the accusations, they were all behind me, dead and buried. And now. *Now* the story lives."

"Sir, if I may. I could get statements from each of them. Written statements, for the record. Do it privately, one at a time. So there is no chance of collusion."

Pilate sat in his chair, out of breath from his rant. "Preposterous. The story they tell, it's preposterous."

"It can be sorted out, I'm sure," said Lucius. "I know these men; I'll know if they are lying."

Pilate nodded, wearily, and waved him away to the task.

The cells where the soldiers were held were in the basement of the Fortress. One of the guards opened the cell of the first soldier to be interrogated, and Lucius entered with an amanuensis beside him to take notes. This soldier, Cassio, was the one in charge that night. He sat with his back against the wall, his hands wringing themselves, his face all sweat and fear, as he gave his account.

"His voice was like thunder . . . the ground, quaking as he walked." He took a breath, hoping it would ease his trembling. "The stone, it rolled away. Just rolled. He shook his head, as if all hope had been drained from it. "We will be executed for this. All of us."

"Not if your story holds."

"My *story*? It will end with a sword, tonight or tomorrow, but soon. The best I can hope for is that it will be swift."

One cell after another clanged open, clanged shut. In spite of his relationship with the men, it was serious business, and Lucius took it as such. He was pointed in his questioning, patient in his listening, and he was most particular that his scribe get everything on record.

Pilate and Lucius were talking privately in the imperial counsel room.

"The accounts are consistent," said Lucius, placing the pile of handwritten accounts on Pilate's desk.

"'Consistent' does not mean they are true. It could mean they are all partner to a lie."

"And you think that conspiracy likely?"

"I think that the men I sent to investigate, I think *their* report is factual, bereft of any emotion that might cloud the evidence. The stone, they found it rolled away, like the soldiers said. The tomb, like they said, empty. The rest, the rest is too incredible to believe."

"Sir, if I may—"

"We *know* the stone was rolled away. The mystery is, by whom."

"In all due respects, sir, it is no mystery to the men."

"A dream? Could they have fallen asleep and dreamt it?"

"No, sir."

"An angel, bright as the noonday sun? You expect a rational man like me to believe such a thing? Do you expect the people to believe such a thing? *Anyone* to believe such a thing?"

"Cassio believes it. So do the others, to the man."

"Maybe *they* moved the stone. Maybe someone paid them to move it."

"Respectfully, sir, they are not mercenaries, they are soldiers. Roman soldiers. Who swore an oath to protect the Empire from its enemies, without or within."

Pilate paused to recalibrate his line of questioning.

"None of them saw the body, is that correct?"

"That is correct."

"All we know then, for certain, is that the body is gone."

"That is all we know for certain, yes."

"Not that it lives."

"Not that it lives."

"Well, that gives us something to work with."

Pilate made sure a rumor was circulated that would exonerate him, should what he called "Cassio's story" ever find its way to Rome and trouble the ears of Caesar. The soldiers had no motive, he reasoned, and so they were not suspect. But the disciples did. They had every reason to steal the body, fabricate some story about a resurrection, and with that ruse keep the enterprise alive. Though there was no evidence to the theory, there *was* logic to it. Logic that rational men could embrace. And so the story of Jesus' resurrection was put to death with that rumor, entombed in a rational explanation, and made secure by the authority of an imperial seal.

7

In time, most of the Passover pilgrims returned to their respective lands. Back to the seaside shores of Galilee. Back to the cedared hills of Lebanon. Back to the ten cities of the Decapolis, beyond the Jordan. As the population thinned, Jerusalem went back to normal. Normal hours for shops. Normal prices for goods. Things went back to normal for the government, too, and for those soldiers who had sworn their allegiance to that government. But nothing was normal for the soldiers who had guarded Jesus' tomb. And nothing was normal for the centurion who believed their stories.

There was still so much he wanted to know about the man he had crucified. And so for the next several days, his duties were done, he rode his horse through the city, section by section, searching. Stopping to check with locals who might know of strangers who had stayed behind. Knocking on doors. Talking to merchants.

And nothing.

After one of those days of searching, Lucius returned to the Fortress and passed the wood shop where rough-cut beams were lying side by side on a heavy table, two carpenters manning a long toothy saw, squaring off the ends. Lucius watched as they went about the work of making instruments for execution.

He turned his gaze from the laborers, and it fell on the results of their labor. In one bin were iron spikes. In another bin, short, cylindrically shaped wooden pegs to hold the crossbeam to the vertical beam. In another bin, short coils of rope to lash down the arms and ankles. It was all so neat and so orderly.

The air was filled with the resined scent of fresh-cut wood. He breathed it in.

Normally, he would have relished the smell.

He relished it no longer.

Later that day, Pilate was at work in a large room with Lucius at his side, poring over a parchment of troop formations unfurled on a table with a wooden pointer lying across it. Maps inked on vellum hung from the high walls. A map of Jerusalem. A map of Judea and surrounding areas. A map of *Mare Nostrum*. And a map of the far reaches of the Empire. Pilate rolled up one of the parchments and picked it up, changing the subject as he did.

"The city is getting back to normal," Pilate said.

"It is."

Pilate picked up the pointer on the table and moved its tip over a map of the Frontier.

"Back to business, for everyone. Back to *mine*. Which is ... I am taking counsel from all the officers. That is why I have asked you here." Lucius acknowledged the honor with a nod. "What say you is the Empire's greatest enemy?" Pilate pointed to Germany. "The Huns?" He moved the tip to touch Gaul. "The Gauls?" He moved it again to another front.

"A great empire has great enemies," Lucius said. "Everywhere."

"The *greatest*," he replied, stressing his point. "Of them all, which is the greatest enemy?"

"Peace."

Pilate looked at him quizzically. "Peace?"

"Peace makes an empire soft, longing for luxuries. A great empire does not need oils and spices. It needs quarries and mines. We have enough quarries here, in Italia. But we need metal, for armaments and for trade. Zinc, to make bronze, necessary for both. Britannia has mines rich in zinc. Vast reserves of peat and coal to heat our homes, fire our furnaces, warm our troops. And wheat fields, farms, livestock. Everything a great empire needs to sustain itself."

"You propose we invade Britannia? Again?"

"Before ease overtakes us, and we by our luxuries be conquered."

8

Later in the week, Lucius once again rode the streets, scouring the city. Here and there he stopped to inquire about the woman, about Jesus' followers, his disciples, anyone who might know something. But nothing. Until a man pointed to a two-story house on the corner, its windows shuttered securely.

Lucius heard muted singing from upstairs. He tethered his horse and tried the door, but it was barred from the inside. He went around and tried opening a shutter, but it too had been secured. He tried another window in back, jostling it until it allowed him to lift the bar that battened it. Once inside, he crept up the stairs, the singing growing louder, the voices more distinct. He eased his weight against the door to the upper room.

It opened into a great room with high ceilings, the floor covered with over a hundred people. When the group saw a Roman soldier filling the doorway, their voices trailed to silence. Voices began murmuring. Some closest to him moved away. He looked around the room until he saw her.

People on either side of Mary inched away from her, leaving her isolated in full view. She made no effort to hide herself.

"I am Lucius Alexander Titus," he said, taking off his helmet, "the centurion who crucified your king."

They all sat motionless.

Mary stood.

"We know who you are," she said, a tinge of defiance in her voice. "Why are you here?"

"I have come," he started to say, but his voice broke.

For a moment, he stood there, silent, his lips trembling.

"I am sorry."

His answer disarmed everyone, softened everyone. A man stood and put his hand on Lucius's back. A woman sitting near him reached to touch his foot. Another man drew near.

Finally Mary drew near. As she did, the people cleared a path.

Now it was just the two of them, facing each other.

"It was your duty," she said, this time with tenderness, "not your decision."

Lucius took a deep breath to compose himself. "I heard stories, from the guards. Is it true, that he is risen?"

"I saw him," she said. "With these eyes." And she pointed to them. "I heard him, with *these* ears." And she touched her ears. She paused to collect herself. "I touched him," she said, extending her hands, "with *these* hands." She touched his shoulders. "The same hands now touching you. When I beheld his body, the ruin wrought by Roman hands, it was gone. His face, the anguish I saw in it when he was on the cross, gone. I looked in his eyes, and I could not speak. I could hardly breathe—"

The words caught in her throat. She wiped the tears from her eyes, and saw those same tears in Lucius's eyes. For a moment, the rest of the room blurred in the periphery, and it was only the two of them. For a long time, it seemed, it was only the two of them.

The next day, Ashuk was up before dawn, as was his habit, preparing a breakfast of boiled grains, stewed with dried apricots and raisins until the fruit was soft and plump. Hearing his master stirring in the next room, he dished the mixture into a bowl. He set the bowl on the table and with it a spoon, a plate of sliced melon, and a cup of water.

Lucius emerged from his bedroom in his undergarments, scratching his unkempt hair. He pulled out a chair and sat at the table.

Lucius plunged his spoon into the steaming bowl and took a bite, not so much chewing it as mulling it over in his mouth.

"You have not made this in a while."

"I warmed it up, from yesterday."

"It is better, the second day."

Which amused Ashuk. "I will warm it again, tomorrow."

Preoccupied, Lucius missed the humor. Ashuk watched even more carefully as he took another spoonful, tasted it, savored it. And then it dawned on the slave.

"You found the woman."

And a smile spread across Lucius's face.

9

D awn in the dungeon beneath the Fortress of Antonia.
Slivers of light piercing the slitted openings in the wall.

Appearing at the cell where Cassio was being held, a guard jangled his keys in the lock. Curled on the floor, a sluggish Cassio looked up.

Lucius standing next to the guard, smiling.

Cassio smiled back . . . rose to his feet . . . and one by one, the other soldiers rose to theirs.

In the days ahead, Lucius found himself drawn anywhere that Mary was. He sat next to her in the upper room that was filled with Jesus' followers, every head bowed, every eye closed. Except his. He looked over the room, taking it all in, trying to understand it.

Late one night, Lucius was sitting with Mary and Jesus' mother around a campfire in the Garden of Gethsemane, where Peter, James, and John were gathered, talking about the kingdom of God.

Early on another day, Lucius found himself sitting next to her again, this time in the upper room to hear Peter preach.

And then one afternoon, he happened upon her washing the body of a lame boy on his mat near the side of the street. She moved the wash rag over him with the reverence of one washing a newborn, swaddled in the mystery of birth. Watching her, he was wooed by her. Their eyes met, and both sensed a sacrament of some kind had passed between them. But neither spoke of it.

Again, he sat next to her at a prayer meeting, every head bowed, every eye closed. Including his.

It was late by the time Lucius arrived at the Fortress, and Ashuk was asleep. He looked out the window, breathing in the night air. He could not get her out of his mind. Every direction his thoughts turned, they ran into her. And running to her, they stopped and stood captivated. Which was a puzzlement. She had done nothing to draw his interest. She dressed modestly. She wore no cosmetics to whiten her skin or to redden her cheeks, as was the fashion of Roman women. She wore no jewelry, no braids in her hair, nothing to draw attention.

And yet, and yet she was impossible not to look at, stare at, marvel at, the way one would gaze upon an exquisitely sculpted goddess adorning the Roman temples in Caesarea.

Thoughts of her lingered, almost translucent in the morning light. Lucius stepped quietly among them, fearful they would be startled and take leave. Ashuk was already up and cooking. Drawn by the aroma, Lucius came into the kitchen.

"A good morning to you, Master."

"And to you."

"A hearty meal this morning."

Lucius took a spoon and sampled the scrambled eggs and bits of meat from the pan. Ashuk dished out a bowl and gave it to him. He took the bowl and sat at the table, where he began eating.

"Breakfast with me," said Lucius.

"If it is your pleasure."

"It is."

Ashuk dished himself a bowl and sat opposite his master, a slight smile on his face in response to the privilege.

It was late in the day when Lucius was sitting with Mary again, this time at a low table near the floor with some of Jesus' followers, where he had been plying them with questions, which they answered with their stories.

"I could not do this before I met him," said one of the men. "*See you*, I mean. I was blind since birth. Left to beg. All I knew was my soiled mat on the side of the street, where other children passed, laughing, playing. Left there, to the passing kindness of strangers. Or to their passing sarcasms. Then Jesus came, walking down *my* street, past *my* mat. I called to him. 'Son of David, have mercy on me!' I was afraid he had not heard, afraid he had passed me by. I called again, louder this time. 'SON OF DAVID, HAVE MERCY ON ME!' This time he heard. He stopped. He came.

"The words that came from his lips, I could feel them, feel his words, kneeling. '"What do you want me to do for you?"'

"For *me*." A tear took a slow path down his face. "That I can see you, centurion, with these eyes—" He wiped the tear. "*He* did that."

An older woman down the table from Lucius spoke next.

"I am a widow. And this," she said, touching the arm of the man next to her, "is my son. My *only* son. My only hope for surviving the years ahead." Her son squeezed her hand. "Not long ago, he died. And we were on our way to bury him, when Jesus saw me. I did not know him. Did not even know *about* him. And so I did not call out to him, did not say his name, did not ask for mercy. Yet he came. To *me*, a poor widow. And he gave me back my son," she said, touching her hand to her son's face. He hugged her, trying to buttress her weight, which was leaning on him now.

One by one, the people at the table shared their stories. And one by one their stories found a place to live in Lucius's heart.

Lucius no longer wore his uniform when he went to see Mary, which attracted undue attention, just his tunic. This time the two of them hiked up the Mount of Olives, outside the city walls.

They walked a footpath toward the summit, where she led the way. The hummock was an uneven surface, tufts of grass sprigging from the rocky soil, shrubs all aleaf, flowering vines cascading down the mountainside.

Cooled by the breeze, Mary took in a breath and sighed it out. "This was his favorite place." She walked to a nearby olive tree, resting her arm on its branch and her head on her arm. She spoke in a more somber voice, adding, "Also the place where the soldiers arrested him."

"Tell me more about your Jesus."

"*My* Jesus? He is your Jesus, too."

"I did not know him," he reminded her. "I only saw him die."

"He died as he lived, giving himself to others. Always giving himself," she said wistfully. "He had a quiet strength that drew you to him. Few words. You always wanted him to say more, explain more."

"A teller of stories, with few words?"

"He told them the way a sower seeds his field, casting them broadly over the ground. Small kernels, full of life. Leaving them to grow in their own way, bear fruit in their own time. Amazing now that I think of it," she said, pausing. "So many hopes he must have had for those seeds, yet he sowed them in such uncertain soil."

"Tell me *your* story, how you met him."

She walked, and he followed her. They came to a pleasant glade on the other side of the hill, where clusters of olive trees were laced with brocades of lilies, hollyhocks, and chamomile. As they walked through cool of the garden, she told her story.

"He came to Magdala, where I lived. My life, it was . . . it was something you stepped to the other side of the street to avoid. People shunned me, children ran from me. Afraid of the demons inside me. Seven of them. They did not all come at once. One by one they crept in, each opening the door a little wider for the next one. One came in my childhood. Another, in my early womanhood. The others came in my adulthood. Sometimes their presence was like a whisper, seducing me. Other times they accused me for giving in to the seductions, telling me how worthless I was, how vile and disgusting."

She stopped walking and turned to Lucius, emotion pooling in her eyes.

"Then I met Jesus. I shrank back when I first saw him, the demons within me cringing. But Jesus did not cringe in their presence. He did not avoid me, and he did not run from me. There was no disgust in his eyes. Only kindness. He had the kindest eyes. Especially when—"

Her voice cracked, and she paused to collect herself.

"He called out the demons, *ordered* them out, told them to leave, to never return. What I could not do for so long, he did in a moment. A mere word. And gone were the voices, the seductions, the accusations, the nightmares. The babbling, the sobbing, convulsing, it stopped. In one merciful moment, it was gone, all of it. In its place—" Tears seeped from her eyes. "No one has ever—"

"How long ago?"

She held up three fingers, unable to get the words out.

"Three years?" asked Lucius, and she nodded.

Lucius touched her cheek and wiped away the tears. Slowly, shyly, self-consciously, she turned her eyes to his. As their eyes met, he leaned into her.

But she turned her head. "We should be getting back."

Back at his quarters in the Fortress, Lucius stared at the moon from his bed, a confusion of thoughts he was trying to untangle. *All she did was smile,* he thought. Was he imagining there were feelings for him beyond that smile? He had tried to kiss her, but she refused. *What do I know?* he reasoned to himself. *What do I really know? She said nothing, did nothing. All I know is that she smiled.*

Mary, meanwhile, was lying in her own bed in an austere, windowless room, looking at a small oil lamp on a table, transfixed by its glowing wick. A strange feeling stirred within her. She felt it, and she feared it. And fearing it, she dismissed it.

She had had her fill of men. She did not need one, did not want one. She only wanted Jesus. Never had she met a man like him. He was not only enough for her, he was everything to her. And there was no room in her heart for anyone else.

Besides, there was no time.

Jesus had risen, as he had promised, to sit at the right hand of his Father in heaven. And, as he had promised, he was coming back. Soon. So there was no time for distractions, least of all the distraction of falling in love.

10

Summoned to Pilate's quarters, Lucius, along with several other officers, dined at his table. By the end of the meal, Pilate raised his goblet. "To the glory of Rome!"

The others followed. "The glory of Rome!"

"You are here because you have caught the eye of the Empire. All of you are destined for greatness, say your superiors. As you know, military advancement comes through valor as a soldier distinguishes himself in battle. But the Empire, save the far reaches, is at peace. Good for merchants, who eye wealth; bad for soldiers, who eye rank. To further the path to your destiny, I have granted each of you a commission to the Frontier."

He nodded to his attendant, who distributed scrolls to each of them. Each was being sent to a different part of the Frontier, where they were likely to see battle. All were eager to receive their orders. All, except Lucius.

When dinner was over, he carried the thought of leaving Jerusalem like a weight. He had never expected to feel that way. Ever since he had been stationed there, he had been eager to leave. Caesarea. The Frontier. Rome. Those were the places of allure. Not Jerusalem. Not Jerusalem. His hopes, his dreams, his ambitions, they were all other places, on other maps.

He walked through the Fortress, a great angst brewing within him until it had fomented into an even greater anger. Soon he was so angry he could no longer hold it in. He knocked over a few, small things that were in his way. Then he kicked in a door to a large storeroom, where he was alone, and gritted his teeth, hurling the scroll that dictated his destiny at the wall.

He started throwing crates around the room, one after another, the crates shattering and spilling their contents everywhere. Seeing an empty wagon, he got his legs under it and pushed it over in one, great venting.

He stood breathless, his chest heaving in and out. Slower now. Surveying the damage he had done. Surprised at the damage he had done. And finally, resolved to do his duty, he picked up the scroll and left.

Entering his quarters, Lucius tossed his imperial orders to Ashuk. The slave looked at the scroll quizzically. The words struck like a blow. He put the scroll on the table, without comment. Lucius detected his feelings.

"I thought you hated it here," Lucius reminded him.

A vulnerable moment for the slave, and an unguarded one. "I have . . . such sadness," he said, pointing to his heart. "It is so heavy, sometimes, the carrying of it." He paused a beat. "I am tired. I do not want to stay *here*. I do not want to go *there*. I want to go home."

His sadness was a deep wound, but although Lucius felt it, he did not give in to it. He was a soldier, a soldier of Rome, and he had been trained to steel himself to whatever destiny was decreed to him, regardless of how he felt about it.

"I, too, want to go home. But I, too, serve a master. And in his service my wants have no place."

An almost palpable silence stood between them. "When do we leave?"

"Soon."

"For long?"

"Yes."

"Tell me what to take, and I will pack it."

The next day Lucius was off duty, dressed leisurely, and walked to the lower city to tell Mary. He knocked on the door of the home where she was staying. A woman answered.

"Salome. Is Mary here?"

"I will summon her."

After a moment, Mary came to the door, surprised to see him.

"Come in," she said, smiling. "Have you eaten?" He shook his head, and she noticed that his eyes had lost their life. Her smile retreated. "What is wrong?"

It was a long walk back. Lucius's mind took many paths along the way, except the one to the Fortress, where an imperial decree had determined his fate. Before he knew it, he was lost in a labyrinth of narrow streets, where he came to a small olive grove. He sat beneath one of the trees, and a great weariness caught up with him. There, under that tree, he bowed his head, closed his eyes, and prayed.

"Why? Why did you bring her into my life, stir these feelings, then send me away? I do not understand. I don't. I am a proud man, unaccustomed to begging. But I *beg* you. Let me stay. Here. With her. Please, let me stay. Grant me this one request, and I will serve you the rest of my life, asking nothing in return. But do not forsake me to the Frontier. Please, God, do not forsake me."

The next day, Lucius met Mary at the gate in the western part of the city, where Ashuk sat waiting in a wagon. He feared it would be the last time they would see each other, but his fears went unspoken. In a bold move, he embraced her. And for a long time he held her. She did not refuse his advance, but she did nothing to encourage it, either.

"So many nights I have dreamed of this moment. Then came the dawn, and you were not there. My prayer is that one day the dawn will come, and you will still be in my arms. Forever and always in my arms."

Ever so gently she pulled away.

He waited for her to return the feelings, but she did not.

"When Jesus was among us, the kingdom of God came near, so near you could touch it. Amazing things happened. Things too incredible to believe. I *saw* those things."

He waited for words to say, something, anything, but words had left him. "My master has told me to go."

Mary knew her words would pierce his heart, and she spoke them slowly.

"And mine, to stay."

An eternity stretched between them, or so it seemed to Lucius. Finally, he turned and mounted his horse.

"He is coming back," she said, and those were her last words to him.

"If he comes, I will return for him. If he delays . . . I will return for you."

And those, his last to her.

Lucius turned his horse and kicked its flanks. Ashuk waved to Mary, whom he had never met, never even seen, until now. She waved back. As they waved, he smiled. She smiled back.

But Lucius did not wave, did not smile, did not look back.

His face, set like flint for Caesarea.

PART II

AD 33–64

CAESAREA

MASSILIA

GAUL

GERMANY

BRITAIN

11

Lucius's thoughts were poor traveling companions. He tried making sense of it all—Jesus' death, the earthquake, meeting *her* on that hill, Cassio's account, the empty tomb, this untimely love, the stories, the sightings, Pilate's orders—but it was an enigma. All of it, an enigma. Especially Jesus.

He had so many questions. So many unanswered questions.

On the road to Caesarea, Ashuk sat in the lead wagon of the caravan and lightly shook the reins to coax the horses. Lucius rode beside him on his horse. Among the soldiers in the caravan were two who had served under him at Jesus' crucifixion, Massina and Antonius. Along the way, Ashuk tried to engage Lucius in conversation, but his answers were short and his voice was without interest. After a while, Lucius trotted his horse to the front of the caravan, where he could be alone with his thoughts.

The road they traveled over had been built by Herod the Great, who, during his forty-year reign in Palestine, had built roads, bridges, the Temple in Jerusalem, and the great port city of Caesarea. The road was paved with cut stone, inset over alternating layers of sand and gravel. As the horses clopped along, the iron-rimmed wheels clinked over the slightest unevenness of stone, and the wood strained at the joints under the weight of the wagon's cargo. Thus passed the time for master and slave, not in spirited conversations but in monotone rhythms—clinks of iron, creaks of wood, the clopping of hooves.

Caesarea lay in the distance as if a great white shell had washed up on the beach; a seamless slate of sea to the west, a great brown barrenness to the east. Every structure in the city had been overlaid with a white marble façade that made the city gleam during the day and at night seemed hewn from slabs of moon. It shone in stark contrast to Jerusalem with its drably weathered, coarsely cut limestone.

Caesarea was everything Jerusalem wasn't. Jerusalem was strictly Jewish with as little of Roman culture as could be tolerated. Caesarea was aromp with gods and goddesses, an impressive temple that was adorned with a seduction of prostitutes, public baths, a spectacular amphitheater, a ten-thousand-seat hippodrome on the seashore, stretching half a mile long.

And overseeing it all, like a benevolent deity, was a colossal statue of the emperor.

When the caravan arrived, it was late afternoon, and the streets still teemed with life—ships unloading exotic cargo, merchants displaying imported wares, teachers tutoring aristocratic students, government officials attending to imperial business, actors rehearsing parts they were to play in the amphitheater.

The caravan made its way to the military fortress, everyone taking in the sights and sounds of the city as it did. When they arrived, Lucius dismounted, and the commanding officer greeted him.

"Welcome to Caesarea, Centurion!"

Lucius clasped his hand to the officer's forearm. With the other one he handed him Pilate's orders. As the officer read the scroll, Lucius gazed over the man's shoulder to the bay where ships were harbored. He took a deep breath.

"The smell of the sea," he said wistfully. "It reminds me of home."

"Where is that?"

"Alexandria."

"Ah, I was there only a month ago."

Lucius's eyes lit up. "How fares it?"

Caesarea was filled with enticements, from physical pleasures to intellectual pursuits to professional ambitions. A world away from Jerusalem. Even farther away from Mary. While stationed there for the summer, until basic training for his men was completed, Lucius sent her letters, each penned on a sheet of papyrus, rolled up, tied with a thread, wax on the knot, stamped with his seal, posted by messenger. Letter after letter he wrote.

She never wrote back.

12

The destiny of Rome was to rule the world, a destiny first espoused by its founders, then by its soldiers, later by its philosophers, and now that destiny has been bred into the citizenry for so long it has become a religious belief, perhaps the most fervent of all their beliefs. And looking down from Olympus, a pantheon of gods practiced their gamesmanship, move by move, to providentially bring that destiny to pass.

Shouldering the weight of its destiny, Rome's back grew strong. She became a nation of warriors. Each citizen was required to serve when and where the Empire needed him. Military service was also a prerequisite for civil service, a soldier needing to serve at least ten campaigns before he could hold public office.

Campaigns were for the purpose of conquest, subjugating their enemies, and expanding Rome's boundaries by taking the enemy's territory. Taking territory, though, proved easier than holding it. There were flare-ups on the Frontier, winds of war that fanned embers in the far reaches of the Empire, embers that had smoldered for generations, now bursting into sudden flame. Usually one legion was enough to stamp out the wildfires. Sometimes two. Seldom more.

The fire now sweeping across the Frontier was in Gaul, the

land north of Italy and west of the Rhine. The Gallic tribes had been pushed farther and farther north ever since the campaigns of Julius Caesar, but they were a stiff-necked people, and they chafed under the Roman yoke.

The general spearheading the campaign in Gaul was Servus Alba Decimus Germanicus, a soldier who had distinguished himself in battle, with the scars to prove it. Having heard of Lucius's skill in using the lay of the land for military advantage, he summoned him.

Having apprenticed in the craft of cartography, Lucius not only knew geography, he understood its importance. He knew which coastlines were suitable for harbors, which were not; which lands were good for growing, which for grazing; where cities would naturally spring up, and where existing ones, solely because of their geography, were destined to wither away.

He also knew its military importance. "Geography determines strategy," he had been taught. In many cases, geography *was* the strategy. A strategic hill could control an entire valley. A narrow mountain pass could be either an army's strongest defense or its Achilles' heel. A small stretch of marsh could bog down an army long enough for enemy archers to decimate their ranks and dispirit those who remained. He knew, almost instinctively, how the incline of the terrain affected the time it took for an army to advance and the tax it levied on the strength of its soldiers. He knew, from geography, how long it would take to attack a fortress, what siege engines would be needed and where they should be placed, how many troops would need to be dispatched and for how long.

"We cannot continue to expand our borders," Lucius told Decimus emphatically, walking to the map on the wall. "Our troops are stretched to the limit, from Britannia," and he took his wooden pointer and touched the island, "across the northern Frontier," and he swept his pointer over the Roman-held border, "all the way to the East, down to Africa and across its northern provinces."

"Our destiny is to rule the world," stated the general in a tone that implied a lapse of some kind on the centurion's part.

"Our destiny is killing us. We have a hundred fifty thousand soldiers. For all *this*. And we're pushing north into Germania as if we had endless resources. And for what?"

"For as long as it takes."

"Why?"

"Because the Huns keep fighting us, relentlessly, generation after generation."

"Why?"

"To conquer us, of course."

Lucius slowed the pace of his words, giving each its space. "Perhaps they fight to keep *us* from conquering *them*."

The statement took the general off guard, and he pondered it. "What do you propose?"

"A wall."

"A *what*?"

"Here," he said, pointing. "If there was a *man-made* boundary, made by their enemy, an enemy they feared. A wall. A wall that stretched across our border, fortified with troops. Here, west of the Rhine. And here, south of the Danube."

"It would take generations to build something like that."

"We have *fought* for generations. We take no casualties when we build; we do when we fight."

"It *would* keep them out," Decimus admitted.

"And us in. If we had a permanent border, it would announce to the world that this is as far as we intend to go. No farther."

"No farther?" the general questioned. The centurion's logic strained his thinking.

"The East, sir, is mostly desert," said Lucius, pointing to it on the map. "All we get from the East is incense and spices."

"Our women love them."

Lucius let the remark pass. "South of our coastal provinces in Africa is desert. The Northeast is tundra, a frozen desert. What kind of world is *that*? And who wants to go there to rule it?"

The centurion's logic had gained a foothold. Other officers, though, were waiting for an audience, and the rest of the conversation would have to wait. "At my meeting with the officers, tomorrow," he said, abruptly changing the subject, "I would like you to tell them what you told me earlier, about geography, how to use it to our advantage. Your thoughts intrigued me." He paused, somewhat awkwardly. "And this other, for now . . . keep it between us."

"If it is your will, it is my command."

The general smiled and draped a paternal arm around the younger man's shoulder as he walked him to the door. "It was a kind providence of the gods to bring you to Caesarea."

"A good destiny to you, General."

"And to you, Centurion."

As Lucius went about the work of preparing his men for the Frontier, Mary went about the work of another kingdom, on a different frontier, nurturing the growth of the church that had taken root in Jerusalem. She worked alongside her dear friend, Salome, and with Jesus' mother and the others who served the emerging church, which had burgeoned from the impassioned sermon Peter had preached after Pentecost. On that day, three thousand were added to their numbers. The converts were a cross section of society: Jew and Gentile, rich and poor, slave and free, male and female, young and old.

It was a joyful chaos.

But it was still chaos.

The sudden and spectacular growth came as a surprise to the relatively small group of Jesus' followers that had remained in Jerusalem after his death. The work that needed to be done was overwhelming. The eleven disciples organized smaller fellowships that met in homes, where they trained overseers to nurture the growth of the new believers. They taught, led worship, and administered the sacrament that Jesus had inaugurated at the last supper he had shared with them.

The women of the church, meanwhile, led by Mary, Jesus' mother, and a number of those who had followed Jesus before his death, discipled the women and children, teaching them about Jesus: who he was, what he did, what he taught, why he died, and where he was now—seated at the right hand of the Father in heaven. And this they stressed most emphatically: that he was coming back from heaven to establish his kingdom here on earth, and that they all must be watchful and prayerful, for he had told them he would be coming soon.

The women moved among the chaos with grace, serving the poor, taking care of widows, looking after orphans. There was a daily serving of meals for widows, where both the men and the women took part, ladling soup into the bowls of those standing in line and tearing off chunks of hearty bread, still warm from the oven of a newly converted baker who had dedicated his business to serve the needs of the church. So many shopkeepers, merchants, landowners, butchers, and bakers not only came to believe in Jesus but came to believe they could serve him *through* their businesses. Nothing was held back. They gave freely, willingly, cheerfully. And somehow, miraculously, it was enough. It was enough to take care of the needs. And it was enough to take care of them.

Mary's daily life was broken up and given to others—a

smile, a hug, a story, a shoulder to lean on or to cry on. From the bread of such kindnesses, people took and ate. And when they left her presence, they went away warmed and filled.

Lucius, meanwhile, was in the training yard, drilling the recruits under his command, most of whom were raw. Today it was hand-to-hand combat. He drilled them, eight at a time. Each was given a wooden shield, woven with willows, twice the weight of the one they would carry into battle. And each was given a wooden sword, a little under two feet long, again, twice the weight of the ones they would fight with. Behind the men were posts that had been driven into the ground, standing six feet high. The size of a Hun. Roman soldiers were shorter. And they were slighter. Because of that, they had to be quicker, they had to be smarter, they had to be better.

The post stood in the ground as the enemy. They were to assault him, delivering blows to its head, its sides, its legs, its ankles. And they were to do it with all their strength, in full fury.

"Watch your enemy," Lucius called so all the men could hear. "Watch his every move. As he raises his sword—which is twice the length of your own—he will hold it thus." Lucius lifted his own sword, high and to one side of him, and held it there. "When he is on the upswing, that is when you strike. Short, quick jabs," he said, demonstrating how.

He held his hand flat toward his men. "A palm's length is all it takes. His organs, front and back, are just a palm below the skin." He sheathed his sword and used his body to illustrate. "His heart," he said, touching his hand to his heart, "his lungs, his stomach, his kidneys, liver, they are all only *this* far from the tip of your sword. That is all you need to fell him. Once felled, finish him."

The men nodded. "Go again. No slashing this time, just thrusting."

They tore into their respective posts, unleashing the fury of Rome, grunting as they did, and they kept assaulting the enemy until Lucius intervened.

"Halt!" Lucius called out. "Better. Not yet good, but better. I want to see you feint, parry, jab, jab, jab. Again."

The men stepped quickly, half a step back, full step in, thrusting their swords in rapid succession.

"Enough. Enough!" He took one of the wooden shields in hand. "If your enemy overwhelms you—" he started to say.

"Never," said one of the men under his breath, inciting laughter.

Lucius plowed his shield into him, knocking him off his feet. The man's sword went flying. He tried to shield himself against Lucius's assault, but Lucius was on top of him, driving him to the ground. The recruit strained under the weight, trying to shield himself, reaching frantically to recover his sword.

Lucius jumped to his feet, went for the man's sword, and held it to his throat.

"Never?"

The man lay sprawled on the ground, defeated, ashamed, silent.

Calmly but firmly, Lucius spoke. "You say nothing, because a dead man does not speak." No one spoke, no one moved. The man nodded. "You learned something, I trust," Lucius said. The man was slow to find words. Lucius wasn't. *Something? Anything?*

"Never let go of my sword?"

"Then why did you?"

"I, eh, I . . ." but he couldn't answer, just shook his head.

"Because you took your eye off your enemy."

"I didn't know—"

"*What* didn't you know?"

"That you were my enemy."

"Get up." The man got up, and Lucius got in his face. "What is your name?"

"Silvanus Trajan Antiochus."

"Silvanus Trajan Antiochus, I am the worst enemy you will ever face. When you go into battle, you will go prepared, or you will not go at all. Treat every drill, every day, not only as if *your* life depended on it, but the life of the soldier to the right of you." He looked at the soldier to the man's right. "The left of you." And he turned to the soldier on the man's left. "Look at *them*. In the eye." The soldier looked at the one, the other. "Tell *them* they will not be coming home, tell *their families* they will not be coming home. Because you, Silvanus Trajan Antiochus, *you* took your eye off the enemy."

"Get your sword," he said. Turning to the others, he spoke. "A day will come—and it *will* come—when you *will* be overwhelmed in battle . . . no matter how close an eye you have on the enemy. On that day you will rise again, to fight again, so that one day you can go home again. You will survive that day because you prepared for that day. Because you trained *harder* than your enemy, *longer* than your enemy, *more often* than your enemy. That is the reason you will survive. The *only* reason."

He took one of the men nearby and used him for an opponent. "If you are knocked to the ground, shield yourself, looking for an advantage." Lucius picked up a sword and dropped to the ground, covering himself with his shield. "If his shins are without greaves, your best strike is there," he said, slicing at the back of the soldier's ankles. "Sever the tendon, and he will fall. Second best strike is the shins. A strong slash against them or a jab, either."

Lucius threw away his sword. "And should you be separated from your sword, smash your hobnails against those shins. Coil yourself like a spring," he said, so doing, "then propel yourself into him, knocking him off balance." Lucius shot upward with such force that it knocked the soldier back. "And charge him with your shield until he falls backwards." The soldier fell to the ground. "Once felled," instructed Lucius, "fall upon him like a badger, all teeth and claws." He fisted his fingers as if holding a dagger. "Savage him with your dagger, to his face, his neck, his chest." His motions were swift and unrelenting. He bolted upright, and the soldier struggled to his feet.

He turned to Silvanus. "Redeem yourself."

He took the man's sword and tossed it aside. "Your enemy has knocked the sword from your hand. And your dagger, you buried it in a bush-faced Hun. But it was not a lethal blow, and he continued to fight with your dagger still in him." All Silvanus had was his shield. Lucius burst upon him, sending him reeling to the ground. He shielded himself, coiled himself, propelled himself. But Lucius stepped to the side, and the man fell over himself headlong.

"Again." Silvanus took the same position, shielding himself. This time, Lucius took a wooden sword and waled against his shield. He coiled, propelled himself, and knocked Lucius backwards. But in doing so, he let down his guard. Lucius rushed him, and pushed the tip of his sword against the man's chest.

"Again." Again Silvanus fell to the ground, again he shielded himself, again he crouched. This time, though, he kicked Lucius's shin with his boot, causing him to drop his shield and grab his leg. As he did, Silvanus rushed at him. He fell backwards with Silvanus on top of him, pummeling him with his shield, over and over and over again. Lucius finally wrestled the shield away and threw it to one side. The soldier hovered over him, his chest heaving, his face dripping with sweat, when suddenly he realized what he had done. He stood and extended his hand, helping his superior to his feet.

Lucius turned to the others. "Remember his name. Silvanus. Trajan. Antiochus. And should he be to the right of you in battle, or to the left . . . consider it your good fortune."

13

With pointer in hand, Decimus addressed his officers in the war room, explaining their mission.

"Gallic tribes have made forays over the Alps, plundering our villages in the foothills. Afterwards, they retreat over the mountains, return to their own villages, wait until winter has passed, then make the trek all over again. Each time they push farther into the peninsula."

He turned to a large map on the wall behind him. "Our mission is to replace four centuries of the 14th Legion, here, on the Danube. Two of ours, from Caesarea; two from Carthage. We will sail to the coast, where the western flank of the Alps slopes toward the sea, joining the Carthaginians at Massilia." He pointed to the coast, then to the Alps. "We will march around them, routing any Gauls along the way." Then he pointed to places on the map. "Massilia, Gaul, Germania. Any questions?"

In Jerusalem, Peter stood in a large room, where leaders of the church were meeting, and delivered the orders that he and the other disciples had heard from Jesus before he was taken from them into the clouds.

"'And do not ask about times or eras,' he told us. 'The Father has providentially set those in place, by his own authority. Wait,' he told us. 'Wait for the Holy Spirit.'" The disciples were sitting on the floor, along with the women who had followed Jesus, all at rapt attention. "He will guide you and direct you." Several of them nodded in agreement. "True to his word, the Holy Spirit came. And when he came, he came with power, with signs and wonders, with dreams and prophetic words, the ones Joel spoke of. And before Jesus was taken up, in fact, the very moment before—he told us what we were to do. 'Be my witnesses.' Told us where we were to go. 'Start here,' he said. 'In Jerusalem. Then go out from here, to Judea. Past Judea, to Samaria. And do not stop until you reach the remotest parts of the earth.

"'Go,' Jesus commanded us. And he promised he would be with us as we go . . . with us even to the ends of the earth."

Peter paused. "That is the map. Those are our orders. He was faithful to his word. Let us be faithful to ours."

He looked from face to face to face, until he had looked at each of them. From the expressions on their faces, he could tell they were determined to do so.

In the same war room where the general and his officers were assembled, Lucius stood to address them.

"I have been asked to talk about geography as strategy." He paused. "If our history has taught us anything, it is this: Terrain is more important than courage."

Skeptical, the others cut their eyes toward one another.

"An overstatement, I know, but not by much, as our own history has taught us. Recall the stories, the military stories, and Varus comes to mind. A name every Roman soldier would like to forget. He commanded an army of three legions—the 17th, 18th, and 19th, along with tradesmen and auxiliary staff. They were camped at the River Weser. Here." He pointed to the river on the map. "They had been there for the fall, and

Varus had planned to lead them to quarters that would shelter them during winter. But Arminius, the Hun who had become a soldier of Rome and a confidant to Varus, through a clever ploy lured him off course, taking him through unfamiliar territory, through terrain that was dark and densely forested, a maze of streams, marshes, and bogs that is known as—" and he pointed to the map—"the Teutoburg Forest.

"The column stretched for miles as it slogged its way through the overgrowth. Then came the storm. A violent downpouring of rain that mired our soldiers in the mud, sucking at their sandals. Their wooden shields, now sodden and heavy. Their bowstrings, now too wet to use. Our men were exhausted, disoriented, and dispirited.

"The Huns hit the rear of the column first. They rose from nowhere, from ravines where they had lain in wait, from behind trees, outcroppings of rock, storming down the hills. They struck with javelins first. Not throwing them but jabbing them. Just beyond the reach of our swords. Our soldiers could not retreat, because of the swamp on one side of them. They could not advance, because of the densely treed hills on the other side.

"Rome had better soldiers, more courageous soldiers, with better training, better weapons. The Huns defeated them all, soldiers as well as civilians. Twenty-five thousand went into the forest; a handful escaped to tell the story. Those who were not slaughtered, either fell on their swords or surrendered. Those who surrendered were taken to a shrine in the forest, where they were burned alive as a sacrifice to their gods."

Lucius put his pointer on the table.

"How could this have happened?" he asked. "The Huns knew how to use the terrain to their advantage; we did not." Then, with emphatic gestures, he stated: "That will *not* be the fate of *our* soldiers. I swear by all the glory amassed behind us, by all the glory that lies before us: We will *know* the land of our enemies, and we will *use* the land of our enemies . . . to *our* advantage."

Having so roused their attention, he taught them what he had learned as a boy, poring over the stories shelved away in the library at Alexandria. There he had studied the campaigns of Caesar into Gaul, memorized his strategy, his tactics, his way with his men. In that library, his imagination had taken him across distant shores to faraway lands, all the while preparing him for such a time as this.

On this day, Mary was walking down the street with children; she had once dreamt of having her own, but never did. Now a child on each arm, clinging to her, stepping and skipping to keep stride with her, almost as if they were dancing. It was a walk she had once imagined taking but never had . . . until now. The lightness of their spirits lifted hers as they flit from one moment to the next in an endless field of moments, dappled by the late-afternoon sun.

With them in that field she had no wants, no needs. There was nowhere else in the world she wanted to be, no one else she wanted to be with. The children adored her. Her eyes were like mirrors that saw only the beauty in them and reflected it back to them so that they saw it, too. It made them feel beautiful in a way they had never felt before.

When the children went home, though, the moment twilighted away and was gone. Now she was alone. And alone was when she realized that moments like this were not enough. When she was alone at night in her room, as she was now, that realization became sharper, clearer; and the pain that came with it, more acute.

She got out of bed, knelt to pray.

"I love you, Jesus. More than life itself. I pray I could love you even more. Grant that I would love you today more than I did yesterday. More tomorrow than I do today. More the day after tomorrow than tomorrow. And may I live that way, every day of my life, for the rest of my life, until at last I see you face-to-face and fall into your arms. I miss you so much. So, so much. Come, Lord Jesus. Please. And quickly."

A knock on the door brought her to her feet. It was Salome, with a letter in hand. Mary sat in bed next to the small lamp and read it.

She treasured every letter Lucius had sent her, every *word* of every letter. But at the same time she loved his words, she feared them. Not *them* really. Rather, she feared the inky well from which they had been drawn—that place called love, where the spills could be blotted but the stains were permanent. She had loved other men, or so she thought at the time. They all had their own words; flattering words, all of them; kind words, some of them; promising words, a few. But all the words in the end betrayed the promises they had made, the kindnesses they had offered, the flatteries they had whispered. She had learned to protect herself from the onslaught of such words, building a wall around her heart, a trench around the wall, and barricades around the trench.

Jesus' words to her were different. Because of those words, she opened her heart to him.

Lucius's words were also different. And letter by letter, their legions breached those barricades. She would reread his letters at night by the soft glow from the wick of an oil lamp. She had not written back because she feared a letter from her would only fan the embers. Better to say nothing and let the fire die than to enflame a passion that could never be.

She broke the seal on the scroll and unfurled it.

I write one last time, Mary, wondering why? Why do you not write? A word would mean so much. Is your heart so impoverished of feelings that there is not even a crust you could spare a starving man?

Your Jesus, who once seemed so near to me in Jerusalem, where I bowed before his cross, now seems so far from me in Caesarea, where I am bound for the Frontier. I hear nothing from him, nothing from you. And the ache of that is greater than I can bear.

You have said he is coming back, but *when?*

Soon, you say.

I cannot steer a course from such a setting.

And what about *you?* What if Jesus doesn't come back soon? What if he tarries? A lifetime could pass. What then? What of all the years wasted in the waiting? Of all the love that could have been but never was? What then, Mary?

Answer me, if you can.

Even if you cannot, I will still be yours,

forever and always,

Lucius

It was shorter than any letter he had written. More direct. And with a tone of finality.

That night she wrote back.

14

Part of the legion's training involved swimming. Every recruit was required to learn, if he had not already learned. In the course of his military service, he would almost certainly need it, whether he found himself on the open sea or on an inland lake or on some of the large rivers he would have to cross.

It was an end-of-the-day routine, when Lucius jogged with his men to the beach. And it was an everyday routine. He had them swim parallel to the shoreline. Antonius led them. Lucius stayed behind for the handful who couldn't swim, one of them being Massina.

"When we are at sea," he told them, "if we get caught in a tempest's rage, your ship could go down. I don't want you going down with it. The sea favors the strongest swimmers. That is what you will become. Understood?"

The men nodded.

"*Understood?!*"

"Yessir!" they responded, in unison.

"Wade to the waist."

The men waded on tentative legs, then turned. The water lapped them, but it was of no consequence. But then a wave of some consequence curled, crashing against their backs. All lost their footing, a couple of them slipping underwater. They came up gasping for air. Massina, caught in a current, paddling furiously, like a floundering child, churning the water, his eyes filled with fear. Lucius waded out to him, showing the man how deep it was. Massina stood up, sheepish and shivering.

"You swim like a dog," said Lucius, dismissively.

"Yessir."

"Don't."

"No, sir. I mean, yessir. I won't anymore swim like a dog."

"Don't slap the water," Lucius said, demonstrating by slapping the surface several times. "Pull, as you would an oar." He reached for a handful of water and pulled it toward him. "Right, then left. Right, left. Watch." He swam a half-circle around them, and they wheeled around to watch. Lucius was behind them now, only his head above water, treading the sea with his arms to stay afloat. "We will do this one at a time. Massina first."

Massina stretched his arms in front of him, trying to summon the courage to take the plunge. "Go," said Lucius. The young man bent his knees but hesitated. "Now!"

Massina dove headlong toward Lucius, slapping at the water.

"Pull your oars!" Lucius said, and he tried to comply. "Lengthen your reach!" Massina obeyed the best he could, looking up to get his bearings. But he swallowed water as he did and panicked, flailing his arms. The others watched nervously. Lucius continued to tread water. They were surprised he did not help. Massina went under. The men watched in horror, looking to Lucius to do something, but he just waved the men back.

Massina shot to the surface, coughing, only to find he was in shallow water. Lucius stopped the motion of treading water and stood, revealing that he had been simply crouching in the shallows to make them think he was in deeper water. The others breathed a collective sigh of relief, and Lucius extended his hand to steady him.

"You were in no danger, save the danger of your fears." He turned to the others. "Fear is a soldier's greatest enemy. Whether you find yourself overwhelmed by the sea or by the enemy, do not panic. It will not end well for you, or for your comrades."

"Try this," he said, demonstrating the arm movements. "It is not as fast a stroke, but it is a steady one, and it will keep your head above water. Think of the way a frog pushes himself through the water." And this seemed to register. "Try it."

They practiced the arm stroke, standing up. One pushed off toward Lucius, the others followed. Lucius was impressed.

"Good! Keep it up!"

They swam to him and, to his surprise, passed him and kept going. A swell lifted them and pushed them back. They turned, fearful, and swam toward shore. As they did, Lucius counted heads.

One missing.

His eye caught a churning in the water. He swam with all his strength, tearing at the sea. The far-off slap of a hand. He swam faster, harder. Fingers breaking the surface, frantically. The others were on the shore, watching. The hand disappeared. Lucius dove. For a few agonizing seconds, nothing.

Lucius shot to the surface, the man's hand in tow. It was Massina, and he wasn't moving. Lucius kicked hard, pulling at the water with his one free hand. Kicking, pulling, kicking, pulling. The others waded in to help. The carried him and plopped him on the beach. He wasn't breathing. Lucius took his limp arm, pulling him up. As he hefted Massina's bulk onto his shoulder, the man folded over it, lifelessly. Lucius jumped, and Massina flounced against his back.

Then he coughed, expelling the sea from his lungs. He

choked, coughed again, and more of the sea spilled out. Lucius let him down, and the others eased him onto the sand. He sat in a heap, his eyes glazed, his chest heaving. Finally, Massina caught his breath and returned to himself.

He looked up, saw Lucius bent over, holding his knees and coughing. Lucius stood erect, trying to catch his breath. Massina lifted his hand to Lucius, expressing his gratitude.

Lucius lifted his in return, along with a nod.

As a training exercise, the soldiers in Lucius's command had set up camp outside the city. While his men were enjoying the camaraderie around the campfire, Lucius was in his tent, reading by lamplight.

A messenger arrived at camp with a packet of mail and one post addressed: Centurion Lucius Titus Alexander, Caesarea. A soldier directed the man to Ashuk, who accepted the letter and brought it to Lucius's tent. He knew it must be a letter from Mary, and that made him happy, because he knew it would make his master happy, and he had not been happy since he left Jerusalem.

"A letter!" exclaimed Ashuk. "I have a good feeling."

"Are *you* going to read it, or should I?" Lucius said, jokingly.

"You." He handed Lucius the letter and stood there, waiting for him to read it.

"Shall I read it to you?"

"I would like that."

"Go. Now."

Ashuk bowed, and he left.

Lucius broke the seal, and he opened his heart, his very vulnerable heart, to her words.

Dear Lucius,

I am sorry I have not written. It is not due to an impover-
ishment of feelings, I assure you. How I wish we had met years
ago. So many nights I lay on my bed wondering about the life
we could have shared. Wanting that life so bad. Aching for it.

I do love you, Lucius. It took me a long time to admit it,
an even longer time to say it. But I am saying it now because
I want you to know it. I also want you to know this. There are
right loves that come at wrong times. Loves that cannot be.

It has nothing to do with you, Lucius. It has everything to
do with the times we are living in.

The time is short, and much needs to be done to prepare for
Jesus' return. If you worry that he may tarry, worry not that the
years spent waiting for him will be wasted. Mine won't, anyway.
Nor will my love. I have no desire to go to Rome, as you do. But
should I go there one day, I am certain its glory will pale beside
the glory I have seen, spilling everywhere, onto everyone, Jew
and Gentile alike, male and female, slave and free.

I have seen so much the past few years.

I wish you could have been with him to see it, too.

I wish you could be with me to see it now.

Eagerly awaiting his return,

Mary

He paused a moment, the way one pauses after a sudden
and unexpected blow to the stomach. Not what he had expected.
Certainly not what he had hoped for. He walked out of the tent,
the letter crumpled in hand, and joined his soldiers. He took
no warmth from the fire and no joy from the revelry. In spite

of their company, he felt something he had never experienced before.

Loneliness.

He had not known it in his childhood, nor had he known it in his adulthood, until now. In his childhood, he was surrounded by scrolled stories, shelved beside one another, stories that filled his imagination with nobility in duty, bravery in battle, endurance in hardship, honor in sacrifice, joy in triumph, and, overarching all of those ideals, the glory of Rome.

In his adulthood, he was surrounded by the camaraderie of his men. Side by side, marching down a Roman road. Shoulder to shoulder, maneuvering on the field. They shared meager meals around campfires, along with small talk, wagers on trivial things, and sarcasms that sometimes led to fists but never to swords. They also shared a communal wineskin that was passed one to another as each drank in soothing fermentations of home.

But this night, around this campfire, thoughts of home were far from him.

"A drink, sir?" asked Ashuk, offering the bloated skin of wine.

Lucius raised the skin and took a long pull. He let Mary's letter fall into the fire, turned from the radius of warmth, and walked into the night.

He walked with the slightest of limps, gingerly favoring the loneliness within. The ache was like a bone shattered in battle that had never quite healed, leaving him with pain sometimes so stabbingly sharp he nearly buckled when he put his full weight on the tender place where her absence was.

As Lucius walked away, he prayed. "I have asked only one thing of you, God. And this one thing you have denied me.

Why? Why do you put a feast before a starving man, to see, to smell, to taste, then pull away the food?"

The tempest within him now raged.

"Say something, *anything*! If you are there, *show yourself*! Every citizen has the right to appeal to Caesar. Am I less than that in your eyes, less than one of them?

"If so, you are less than one of the gods in mine. How are you different from them with their torturous pastimes they pass off as fate?"

Mary lay in bed, Lucius's letters beside her, the room dark, save for the warm glow from the oil lamp by her bedside. As the lamp flickered, it threw shadows on the walls. As she watched, the shadows, shy as they were, seemed to be dancing. A flame, and they embraced. A flicker, and they parted. Anxious in the parting, she thought, passionate in the embrace. Together. Apart. Together. The flicker dimmed, the shadows shrank, the spell broke.

She turned to the earthen lamp, touched her fingers to her tongue, and extinguished the wick.

15

B asic training was over. Only one duty remained. The *sacramentum*.

The *sacramentum* was a sacred oath that every soldier pledged. It was an oath of loyalty, first to the emperor, to the citizens of Rome, to their military superiors, and finally to their fellow soldiers. In doing so, the soldier bound himself to serve the emperor exclusively. In return, the emperor bound himself to them, promising reward for faithful service in terms of land, money, and other gifts, according to the service they had rendered.

The oath was formal, solemnly spoken in a communal setting with their superiors and fellow soldiers. A variation of the oath was given less formally among the soldiers themselves. It was this *sacramentum* that Lucius and his men had gathered to pledge.

Lucius had mustered his eighty men into formation. They stood before him, steadfast in their commitment, not just to the emperor or to Rome or even to their legion, but to him.

Centurions were the backbone of the army. Every legionnaire knew that and respected that. If they were prepared for battle, it was their centurion who had prepared them. If they survived the battle, he was a big reason why. And whatever

victory they won, credit in large measure went to him. He was
the one who drove them the hardest, protected them the fierc-
est; first to lead the charge into battle, last to leave the field in
retreat. He was the soldier they all aspired to be; the man they
aspired to be; the friend.

"I, Lucius Alexander Titus, bind myself to you, my com-
rades, unto death.
I will not forsake you, for fear or for flight.
Nor will I leave my place in your ranks,
Save to retrieve my weapon, or to strike the enemy,
Or to save a comrade."

His words almost shook the ground beneath them, such
was their force. And he spoke with such resolve that it not
only ennobled them where they stood, it emboldened them for
whatever they would face on the Frontier.
Lucius waited as Antonius came and stood beside him.

"I, Antonius Crassus Scipio, bind myself to you, my com-
rades, unto death.
I will not forsake you, for fear or for flight.
Nor will I leave my place in your ranks,
Save to retrieve my weapon, or to strike the enemy,
Or to save a comrade."

Next came Massina, standing beside them both.

"I, Massina, the Syrian, bind myself to you, my comrades,
unto death.
I will not forsake you, for fear or for flight.
Nor will I leave my place in your ranks,

Save to retrieve my weapon, or to strike the enemy,
Or to save a comrade."

Then another.

"I, Silvanus Trajan Antiochus, bind myself to you, my comrades, unto death.
I will not forsake you, for fear or for flight.
Nor will I leave my place in your ranks,
Save to retrieve my weapon, or to strike the enemy,
Or to save a comrade."

Then came Sergius. After him, Flavius. Then another. And another. Until all of them had spoken. And thus the ties that bound them as one were knotted and cinched.

In Jerusalem, another *sacramentum* was being shared.

Peter stood behind a table, on which stood a goblet of wine and a plate of unleavened bread. The rest of the disciples, Jesus' mother, Mary, the other women, and a crowd of converts stood in the great room, listening to him.

"On the night in which he was betrayed, our Lord vowed he would not leave us orphans but that he would come for us. Before he left us, he bound us to himself with the most solemn of oaths.

"'Take and eat,' he said, and Peter lifted up the flatbread. "'This is my body, which is broken for you. Do this in remembrance of me.'" He broke off a piece and shared it with the person closest to him. "So share it with one another."

The bread passed from hand to hand, each person breaking off a piece and placing it in the mouth of the person next to them. When it had traveled through the crowd, Peter spoke again.

"In the same way, after the meal, he took the cup and said, 'Take and drink, this is the new covenant of my blood, shed for you for the forgiveness of sin. Do this in remembrance of me.'"

He took the cup and passed it to the same person. He, in turn, spoke solemn words to the woman next to him, then tipped the cup so she could drink. And so passed the cup until the last person had received the sacrament.

The soon-to-be deployed troops spent their last day enjoying the city that many of them would never again see. Most offered sacrifices in the Temple of Venus, a strikingly beautiful deity, revered by Romans as the goddess of the sea and protector of the seafaring. Although Lucius did not believe in the gods, he accompanied his men as a show of solidarity. Together they brought offerings of incense, wine, cakes, and various animals for sacrifice, from the most unceremonious of pigs, squealing as it tried to wriggle free of its fate, to the most ceremonious of oxen, sure-footed and stately, adorned with garlands on its head and gilding on its horns.

With their offerings behind them, the soldiers took to the baths for one last plunge into the deep end of the pooled pleasures they would be leaving behind. The baths were public, for everyone to enjoy. As such, they represented the purest expression of democracy in the Empire. Young and old, rich and poor, male and female, slave and free, all were welcome. And all, at least for the brief time they came together under its dome, were equal.

Public baths in the Roman Empire, especially in the larger cities, were vast complexes that spanned ten, twenty, thirty acres, sometimes more. Under one roof, their patrons could enjoy massages and baths, work out with weights, wager on sporting events, shop, eat at their restaurants, read in their libraries, admire art in their galleries, lounge in their gardens, listen to lectures in their courtyards, or indulge themselves with prostitutes, who led them away to brightly colored but dimly lit rooms, redolent with incense.

The bathhouse Lucius entered had a threshold with the words *BENE LAVA* inlaid with small squares of tile. He took off his sandals, and a servant put them away for safekeeping. Another servant took his clothes, handing him a Mediterranean sponge and a towel. A number of his men were getting massages, their bodies slathered with aromatic oil. After a good rubdown, the attendant used a *strigil,* a curved metal instrument with a wooden handle, to remove the oil before he patted down the skin and dried it off with a towel.

The main pool sat under a domed enclosure. As the steam rose, it condensed, trickling down the curvature of the structure to gather in gutters, where it was channeled away. It was designed this way to keep the cool droplets from falling onto bathers.

Wrestlers squared off at the far end of the pool, where others were lifting weights. At this end, a few wandering minstrels piped their music lightly so as not to disturb the conversations that were going on everywhere around them. Lucius stood, taking all this in. As he did, his most ambitious soldier approached him. His name was Flavius, and he came with a smile.

"Is it true what they say, that at the bathhouse we leave our rank at the door?"

"So I have been told," said Lucius.

"Spar swords with me?"

"I am ten years your senior," Lucius replied dismissively.

Flavius turned to the soldiers who had begun to circle them. "A riddle of a man stands before me." Then he turned to Lucius. "Ten years my senior. Mmm. I wonder. Are you exalting yourself . . . or making excuses for yourself?"

The remark caused his fellow soldiers to snicker, though they were careful not to let the centurion hear. After all, he outranked them, regardless of what the bathhouse traditions were.

"Here," said one of them with two straws in his hand. "The long one gets to be the Roman; the short one, the barbarian." He extended his fist to Flavius.

"I defer to my elder," he said, smiling and bowing.

When the soldiers saw the centurion smiling, they laughed. The hand was now extended to Lucius.

Lucius pulled the straw, which was the short one. The betting began. A soldier threw them swords, and they caught them by the hilts. Once with swords securely in hand, the men stepped back from each other, studying each other's feet, hands, eyes.

"Remember, you are no longer my subordinate," said Lucius.

"And you, no longer my superior."

"Just barbarian against Roman."

As bets were being placed, the men maneuvered for position, stepping into their roles.

"Why do you covet Roman soil?" demanded Flavius.

"It is not soil I covet."

"Then what?"

"Glory."

"Come and take it, if you dare," taunted the soldier, motioning him forward. Bets changed hands again, this time favoring Flavius.

"You can make this easy on yourself," said Lucius.

"How?"

"Surrender," he said with a smile, exciting another round

of laughter and another round of betting, this time in Lucius's favor.

Flavius brought the hilt of his sword to his chest, offering an oath. "Caesar is my only king; the glory of Rome, my only ambition."

Lucius shot him a suddenly serious look. "Say it like you mean it."

This time he shouted. "Caesar is my only king; the glory of Rome, my only ambition!"

"We Huns will rout your soldiers, ravage your daughters, raid your coffers."

"You will have to step over my back to do it," Flavius said as he brandished his sword.

"The backs of your soldiers will pave our way to Rome."

One of the soldiers spoke up. "Battles are won with swords, not words."

Flavius was not the strongest soldier in Lucius's command, nor the swiftest, but he *was* the most cunning. He feinted one way. Lucius jabbed at nothing but air. And with that parry, the contest began. Swords clashed, and the sound of steel sliding against steel rang through the cavernous bath. Those on the massage tables sat up. *Strigils* were laid down. Weights were dropped to the floor. Flutes were lowered.

The match went on for several sweaty minutes, and it seemed as if the contest would end in a draw. But then Lucius, in a masterfully wielded backhand, knocked the sword from his opponent's hand.

Flavius stood before him, defenseless. The circle watched with held breath. Lucius drew near, edging the tip of his sword toward the soldier's throat.

When the tip was inches away, Flavius used his forearm in

an uppercut against the flat of the blade, sending it clanging to the floor.

Lucius turned to retrieve it. As he did, Flavius plunged into him, slamming him to the ground. Lucius's breath was knocked out of him, and he was slow to move. Flavius seized the advantage, pressing his foot firmly against his neck. He held it there a few seconds, constricting the flow of air as the color in Lucius's face changed.

"Yield," ordered Flavius.

But Lucius did not yield. His face turned red.

"For the sake of the gods, yield!"

His face turned blue, his eyes bulged, and the veins in his forehead seemed on the verge of bursting.

Finally one of the soldiers shouted. "Mercy!"

The plea was echoed by several of the onlookers. "Mercy! Mercy! Mercy!"

Flavius stepped away, and the soldiers began settling their bets, some of them congratulating him, patting him on the back.

As they did, Lucius crouched, then charged, throwing his full weight into Flavius, driving him into the pool.

Lucius steadied himself at the lip of the pool. He turned, standing breathless but erect. As the humiliated soldier stepped dripping from the pool, Lucius spoke sternly to his men. "Mercy is the prerogative of emperors, not soldiers. We are the hobnailed boot of Rome, sent to tread on the neck of its enemies. Those who tread lightly will face the same enemy again."

It was a mid-September morning when Ashuk packed his master's belongings into trunks and trundled them to the docks, where ships were being loaded. It had been a restless night for Lucius, and he woke early.

His last day in Caesarea.

His first day in open waters.

Yet the sails within him were not full but slackened. He stood at his window, where he saw the sun rising on one side of the sky and the moon falling on the other. The sun was all fire and heat, as if fresh from the forge; the moon, all coolness and translucence, as if a finished piece of glass. He stood there, without thought. As he did, a great emptiness opened within him. An emptiness he could not name, could not understand, could not overcome.

When Lucius left Caesarea, he made a vow that came from a place so deep within him it was beyond the reach of words. He would never allow himself to be gullible again, bewitched by the words of some dying man he did not know, a man who existed only in other people's stories and in the brief encounter he had with him on that godforsaken day when the veil of heaven parted a moment, and he saw, or thought he saw, something divine spilling out.

Had he seen anything that day? He was certain then. Now he wondered.

Each step took him further from the day when the earth shook beneath his feet. Was it a tremor in his soul he felt that day, some spiritual experience that shook the bedrock certainties upon which his life had been based? Or was it merely the natural shaking of the earth, over which he had imposed some supernatural interpretation?

Regardless, he had walked away from it. Away from faith. Away from hope. Away from even daring to hope again. He had walked away from love, too. Away from ever allowing himself to be vulnerable again, hurt again, humiliated again.

16

Port of Caesarea. Dawn. An auspicious morning, according to the official augur who gave his blessing for the voyage.

Two merchant ships, each carrying a century of soldiers and a full belly of supplies, sat heavy in the water as they pushed off from their moorings. A dock full of gulls took flight after them, darting in and out of the rigging, squawking as they did, hoping some morsel might fall their way as they hovered. None did, and a few at a time peeled off toward land until the last of them were gone.

Before the two keels were out of the harbor, their square linen sails flapped in the breeze, as if the wind were testing them to see how seaworthy they were before snapping them taut and putting them to work. And so, with robust sails, the ships picked up speed, their prows parting the water, smoothly and effortlessly, an endless sea stretching before them. The eastern sun cast great handfuls of freshly minted coins into the sea, which it caught in its scalloped palms and used to pave the way to open waters.

Lucius stood on the foredeck, hands on the railing, the wind in his face. The captain came alongside him and asked, "First time at sea?"

"First in open waters. Other times we hugged shore."

"We usually hug shore, too, but if we are to reach Massilia before winter, we have to take a straight route." Massilia was a port west of Italy where the western end of the Alps sloped to the sea. These two centuries were mustered there to join two other centuries in order to replenish one of the legions that was fortressed on the Rhine. "It is a bold endeavor," he continued. "Pray Neptune does not see it as an affront and stir the sea with his wrath."

Lucius had long shed his boyhood belief in the gods. It was treasonous to deny them, though, so he never spoke of them. And he did not speak of them now.

Ashuk had his head over the rail, throwing up his last meal.

Lucius came by and patted him on the back. "Nothing like the smell of sea for one too long on land."

Ashuk pulled himself back from the rail, trying to steady himself. "Or the smell of land for one too long at sea." Before he could smile, he folded himself over the rail and threw up again.

Below deck, Lucius's men were amusing themselves with knucklebones and other games of chance and feats of strength like wrestling. The mood was ebullient, made more so by an amphora they tilted to pour wine into their tin cups. The occasional creak of timbers in the hull caught their attention. Though no one spoke of it, all felt uneased by it.

The bottom of the hull was full of sand, ballast to steady the ship. Above it was a floor of thick, pine timbers that held the cargo: tents, weapons, equipment, along with supplies for the voyage. Livestock was penned in the hold: sheep, pigs, a cow, along with a tenement of wicker cages, housing chickens to supply them with eggs. But the chickens were on board for more than their eggs, for they held a sacred place in the religion of the Romans.

Romans were a particularly superstitious people, uncertain of the moods of their deities: the gods' longstanding jealousies, their petty power struggles, their short-tempered spats among themselves. They were a covetous lot, too—one eye filled with lust, coveting the wives of mortals as well as those of other gods, the other eye filled with greed, coveting everything from fame to fortune to the finer things of life. Mortals who lived under the jurisdiction of their caprice were always looking for omens and prophecies to help them navigate the uncertain sea of circumstances that determined their destiny. Before a voyage like this one, for example, an augur was consulted to foresee the fate that lay ahead of them, followed by sacrifices to appease the gods that looked down on them.

The captain was an especially superstitious man and brought his own personal augur on board all of his voyages, especially on ventures into open water, ventures most captains were hesitant to take, many of whom would only sail within sight of the coastline.

There were two categories of augurs: those who specialized in discerning signs in the skies and those who specialized in discerning signs from the birds that flew in them. "Taking the auspices" was the term that described what they did. One of those auspices involved chickens. If chickens ate well, it was a good omen. If they stopped eating, it was a bad one. Who knows what the bad was or how bad it would get? It was this ambiguity and the augur's skill in interpreting it that kept these people in business. And business was good.

The moment the captain introduced his augur, Lucius disdained him. Too many trinkets, too many platitudes. Lucius avoided the man and all he was selling. He stood at the rail, his eyes resting on the horizon. The sun was low in the sky, like a peach hanging heavy on the branch, its yellow ripening to deeper yellow, to orange. Then it was gone. A final flourish of orphaned light on the clouds. Pink. Purple. Gray.

As compensation, the sea proffered a moon, pale and demure. Part of the crew stayed above deck to navigate by starlight, keeping the sail trim and the rudder held fast, while Lucius and his men, along with the other sailors, went below for the night.

The hull of the ship was cavernous, the darkness pushed to the periphery by some large oil lamps hung from a beam. Soldiers as well as sailors were drawn to the light to hear the story Lucius was about to read them. It was one of the stories he had savored as a boy. But before he read, he spoke.

"It will be a long voyage. A few stories will shorten it. We will begin at the beginning. Romulus, Remus, twin boys left to die on the banks of the Tiber. Found by a she-wolf, who suckled them. Visited by a woodpecker, who fed them. Or so the story goes," he said with a smile. "As the boys grew, so did their ambitions. And they sought to found a city that would one day rule the world. This much you know. But there is more to the story, which some of you may not know. The brothers, it is said, descended from a prince named Aeneas, a fugitive of Troy after it was burned. The reason he survived was because of his destiny. That destiny was to be the founder of Rome."

Lucius opened a codex. "Herein lies the story—The Aeneid, by Virgil." And, by the soft circle of light that gathered them all, he read.

> I sing of arms and the man, he who, exiled by fate,
> first came from the coast of Troy to Italy, and to
> Lavinian shores—hurled about endlessly by land and
> sea, by the will of the gods, by cruel Juno's remorseless

anger, long suffering also in war, until he founded a
city and brought his gods to Latium: from that the
Latin people came, the lords of Alba Longa, the walls
of noble Rome. Muse, tell me the cause: how was she
offended in her divinity, how was she grieved, the
Queen of Heaven, to drive a man, noted for virtue, to
endure such dangers, to face so many trials? Can there
be such anger in the minds of the gods?

Twilight. Above deck the moon was a cameo in the deep
blue sky. A lone planet shimmering on the horizon. The first
speckling of stars. A steady breeze filling the sail, its proud
chest awash in moonlight.

The story below deck continued. Lucius had a strong voice
but not a dramatic one. He read straightforwardly, without
rhetorical flourish, allowing the writer's words to speak for
themselves.

"Juno now offered these words to him," he said.

Aeolus, since the Father of gods, and king of men,
gave you the power to quell, and raise, the waves with
the winds, there is a people I hate sailing the Tyrrhe-
nian Sea, bringing Troy's conquered gods to Italy:
Add power to the winds, and sink their wrecked
boats, or drive them apart, and scatter their bodies
over the sea.

Above deck the captain consulted the augur.
"How flew the birds today?"
"I saw no birds."

"A good sign, or ill?"
"Birds are first to sense danger. *Always* the first."
The captain was quiet, pensive, his brow furrowed.

As Lucius read, every eye was fixed on him, every neck craned, every ear cupped.

> Neptune, meanwhile, greatly troubled, saw that the sea was churned with vast murmur, and the storm was loose and the still waters welled from their deepest levels: he raised his calm face from the waves, gazing over the deep. He sees Aeneas's fleet scattered all over the ocean, the Trojans crushed by the breakers, and the plummeting sky. And Juno's anger, and her stratagems, do not escape her brother. He calls the East and West winds to him, and then says: "Does confidence in your birth fill you so? Winds, do you dare, without my intent, to mix earth with sky, and cause such trouble, now? You whom I—! But it's better to calm the running waves: you'll answer to me later for this misfortune, with a different punishment. Hurry, fly now, and say this to your king: control of the ocean, and the fierce trident, were given to me, by lot, and not to him. He owns the wild rocks, home to you, and yours, East Wind: let Aeolus officiate in his palace, and be king in the closed prison of the winds." So he speaks, and swifter than his speech, he calms the swollen sea, scatters the gathered cloud, and brings back the sun.

Lucius closed the book, to the groans of his men. "The morrow is best seen with rested eyes. I bid you all a good night."

The morrow came, and all were on deck to see it. The day passed uneventfully. And the next.

Until the fourth.

Something about the fourth day did not seem right. The sail was slack; the sea, like glass. Some of the men had slept fitfully, troubled by nightmares. Not a good sign, according to the augur. He saw no birds in the sky, and he was wary of that as well. He checked the chickens in their cages. The grain in their troughs had not been touched. He hurried to find the captain.

"The chickens have not eaten."

The captain knew what that meant. "Since when?"

"Yesterday."

"Blanket the cages. Tell no one."

The captain moved calmly but purposefully, telling a few of the men to secure the cargo; a few others to check the knots on the rigging; still others to inspect the hull for weak spots. He checked his map, seeing that Crete was not far off.

It was serene the first half of the morning, eerily so. Sailors murmured among themselves, then began speaking to the soldiers. By midmorning, the wind had picked up and worried the sail, with the ropes securing it stretched to their limit. The sky grew dark, like a pall. The sea frothed with whitecaps, jostling the ship one way, then another.

"Land!" yelled one of the sailors. All looked up, many moving to the starboard side for a better look; a few were seasick by now, hurling their stomachs overboard.

"Crete!" the captain called triumphantly. "Rudder her way!" he shouted to the men astern. "Turn sail!" he called to the men at the riggings. The wind was driving them shoreward. A hopeful sign, and everyone felt it.

Then came the rain.

It came suddenly; first, a pelting of beads; then the beads becoming needles, piercing their skin. The onslaught was relentless, one volley after another after another. The sky was a clash of titans, their swords striking each other with such fury their sparks lit up the night.

A gust of wind hit the sails, flapping the linen so hard it tore one of the seams.

A great swell of sea slammed against the ship, sending everyone sliding across the deck. The wave swept one of the sailors overboard, his screams drowned out by the howl of wind; another nearly went with him, but he got caught in a tangle of rope that tethered the mast and was saved. As the men regained their footing, a lash of water snapped across their backs, and they all fell forward.

The wind unleashed its wrath, holding nothing back. The mast strained so hard it seemed it would break. "Lower the sail!" shouted the captain. Several of the sailors wrestled the ropes. Once the sail was lowered and tied down, the captain shouted. "Sailors on deck; soldiers below! Make haste!"

There was nothing for the soldiers to do, except ride out the storm. Their only hope now was Neptune. If only he would show favor, plunging his trident into the sea to still the tempest and call on the Winds to harness their fury.

But Neptune had forsaken them. As had the Winds. Even Fortune herself.

Below deck was chaos, the men stumbling, tripping over each other. A frenzy of chickens, beating their wings. A bleating of sheep, sopping wet. A squeal of pigs, slipping in their stall.

A wave washed over the deck, and some of the men below

were slammed into support beams and stores of cargo.

The sea rammed headlong into the side of the ship, almost capsizing it, knocking everyone off their feet. Ropes that held cargo snapped, spilling a stall full of five-foot-long posts. The joints strained but held. As the ship righted itself, a back slosh of debris washed over the soldiers and crashed against everything still standing.

In a desperate attempt to save his men, Lucius opened the gate to the stall that held the pigs and waved to his men—all eighty of them. "Every man, here! Over here!" The men rushed to the stall, slipping and sliding as they came. One by one they made it. Except two. One was sprawled on the floor, unable to get up; the other was unconscious. Lucius went after them, helping one to his feet and bringing him, limping, to the others. The other he dragged by the arm, and the men revived him.

Crammed together, the soldiers could hardly breathe. With each wave their bodies pressed against each other, expelling a collective moan.

The hull strained against the storm. A loud crack, and water sprayed in from a broken seam. The sea threw its heft against the hull, and the wood groaned in trying to hold it back. Seam after seam leaked water.

Lucius's eyes darted from one end of the hull to the other. Water was everywhere, two feet deep now, pieces of wagons and siege engines strewn over the surface. Fence posts were everywhere, floating on the water that was fast filling the hull. The animals were mostly dead, save a few chickens that had flapped their way to higher places. The few craftsmen on board were all dead. The cooks, dead. The augur, dead.

The wind ripped off the hatch to the top deck, screaming into the hold, spitting rain as it did.

The fury had found them.

Lucius looked for some way out, but their fate seemed inescapable. He spotted ropes uncoiled on the water, and an idea lit his eyes. He vaulted over the gate, took his dagger and began cutting lengths of rope. He tossed one into the stall, then another.

"Tie it around your comrade's wrist. Lash the other to one of those posts. Assist each other until the last one is secure."

He continued cutting the rope until everyone had a piece. The final one he cut for himself. The work of securing pieces of wood that would keep them afloat was cumbersome, but they assisted each other with fierce determination until the work was done.

"Follow my lead above deck," Lucius shouted above the roar. The men's eyes were filled with fear. "We will hurl ourselves into the sea, *together.*" He looked into their eyes, resolved. "And *together* we will come out of it."

He saw Massina shivering, his eyes filled with terror, his teeth chattering. He took hold of Massina's timber and held it to his face.

"This is your post. Do not abandon it."

Massina nodded.

Standing next to Massina was Ashuk, his eyes filled with fear. "I cannot swim."

Lucius cut him loose from his timber. Ashuk's eyes widened. Without a word, Lucius lashed his servant's wrist to his own timber.

The centurion led the way up the stairs. A gush of water cascaded on them from the open hatch. They stopped to grip the rail, then climbed as fast as they could before another wave found them.

All were above on a deck now empty, the sailors having been all swept overboard.

Against the wind, Lucius shouted. "A wave drives you

under, hold your lungs till they burn! *Past burning till you feel they will burst!* The wood will take you to the surface! Trust it!"

A blinding light, a deafening crack.

The mast buckling, aflame, falling, crashing.

The strike was observed by the captain in the other boat, the white flash lingering long enough to reveal the ship pitching the men overboard.

A moment later, the ship ran aground on a reef, where a great arm of sea lifted it and crashed it against the rocks, its keel breaking like a twig under a soldier's foot.

Debris was everywhere. Shattered, splintered. Bobbing on the water. Slamming into itself, into the men.

A piece of flotsam hit Lucius's forehead, knocking him out. His face went into the water. Panic on Ashuk's face as he pulled his master's head out of the water, cradling it with his free arm. A splash of water in his face, and Ashuk coughing out the water, losing his grasp as he did. More panic. Struggling to pull Lucius's free arm over the timber.

A wave curled into Silvanus and pushed him under. Deeper. Deeper still. His lungs burning, about to burst. Bubbles seeping from his nostrils. The timber shooting upward with him in tow. Bubbles escaping from his mouth. His head, breaking the surface. A great gasp for air.

Antonius clutching wood, a wave picking him up from behind and tossing him headlong over it.

Flavius plummeting into a valley between swells.

Massina on the periphery, struggling to keep his head above water. Fear on his face. His knot starting to loosen. His hand slipping out.

Lightning made an etching of the coastline.

And in its afterglow, an etching of Massina's post, abandoned.

17

The storm lasted the night. As the night waned, so the storm. The winds fled. The waves tired. The captain peered into the grayness before the dawn.

Remains of the ship littered the sea.

A few timbers with only limp hands above the water. Two timbers had ropes but no hands. One of the men, bludgeoned and lifeless. Another, bloodied but alive.

A shout from the sea. Echoed by another. Men waving their free hands, wildly.

The ship turned its rudder and plowed toward them.

The same men smiling, laughing, cheering. Kissing their timber. Praising their gods.

When the other ship pulled alongside them, one man at a time was thrown a rope with a slipped knot that he pulled over his timber, cinching it tight. The sailors pulled each one to the side of the ship, upward, over the railing, onto the deck.

The rescue took the better part of the morning.

When all were on board, Lucius stood before Antonius for his report. The blood on his forehead had dried. "Your tally?"

"Shy twelve."

Lucius's countenance fell.

"Massina?"

Antonius shook his head.

"I failed him. Failed him before we ever set sail. I should have trained him better, pushed him, harder. I should have—"

Antonius interrupted. "Sixty-eight, sir."

Lucius looked at his men, lying on the deck, exhausted. Some lying facedown, resting. Others lifting their faces to the sky, warming themselves.

"Sixty-eight came out of the sea," said Antonius. "*Together.*"

After the storm the men thought themselves more religious. Lucius merely thought them more superstitious. One thing was certain, though. The bond between them held. And it held fast.

Ashuk cleaned Lucius's wound and dabbed his forehead with oil, wrapping it with cloth when he was finished. "It will be a good scar," he said. "And someday, a good story."

Lucius took off the cloth and tossed it aside. "It will never be a good story."

When the ship docked at the port city of Iepetra on the island of Crete, the men stumbled over themselves to get off the ship and kiss the ground, praising the gods and celebrating their good fortune. Immediately they set off to find the local temple so they could make sacrifices.

Timithius, the other centurion who had made the voyage, got off the ship with Lucius, followed by Ashuk.

"The gods were against us," Timithius said.

"The *sea* was against us."

"And who rules the sea but the god of the sea, Neptune?"

"No one rules the sea," Lucius said. "*No one.*"

"I am going with my men, to the temple. Come. It will do you good."

"I will secure us quarters for the night," he said, "which will do us *all* good."

The centurion left to catch up with his men, and Lucius turned to Ashuk, smiling. "Gods or no, we are lucky to be alive."

Before Ashuk could say anything, Antonius came running toward them, a bedraggled man in tow. "Look what the sea washed up."

"Massina?" The ragged man nodded, and Lucius embraced him. "How, how did—"

"I swam. Like a dog, but I—"

"You survived! Matters not how!" Lucius looked at him, speechless, incredulous. "But how?"

"I held on to my post, like you ordered. But the sea tore it from my hands. I prayed to every god I could think of—Neptune, Mars, Mercury, even Jupiter himself. Nothing. For a long time nothing. Then I cried out—'Jesus of Nazareth! King of the Jews!' Louder and louder. *Jesus of Nazareth, King of the Jews!* Still nothing. When all hope deserted me, I whispered, like this: 'Remember me when you come into your kingdom.' Then *something*. A swell of sea lifted me. It was like . . . like I was cupped in its hand, and it carried me. The next thing I knew I was on the beach, my strength spent, but alive. *Alive!*"

Lucius and Ashuk stood there, amazed.

"It is some story," said Massina, "is it not?"

Lucius had no response, and stood without words.

"It is," said Ashuk, affirming him. "Truly it is."

While the men recovered from the ordeal at sea, they filled their pockets with amulets and tokens of devotion to the gods for the voyage ahead. Lucius and Timithius sought to find a ship and crew willing to transport them to Massilia. Once they did, they stocked it with food and supplies.

The two ships left Iepetra. Before them lay a burnished

shield of sea, hammered by an even wielding of wind. For the rest of the voyage, Fortune was with them, and they sailed without moodiness of sea or inclemency of sky. The ships stopped at island ports along the way, Syracuse in Sicila and Caralis in Sardinia, but, after two months on open waters, the men were weary of it and longed for the solid feel of earth beneath their feet.

Lucius was at the bow, searching the horizon for traces of land. The first trace was a seagull. The gull hovered over the waves, hoping a hand of sea would feed him fish. But the sea was a miser that day. Lucius took a crust of bread from his pocket and tossed it to the bird—a fondly remembered sacrament from his childhood along the coast of Alexandria. The gull swooped to catch it, landing on the railing to swallow it. It moved toward Lucius in swift, bold steps that turned slow and cautious the closer he got. Lucius tore off another piece, extending it, but the gull did not move, save its head, which necked forward and back, forward and back. Lucius pushed the offering toward the bird, which shuttled a step in his direction. Then another. It seemed a stalemate until the gull made a daring move, beaking the bread as it took wing. Lucius smiled. The gull circled back, hung in the breeze next to him, eyeing him, waiting for another crust that never came. Impatient, it curled off to skim the waves.

At last, land came into view.

"Massilia!" shouted the lookout, pointing to a scrawl of coastline, which incited a riot of enthusiasm on deck.

18

Massilia's harbor was a large rock formation shaped like a theater that looked out to sea. The walled city of six thousand was strategic for trade, catering to traffic to and from the west end of *Mare Nostrum* and serving as a gateway to the Frontier, fanning out to Gaul and on to Germany in the northeast. The ships docked in harbor came from the far reaches of the empire—Tyre, Sidon, Numidia, Alexandria, Spain, Italy. And in the town square, signs in shops were written in four languages—Latin, Greek, Aramaic, and Gallic.

Many in Massilia made their living from exports, doing a brisk business in wine, olive oil, and fish, as well as pottery. For this Roman province, though, the backbone of the economy was its trade with the military. Shipyards, where sails were mended and repairs made. Storehouses, where equipment such as weapons and seigeworks was inventoried. Supply houses, where anything for the Frontier could be bought off the shelf, from tents to pickaxes. Stables, where horses and tack were sold. Blacksmith shops, where ironworks could be fabricated. And a hundred other shops, selling everything from common necessities to coveted luxuries.

The city also had a vibrant economy in all things religious.

There were silversmith shops, where images of the gods were for sale, along with amulets to curry their favor. On a hilltop overlooking the city were two temples, one for the cult of Apollo and the other for the cult of Diana. It was a prestigious center for oracles. People of prominence, from wealthy merchants to war-hungry generals, made pilgrimages there, bringing gifts of tribute to gain favor with the gods and with the oracles that spoke on their behalf. Like lesser constellations in the night sky, a dim array of seers and soothsayers was spread throughout the city, sharing what little light they had, or thought they had.

Shortly after the two centuries from Caesarea arrived, they met with the other two centuries that had sailed from Carthage. The four Roman centuries had to travel through the territory of Gaul—not so much a country as an alliance of tribes and families—to reach their assignment on the Danube. The Gauls were a mixed race of Celts and Ligures. They were tall and strong, robust and rough-voiced, with blue eyes and either blond or chestnut hair. Their hair was long; their beards, full. They were also heavy drinkers, which emboldened them for battle.

It would take all winter to pass through their territory, a tenuous journey at best. The day before they left Massilia, the soldiers loaded wagons with equipment and supplies. The first day's march started in the dark chill before dawn. The men were quiet, groggy from a long last night in the city. The only sounds were their boots on the road and the wheels of the wagons that accompanied them. Three centuries led the line of wagons; the fourth brought up the rear.

After an hour, the blackness softened to gray. Soon tethers of pink were flung across the sky, pulling up the sun. The men did not stop, either to eat or to rest, until they had put twenty miles behind them. Scouts rode ahead, looking for signs of renegade bands that might be lying in wait. Midmorning, surveyors rode out, looking for a suitable place to set up camp.

Never did Roman troops sleep under the stars, unprotected. They always set up camp. The Roman camp was without precedent. No army in history had been so strict in its protocol of setting up a fortified camp, without fail, even if it was only for a night. This discipline was carried out in peacetime as well as in times of war.

For two weeks they marched without incident, without even so much as an ill wind against them. One day, one of the scouts galloped back to report his findings. Sensing urgency, the four centurions ran to meet him. The rider dismounted with great eagerness.

"I saw an eagle! At forest edge!"

"How far?" asked Timithius.

"Quarter-march."

"A good omen!" said Timithius. Sightings of eagles were always viewed as good omens, since the eagle was Rome's most esteemed bird. It was so revered that a golden image of one with outstretched wings was placed atop every legionary standard as a reminder of their destiny and a predictor of their fortune.

The centurions met the news with elation. Except Lucius, who stood silent.

As the scout continued his report, eyes from the forest watched. Two scouts, hiding behind an outcropping of rock that was guarded by a sentry of pines. Neither moved. Neither spoke. Crouching low, they peered to tally the ranks of their enemy.

"We should make camp," said Lucius.

"The most auspicious spot would be where the eagle was sighted," said one of the centurions. The others voiced their support.

"We will lose the sun," countered Lucius. Two of the centurions looked to Timithius, but he was silent.

"Double-time," suggested one of them.

"And wear out the men?" snapped Lucius. But nothing he said persuaded them. He took another tack, a more conciliatory tone. "It is a risk."

"The greater risk, as I see it," concluded Timithius, "is to ignore the omen."

The others nodded, and it was decided. The march continued, double-time.

Along the way, a network of spies watched from a distance, studying the procession, one perched in a tall tree, another hiding behind a stand of trees, still another crouched low in a patch of weeds. They communicated with each other with hand signals until the relay reached deep into the forest to a rider who rode to report to the tribe.

As the men marched, the forest to the right of them grew thicker, darker. Shafts of afternoon light filtered through the pines, drawing Lucius's attention. As he watched, a fresh shaft angled through the branches, a distance away, and he thought he saw movement. He waved to two of his scouts and pointed in the direction of the movement. They rode hard to the forest, slowing at its edge, separating, and moving with caution.

One of them saw something suspicious in the shadows and waved the other scout to his side. Together they rode to investigate. Nothing. A sudden movement in the periphery. The scout who saw it whipped around. Again, nothing. The other scout dismounted and studied the ground. Behind a tree, footprints.

He followed them a few feet, but the forest floor was a thatch of pine needles, and the footprints disappeared. He touched the prints and found them fresh. He mounted his horse, and the two reined their horses around, riding as fast as they could back to camp.

19

The centurions saw the scouts riding toward them and were there to greet them when they arrived.

"A handful at most," reported the one rider.

"I say, rout them," said a centurion, "while we have the sun at our backs."

"They know the woods," said Lucius. "We do not."

Timithius weighed the alternatives. "Say nothing to the men." He looked to Lucius. "Where should we make camp?"

He pointed. "There, with the river at our back. One less trench to dig; one less wall to defend."

Camp was set up quickly. The procedure for setting up camp was always the same. First, a spot was chosen that would provide the best defensive position available, on high ground, preferably, with good drainage in case of rain and with as full a view of the landscape around them as possible. Then the walls were constructed, one deep-set log at a time, buttressed on the inside by stepped ramparts; on the outside it was encompassed with a trench, nine feet wide and seven feet deep. Finally, when the tents were all set up, everyone ate. Afterwards, a watch was kept, men who spent the night on the walls, peering into the darkness for any movement, however slight, that might prove hostile. Watchmen were flogged for the slightest dereliction of duty, even killed for more flagrant violations.

Lucius and the other centurions consulted with the surveyors and determined that the best position for their encampment was an open plain, far from the forest. Lucius unfurled a vellum map on the ground and gave instructions to those charged with overseeing construction. Soon the surveyors were laying lines for the walls, and the engineers directed the digging of post holes for timbers and the trenching of a perimeter outside them.

As posts were being planted, Lucius gave instructions regarding the trench around the walls. It was to be dug in the shape of a U, open to the river. When all the walls were up and all the equipment within the walls, he had the trenchers cut into the river, channeling it to form a moat. As the sun sank low on the horizon, it sent shafts of light through the forest, deterring any chance of an attack.

The soldiers had not eaten all day, and Timithius instructed several of his men to cook for them. Soon cauldrons of grain were tripodded over fires—a bubbling mush of corn and oats with handfuls of dried fruit thrown in. The grains were coarse and hearty and boosted morale. After the meal, Timithius gathered them to alert them of the threat, urging a good night's sleep the best preparation for battle, should there be one.

"Double the watch," Lucius told the watchmen assigned to the walls.

As the men slept, the centurions convened in the officers' tent. Inside, they were hammering out a fretwork of strategies. All four stood around a tall table, where a papyrus had been unfurled. Lucius had marked the camp with charcoal, etched in the river, the forest, the road before them and behind them.

He gave the charcoal to Timithius. "Sir."

"We let them come to us. Here," he said, marking the map.

"This is where we will make our stand, three centuries, fighting one at a time. Lucius, your men will lead. At the sound of the horn, the first century falls back and the next one engages. At the sound of the second horn, the second falls back and the third engages. At the same time, the fourth century does a flanking maneuver." He sketched the movement on a page of papyrus.

While the senior centurion was mapping out his strategy, an arrow pierced through the top of their tent, impaling itself on the table. The men recoiled, and another landed behind them. From all over the camp, men shrieked in pain. The officers threw open the tent flap. Several men were hobbling from their tents, bumping into each other, writhing in agony. Lamps were lit, campfires were stirred, and soon the entire camp was awash in light.

As the chaos subsided, Lucius grew angry, his rage seething in his neck, his jaw, his eyes, and gathered in his voice. "Why was there no call from the watchmen?"

As soon as he said this, two soldiers brought a watchman into the tent and dropped him on the ground, two arrows in his chest.

"The others?" asked Lucius.

"Dead."

"Rally the men," ordered Timithius, then paused. "No. They will be expecting that, perhaps *wanting* that. Tend the wounded. First light, we strike."

"A night attack," said one of the centurions. "Cowards."

"Cowards," said Timithius, "or else outnumbered."

The men were wakened early, two hours before the sun, and readied themselves for battle. Before first light, they were already on the field, all in formation, waiting for the enemy to emerge from the woods.

Lucius paced the formation and spoke to his men. "Remember, long swords need a long swing. Bunch them up, and they'll have no room to wield them. One thing more. The oath you made to the emperor, it is the same you made to each other. For today, forget the emperor. Fight for the man to the right of you, to the left of you. It is within no one's power to live long, but it is within everyone's power to live nobly. If this day your life is cut short . . . let it end nobly."

The first of the day's light stole through the trees. As it did, the soldiers could see a silhouetted line deep in the forest. Moving closer. Until their shapes could be seen. Closer still. Until their colors could be seen. Even closer. Until their faces could be seen.

The enemy stepped out of the forest, where they taunted the Romans, lifting their swords in the air, their spears. Chanting. Louder. And then . . .

Silence.

A storm of arrows rained down on Lucius and his men, but they sheltered themselves under their shields, surviving the downpour.

"Archers, fill your bows!" shouted Lucius.

The front line knelt and shielded themselves as the row of archers behind them drew arrows from their quivers and pulled back their bowstrings.

"Let fly!"

With his order, their arrows dropped the enemy's frontline. They again sent their arrows flying. And again, the next line fell.

The enemy charged.

As they drew near, Lucius called to his men. "Stand fast!"

The wall of warriors crashed against their shields. For a

few minutes, the soldiers stood fast, and the line held. As the Gauls drew back their swords, the Romans jabbed and thrusted, jabbed and thrusted. More of the enemy fell.

But the crush of the onslaught pushed the soldiers back, and the formation broke.

Lucius threw himself into the fray, running his sword through his opponent's stomach. Another warrior wielded his mace, bringing it down on him. But Lucius rolled out of the way and, with a backhanded slice, severed the man's tendon. The warrior buckled. Lucius moved over him to finish him off, but as he did, a sudden sword opened his arm. He wheeled around, and, as the enemy drew back his sword to strike, he switched his sword to his other hand and jabbed the man's throat, severing his windpipe.

A javelin hit Lucius's thigh, an arm's length of its shaft exiting the other side. He fell, first to his knees, then on his side. Silvanus stepped in front of him, forming a wall between the centurion and the enemy. He pushed his shield against the onslaught, knocking man after man off his feet, where they were put to a quick end by the swords of other soldiers who had rallied behind their fallen comrade.

The fight was blade against blade, the ringing of steel against steel. The banging of shield against shield. The clanking of mace against helmet.

The perimeter that had formed around Lucius was crumbling. A soldier fell to the right, opening a gap, but as soon as he did, another filled it in. Another fell to the left, but as soon as the gap opened, the soldiers closed ranks.

A warrior slammed his sword against Silvanus's shield with such force that he lost his footing. The enemy was about to finish him when an upward thrust javelin pierced the Gaul's rib cage, and he fell forward, pushing its tip out his back.

Silvanus looked at the bloody shaft, following it to Lucius, who, in the thick of battle, had pulled the javelin out of his thigh and thrust it against the enemy.

A horn sounded the retreat.

The first century fell back, allowing the one behind them to fight. The fresh troops hacked a swath through the enemy like harvesters in a wheat field. They fell like so many stalks, lying on their sides.

A horn sounded the second retreat, and the century fell back, giving way to a fresh group of soldiers, eager to fight. As they engaged the enemy, the fourth century flanked the mish-mash of warriors, maneuvering behind them. The two centuries squeezed the enemy like a tick.

In a final flurry of swords, the battle was over.

The field was thick with smoke and humid with the smell of sweat mingled with blood. Then, as if a beneficent gesture from Mars, the rain began. It was a cleansing rain, rinsing the victors' skin, the acrid sky, the bruised grass, the blood-soaked earth.

Soldiers picked their way through the carnage, making a quick end of the enemy's wounded. Other soldiers tended their own wounded. Still others removed the dead.

Antonius, Silvanus, Massina, and Flavius fanned over the field, searching for their leader. Silvanus stopped. "Over here!"

The men came running, slowing as they saw him.

Facedown.

Not moving.

20

They turned the centurion over to find the front of him slashed and bloodied. Their hearts stopped at the sight of him. They knelt beside him and were relieved when they saw that his life had not left him.

The four carried him back to camp, where they laid him on a table inside a tent. When Ashuk saw the limp body, he immediately went to work. "Fetch a hot iron," he told Massina, and the Syrian ran to check the campfires.

Those tending to Lucius did what they could to blot the blood, which was all over him. Ashuk took a washcloth and gingerly moved it over his skin, then rinsed it in a wash basin. Once the skin was washed of its blood, Ashuk poured wine onto a cloth and dabbed the wounds.

Massina, meanwhile, found the glowing orange end of a tripod sitting in the coals. He broke the three iron rods apart and picked up the cooler end with a scrap of leather. When he returned, Ashuk pressed the iron against a wound. The blade hissed, and the smell of burnt flesh filled the air.

The biggest wound was a gaping hole in the thigh, too big to sear. The only way Ashuk could treat it was to stitch it. He opened a box and found a large, curved needle and some thick thread.

"Hold him," he instructed. Each of the men took an appendage and anchored it with their weight. As Ashuk stitched him, Lucius grimaced, moaned, flinched, but did not regain consciousness.

That night, as Lucius slept, Ashuk sat next to him, keeping vigil. As the slave watched, the bruise on his master's face swelled and ripened. The hours passed slowly; and for Lucius, fitfully. Toward morning, fever set in, and he began to sweat profusely. While he slept, a blurred chaos of nightmarish images charged him. Hemmed in, he fought them off furiously, mumbling to himself, then shouting orders to his men on the field.

Ashuk draped wet cloths across his forehead and over other parts of his body. He put a cup of water to his lips, but the water just spilled down the sides of his mouth.

Lucius hovered between life and death, his fever rising one hour, falling the next, rising, falling, until two days had passed. Ashuk re-dressed the wounds, touching them with a soft cloth soaked in olive oil mixed with herbs.

Finally, the fever broke. Lucius's eyes slitted open, then squinted. As they adjusted, they saw Ashuk's face, and the beginning of a smile. Lucius tried to part his lips and form a word, but they were too parched. Ashuk took a tin cup of water and tipped it to his mouth. Lucius touched his tongue to his lips, desperate for every drop. Ashuk gave him another drink. This time he gulped it.

"H . . . how . . ." The effort to speak exhausted him. "How long . . . did I—?"

"Three days."

Lucius tried pulling himself up, but his wounds tethered him, squeezing a sigh from his lungs. He gathered strength for a cough, pressing his arm against his ribs to hold in the pain.

As he coughed, he felt stitches pulling apart and the cauterized wounds breaking open to seep fresh blood. He gritted his teeth and lay back down, surrendering to the pain, closing his eyes as he did.

"Losses?" he asked, the words rasping his throat.

"Including the watchmen, thirty-two."

The next word came slow and hard. "Mine?"

"One."

He labored to ask, "Who?"

"Quirinius."

"His wounds?"

"Twenty-three."

"Where?"

"All in front."

Which pleased him.

"Their losses?"

"All of them."

Which pleased him even more.

Lucius fell back asleep. While he slept, Ashuk fashioned a primitive crutch and leaned it against the table. When Lucius awoke, he propped him up, fed him broth, and gave him wine for his pain.

The next day Lucius sat up on his own.

"I will get you what you want," said Ashuk.

"I want to get up."

He stood on tentative legs, favoring the wounded one, and hopped to the table where the crutch was. He groaned as he put his weight on it, the side of his face throbbing so much he felt it would burst.

"I will help you."

"I do not want your help."

As he crutched toward the opening of the tent, Ashuk

followed. Lucius felt light-headed and stopped. But his balance betrayed him, and he started to fall. Ashuk caught him, steadied him, and walked him out of the tent. Exhausted, Lucius stopped. He waved Ashuk away. He stood a long time, leaning on his crutches, savoring the sight of soldiers, hard at their duties. Nodding his approval. He took a deep breath of crisp air. Let it out. Smiling into a winter sun that was shawled in low clouds.

The other two centurions visited Lucius as he convalesced. One of them had a bandage over his hand and one around his forearm. The other had an arm in a sling.

"You fought well," said one of the centurions.

"We all of us fought well," said Lucius. "Where is Timithius?"

"He died on the field, nobly."

"We have decided to winter here," said the other.

"Why was I not consulted?" Lucius asked, and he could feel the blood rising from his chest to his neck to his face.

"You were in no shape to—"

"We are not needed *here*," objected Lucius. "We are needed on the front."

The centurion stood resolute. "You are not the only man wounded. And you are not the worst of the wounded. Winter is at our heels. The ground will soon grow hard."

"Our men will grow harder," said Lucius. "Let winter soften our enemy; let it not soften us. Any of us. Even the wounded."

21

They broke camp in the cold dark of the next morning and marched into dawn. The seriously wounded were placed in wagons. Ashuk traveled with Lucius in his. Although he grimaced with every rock and rut in the road that the wagon found, each grimace was followed by the reassuring thought that they were on their way to the front, and nothing, least of all *his* wounds, would deter them.

Each afternoon camp was set up; each morning it was taken down. The pace was twenty miles a day, except when the weather was against them. Winter was nipping at their heels as they marched. The days grew shorter; the weather, colder. Driving rains turned to sleet; eventually, to snow.

The road ahead took them in a northeasterly direction, a route that traced the toes around the foot of the Alps, which now had a cape of snow draping its shoulders. Each mountain in the range faded from the one before it, until the range itself dissolved in the distance.

Today the morning sun was obscured by a ubiquitous covering of gray, the only evidence of its existence a pale circle of diffused light in the east.

Then came the snow.

It came as a light feathering of goose down, which soon

became a blanket that covered the countryside. Ashuk brushed the flecks from Lucius's face. As he did, the wagon found a hole in the road, flouncing them, tearing at Lucius's wounds so strongly he could not suppress the pain.

Then came the wind.

It came playfully, as a child kicking up the freshly fallen snow. It was not much of a wind, but it was enough to impede visibility, forcing the train of wagons, mules, and soldiers to stop. Orders were given, and camp was set up quickly but hastily. No trench, no ramparts. It was a risk, but a calculated one due to the weather and the flagging morale of the men. Besides, they thought, what enemy would attack in *this* kind of weather?

Ashuk helped Lucius from the wagon, shouldering his weight as he hopped on his good leg. He eased him onto a bed in his tent, where the soldier slumped from exhaustion. He motioned for the wineskin. He drank deeply, draining the skin before tossing it aside. He said nothing. His face was expressionless; his breathing, labored. He started to lie down, a painful movement at a time. Ashuk lifted his legs onto the bed and covered him with a blanket.

Then came the storm.

It came like a pack of wolves, descending on them from the mountain, howling, biting. It ran through the tents. Those that had been quickly erected just as quickly collapsed.

Thus passed the night.

Savage in its passing.

Every effort was made to hold the savagery at bay, the men driving stakes through the flapping ends of their tents into the cold, hard ground. Each soldier burrowed into his blanket to ride out the storm.

And then, somewhere in the night, it was over.

The next morning, the sun rose cool in the sky, glistening over the endless swells of snow.

Over the weeks ahead, Lucius's wounds grew smaller until at last they became scars. His thigh healed, though he walked with a limp. The swelling in his face went down, and the eggplant bruise lightened to a yellowish brown until finally his complexion returned to normal.

The seared skin and the scars, though, would remain with him forever. So would the memories of that day on the field. He would remember the long-haired look of the enemy at a distance, the full-throated sound of their battle cry, the terror of their charge, the fierceness of their blue eyes, the relentlessness of their weapons.

He would remember the volley of arrows, the clash of swords, the bite of the javelin.

First battle, first blood, first taste of glory.

It was different from how he imagined it would be, as a boy. *He* was different from how he imagined he would be, when he imagined such things, with an imagination that had not spilled blood or had it spilt.

22

It was a cold day when the Danube River came into view, eliciting cheers from the road-weary soldiers. Not far away was their destination: *Carnuntum*, a Roman camp near a bridge, making it strategic both militarily and economically.

The legion they were joining was the 14th Legion Gemina, first levied by Julius Caesar for his campaigns into Gaul. The legion was later massacred at Atuatuca by the Belgian king Ambiorix. In a lapse of vigilance and a naïve trust in an enemy that guaranteed their safety if they would only leave the fort in retreat, the Roman legion fell victim to the ruse and was slaughtered in an ambush.

Ever after, the reputation of the 14th bore the stigma of that defeat. Instead of burying the shame of the legion with its fallen soldiers, Caesar resurrected the legion, filling it with new recruits. Later that year, though, the 14th fell again, this time to the Hun. Inexplicably, Caesar kept the legion's name and replenished its ranks.

This was the legion that Lucius and his men were joining. He knew the stories. He had read the accounts in Caesar and Tacitus. He had discussed them with his superiors. The legion was not one a general would lead into battle. It was one he would leave behind, to guard the camp, the livestock, the stores of grain.

Lucius was determined to change that. He would train the men hard; ruthlessly, if he had to. His discipline would be strict, impartial, unyielding. If the 14th were ever to rise again, to fight again, he would be there in the first cohort, on the frontline, leading the charge.

When the long column of replacements came within sight of the fortress at Carnunuam, a delegation from the 14th Legion rode out to meet them. Lucius was walking by now, though with a limp, and he joined the other two centurions to meet the delegation.

"Welcome to the Danube!" said one of the officers, dismounting to clasp their hands. "Your arrival has been much anticipated."

"By us, as well," said Lucius.

Inside the fortress, Lucius and his men were amazed at its enormity. There was a huge altar for sacrifices. Stables for mules and horses. Storage rooms for grain.

Spring is when armies went to war. Winter is when they prepared for it. This winter day they were hard at it. Blacksmiths pounding iron on anvils. Tanners cutting hides from deer hung by their legs. Cobblers working to resole sandals. Apprentices honing the edges of swords.

In the center of camp was a hospital, staffed with doctors and surgeons, able to treat everything from boils that needed lancing to legs that needed amputating. As the incoming soldiers passed the hospital, they looked in, taking a measure of comfort in it.

They passed the elaborate quarters for the commander of the legion and his officers, and that is where the three centurions were formally introduced. Meanwhile, the men were led to their quarters, which were austere wooden huts, thatched with straw, each housing eight men. Each centurion had his own private hut, as well as an adjacent hut for a servant or two.

The fresh troops were greeted with elation, as their arrival meant that those who had put in their full measure of service could now go home.

Home.

Some of the men had been on the Frontier so long they had forgotten what it was like. They had forgotten the routines of home, of rising up and lying down, without having to build a wall or buttress it with a rampart, without having to dig a trench or to keep watch over it. They had forgotten the serenity of home, of a fire crackling at the end of the day, cozy against the night. They had forgotten the smells of home, too, of a hearty stew bubbling in a pot or a succulent chicken roasting over a fire.

The Frontier, especially this time of year, was dark and cold. The staple of the Frontier, especially when on the march, was grain each soldier ground for himself and cooked for himself. A meal of mush, day after monotonous day. The arrival of the four centuries meant that some of them, at least, would be able to live the life they had only dreamed of for the past sixteen or twenty years. They were going home.

The fresh troops were given towels, soap, sponges—gifts from the gods could not have been more treasured—and they were led to the legion's bathhouse, where they soaked away the rigors of the road. Before long, they caught the smell of pigs roasting on spits and breads baking in earthen ovens.

The night was given to celebration, to eating and drinking, to the bartering of stories and the toasting of gods. The next day was given to offering thanks and sacrifices at the legion's altar. Solemn words were spoken, sacred oaths were affirmed, simple rituals were enacted, and all the reinforcements felt the bonds of brotherhood strengthened and their faith renewed.

The night was crisp and clear, a jeweler's boast of stars spread across it. Soldiers trying to keep warm in their huts rubbed their hands and placed them in the pits of their arms to fight off the chill. Those keeping watch paced to keep the blood flowing to their feet.

The only sounds were those of a lone wolf howling to other lone wolves, keeping their own watch over the vast whiteness. A few tracks crisscrossed the snow—rodents and scavengers, each searching for prey, all eventually becoming that for the larger animals that skulked the nocturnal wasteland.

23

Discipline in the Roman army was swift, stern, severe. A soldier's superior had life-and-death authority over him, even if he was a Roman citizen, for when a citizen joined the army, he relinquished all civil rights.

Infractions included disobeying an order, speaking against a superior, desertion, falling asleep on watch, inciting mutiny, betrayal of an oath, undermining morale.

Discipline for such infractions could be beating, shunning of the soldier by having him live outside the camp, a demotion in rank, dishonorable discharge, death, and the worst possible form of discipline—decimation.

Decimation was a killing of every tenth man, usually restricted to a cohort. It was imposed only for extreme infractions, such as a mutiny. In such a case, every tenth man was randomly chosen by lots, and was either clubbed to death or beaten to death by the hands of his comrades. That was the worst of it. Not death. Death at the hands of one's fellow soldiers, men he had served beside on the battlefield, men he had celebrated with in victory or had cared for in defeat, men he had shared a tent with, stories with, a life with. The shame he suffered facing these men was worse than facing their fate.

The longer Lucius lived on the Frontier, the stricter a disciplinarian he became, often using his centurion's rod to beat those in his century who were delinquent in their duty. Like one of his men he found asleep while on watch.

Lucius was up before sunrise on a frigid winter morning, walking the inner perimeter of the camp to warm himself, his rod in hand, when he saw Flavius wrapped in a blanket, asleep on the rampart. Enraged at the dereliction of duty from one of his own men, he bounded up the steps and began beating him. The commotion woke the men in nearby huts, and they spilled out of them, wondering what was going on.

Flavius recoiled from the rod, shielding himself with his hands, his arms, squirming on the floor, the sting of the wood raising welts and drawing blood. When it was over, Lucius stood over him, out of breath.

"You ever . . . you fall asleep . . . at your post . . . again . . . I will kill you . . . with my own hands."

Flavius cowered beneath him, waiting for the berating to continue, but it did not. Lucius turned, his chest heaving, and walked down the steps.

Later in the day, Ashuk was at the woodshed getting kindling. Massina was by his side, fetching his own.

"Does he ever speak of that day?" asked Massina.

"Used to," said Ashuk as he picked up a piece of wood. "A lot." He picked up another piece, inspecting it. "Less after leaving Jerusalem." He tossed the rejected piece back. "Now, not at all."

"Why?"

"That is for a friend to answer, not a slave."

"Who is his friend?"

Ashuk put a piece of kindling in Massina's arms. "He drinks alone," he said, adding another piece of kindling. "Since leaving Jerusalem." And then gave the man a final stick. "He *always* drinks alone."

24

AD 34

Nights on the Frontier grew shorter, and ice on the Danube grew thinner. Everything was athaw and adrip. The ground drank in the melt, then dried. Sap rose, and trees put out their buds. Birds returned to nest. Wildflowers frothed on endless seas of green. Animals stretched out of their burrows, hungry and eager to mate. Tall, lithe stalks of grain swayed in the breeze that blew across the land. Great armadas of clouds sailed overhead, fleeting moments of shade mottling the countryside.

On that countryside, the legion was practicing maneuvers. The men started early in the day, broke for lunch, then returned to the field. Drill, drill, drill. The routine was relentless. It never stopped, never let up.

Ashuk and the other slaves stood on the rampart inside the wall of the fortress, their backs and feet bare, watching as slingers practiced their aim at soldiers who ran across the open field, crouching behind their shields as they were pelted with rocks.

The slaves were clearly impressed, nudging each other, commenting to one another.

"They are good, no?" commented one of the slaves.

"They are good," Ashuk replied.

Next, light infantry on the run hurled wooden javelins, twice the weight of the ones carried in battle, at stationary wooden targets.

The same slave looked to Ashuk for his assessment. "*Very* good," he said.

The cavalry drilled as a separate unit, three hundred strong, dividing at the sound of a trumpet and rehearsing a flanking maneuver, throwing untipped javelins at targets on the field. Part of the legion played the role of a barbarian horde massed against them. The heavy infantry, at the sound of a trumpet, advanced toward them. At the sound of another trumpet, they launched their mock wooden javelins. Another trumpet, and they engaged the enemy with their swords and shields. The first line fell back to the rear, allowing fresh troops to engage. Another whistle, another group fell back, and another took its place.

The slaves craned their necks to watch the spellbinding display, feeling some unnamed something rise within them, race through them, invigorate them. Their eyes wide. Their mouths agape. Their faces full of life.

The sight of the entire legion on the field was awe-inspiring. Such power, such precision. Then there were the siege engines. Great catapults that hurled boulders, fireballs, sometimes logs. Huge launchers that shot oversized arrows, taking out three, four of their opponents at a time. Massive slingshots that propelled iron balls into the enemy's ranks.

"I know one thing," one of the slaves said. "I would rather serve them than fight them."

Several of the others nodded.

But not Ashuk.

Not Ashuk.

He stepped back from his place on the wall. Took another step and stood in that place, looking at the backs of his fellow slaves. Some black skinned, some brown, some pale skinned. Their skin, glistening in the sun. Their backs, crisscrossed with scars.

And while the others stayed at their places, he quietly left his.

25

AD 38

For four years the army trained. And never a battle. They did not make forays into territory held by the Huns, nor did the Huns make forays into theirs. It was a tenuous peace, but peace nonetheless. Who knew if it would hold?

There were sightings, of course. And causes for alarm. Sometimes trumpets summoned the soldiers to their posts. But never an engagement. Four years, and not one incident. Still they trained in the field. Still they sentried the walls. Still they watched the river. For they knew that the only thing that separated civilization from barbarism was that river. That river and their readiness to defend it.

The barbarian mind was a mystery to the soldiers standing watch on the Rhine. The Huns were everything the Romans weren't. They were not builders of cities, as the Romans were, nor were they tillers of soil. They had no empire, no provinces that had sworn their allegiance, no senate to govern them, no emperor with unbridled power to rule them. Rather, they were a loose alliance of tribes, headed by a king of limited power. They had built no temples where rituals of worship were performed, while Rome was rife with them. Instead, they had sacred places in the woods where sacrifices were made and incantations were offered.

Huns were ponderously large men, their blazing blue eyes framed by a tangle of red hair on their heads and faces. Romans stood five foot five, five-seven at most. And they were fastidious about their appearance, their faces clean-shaven, their hair neatly groomed.

Huns bore no resemblance to Romans. They were not a disciplined fighting force. They were wild and unpredictable, fearsome to behold, and as furious as a bear robbed of its cubs, but unlike the soldiers of Rome, who had been forged into an efficient killing machine, the fury of the Hun, regardless of its cubs, had little endurance. Their environment had honed them to endure cold and hunger for long periods of time, but they wilted in the heat and could not endure thirst.

At dusk, Massina was in his hut with seven other soldiers, cooking a cauldron mush over an open fire.

"Again?" asked one of the soldiers, a weariness in his voice. "Do you have to tell the story *again*?"

"You have a better story?" said Flavius to the soldier. "Are you saying, Massina, that you *don't* believe in the gods?"

"All I am saying is that it was not Neptune who heard my prayer; and it was not Neptune who saved me from the storm."

"You want us to believe that a dead man saved you?" Silvanus asked skeptically.

"He did not remain dead."

"You saw him, talked to him?"

"I was there when he died."

"But after. Did you see him *after* he died?"

"I heard the stories."

"And you believed them?"

"I believe them now."

Early spring, early morning. A detail of two centuries marched out of camp, crossed the wooden bridge, and ventured into the woods north of the Danube to hunt, gather fruit, and collect firewood. Scouts rode ahead of them, searching for traces of the enemy. One of the centuries stood guard while the other century went to work. The hunters went quietly into the forest in one direction, the foragers in another direction, and the woodcutters in still another, their axes resting on their shoulders.

Here and there, they thought they saw something.

Now and then, they heard something, or thought they did.

More and more, they felt uneasy.

Until ...

Huns hiding in the forest descended on the soldiers like hawks swooping down on unsuspecting rabbits, sinking their talons into their fur, carrying them off, tearing at them with their beaks.

It was that sudden, that savage, that one-sided.

They had no chance, only choices. They could run, they could stand their ground, they could surrender. Those who ran were chased down, one by one falling with an arrow in the back, a javelin, a hatchet. Those who stood were hacked to death with swords, skewered with spears, savaged with pitchforks. The slaughter was so brutal and their fate so final that some of them did surrender, thinking they would become slaves but hoping the legion would come for them, exact its vengeance, and rescue them.

In all, eight surrendered.

They were tied to a long rope and led through the deep woods. The farther they walked, the denser the forest. At last, they came to a clearing.

What they saw there filled them with terror.

26

A huge pit filled with timber, large trees on either side of it. A log running over the pit, twenty feet high, the ends of the log resting in a crook on each tree.

A heap of large wicker baskets.

Their captors, circling the pit.

A holy man of some sort, chanting.

An antiphonal chant, the others echoing chants back to him.

A bear of a man working feverishly to light a torch.

One Roman being tied to a tree, singled out to watch.

The others, one by one, being shoved into wicker baskets.

The baskets, one by one, being tied shut.

One by one, being hoisted by ropes over the log.

All of them dangling over the pit.

The soldiers losing heart, pleading, cursing.

The man with the torch touching the timbers.

Flames leaping.

Snakes of fire, twisting in the air, licking the baskets.

The soldiers screaming.

The bottom of the baskets smoking.

The baskets bursting into flame.

Screams echoing through the forest.

One by one, the screams dying out.

The wicker, crackling.

The bottoms giving way.

Bodies falling into the pit.

Cinders flying, curling in the air above them.

The face of the soldier tied to the tree was stricken with terror. The Huns, wild with ecstasy, untied him, their faces pushing toward him, a crush of hellish images. They hefted him onto a horse. Intoxicated with a victor's swill, they laughed as they slapped its flanks, and sent him on his way.

The horse sprinted through the woods, as if chased by demons.

A watchman on the rampart saw the rider and signaled the bugler, who sounded a call to rally the men. The gates opened, and the soldier told his story to the commander and his officers who were huddled around him. The story struck terror in them all, leaving them speechless. They looked to their commander, who decisively assessed the barbarous act. "The sacrifice was an offering to their gods, in preparation for battle. They will strike soon. Tomorrow, my guess."

"First light?" asked one of the centurions.

"Likely," said the general.

"Then we have much to get ready," said Lucius.

"Centurions," said the commander. "Muster your men to the altar, lest the devotion of our enemy to *their* gods outshines our devotion to *ours*, and feeling spurned, they withhold their favor on the battlefield."

Not the order Lucius was hoping to hear, but the other men welcomed the resolution with enthusiasm.

Soldiers soon streamed into the altar area, each offering a sacrifice of some kind—a chicken, a rabbit, a sheep. Some brought coins to lay at the altar. Others brought sacks of grain.

Still others brought a necklace, a ring, or some other token of their allegiance.

Two priests worked the altar, taking the sacrifices and placing them on the grillwork that extended over the fire. Smoke from the offerings rose in the sky, each person praying the aroma would reach Olympus, home of the gods, and be savored by them. No Roman soldier went into battle without seeking the gods' favor. It would be cavalier to do so, an act of hubris so brazen it would certainly incur their wrath.

Massina stood at the entrance, engaging the men in conversation and imploring them with great zeal. One of the men pushed him away. Still, he persisted. Another, clearly impatient, tried to dismiss him. "Paradise, Elysium, what difference? A place is a place, regardless the name on the map."

"There *is* a difference between our gods and his," chided the man behind him. "A *big* difference." Then to Massina, sternly. "Watch yourself."

Later that night Lucius appeared at the door to Massina's hut, ending a conversation he was having with his comrades.

"A word, Massina."

Outside the hut, Lucius confronted him. "I have been asked to report on you." Massina looked puzzled. "It has been brought to the commander's attention that you spoke against the gods."

"I only—"

"He believes the fate of the legion has been undermined."

"Is that what *you* believe?"

"I believe we make our own fate. The strongest hands, and in those hands the strongest weapons. In the end, *that* is how battles are won, how history is made, how it is written. By the victors, not the vanquished."

A respectful pause, and a counter.

"What if the history that has been written is wrong. Not in its stories, but in the way it *measures* its stories?"

An unexpected reply, taking Lucius off guard. "It is talk like that—"

"Beg your patience, sir, to hear out a simple Syrian." Lucius stood silent. "What if the stories we have told each other, the ones that make up our history, cobbled together by the Caesar you read, the Plutarch, the others . . . what if the stories of the strong, *in the end*, are not the stories that matter?"

Massina's words hemmed him in, without room to advance or to retreat. Lucius stood without so much as a dagger of a defense. Instead, he answered the question with one of his own, his tone softening.

"What stories, in the end, really *do* matter, Massina?"

"*His* story."

"The story of far-fetched promises and prayers gone begging, that one?"

"But you were there. You saw it, at least, that part of his story. I saw it, too, and at first did not believe it. *Him*, a king? But then came the storm, and I called to him, and he—." A catch in his voice stopped him. He paused to collect himself.

"This I have come to believe," said Massina, humbly but with conviction. "If the story of Jesus is true, then, in the end, nothing else matters."

"And if it isn't?" countered Lucius. "What if his story is *not* true?"

"If it is not"—the alternative gave Massina pause—"nothing else matters. In the end."

A silence, almost palpable, stood between them. But the centurion did not yield, instead leaving the field of words with these.

"We have a battle to fight, and more important things to occupy our thoughts." His tone turned resolute. "Believe what you want. Keep it to yourself."

27

The commander was a deeply religious man, solicitous of the favor of the gods, and careful not to act without some sign confirming his plans. Having come to the legion's priests for advice, the commander was in their tent, watching as the one cut open a pheasant and spilled its entrails onto a slab of white marble. The two men studied them. They looked at each other.

"Do the gods decree a course of action?" asked the commander.

The priests nodded, and one of them spoke. "One that will appease them."

"And secure victory?" he asked.

"So say the auspices."

This brought a great relief, and emboldened the commander.

All the legion crowded to the front of the fortress, where the commander stood, flanked by the two priests. Massina stood before them, a soldier on either side of him. The commander nodded, and they turned him to face the crowd. Lucius and his men were in the front rows. Ashuk was to the far side of the drama, along with a gallery of other slaves, watching it unfold. In a stentorian voice, the commander called out the crime. "To unsettle the faith of a fellow soldier, especially on the eve of battle, is a treasonous act. An egregious breach of oath. Angering the gods. Undermining morale. Putting the legion at risk."

The legion listened intently, awaiting the verdict.

"Death," decreed the commander. "By the hands of his comrades." The legion erupted in almost unanimous approval. Under the noise, he spoke to the soldiers guarding the condemned. "His body, outside the camp. And trouble not the ground to welcome it."

Ashuk could not believe what he had heard. He felt as if he were in a terrifying dream in which he could not move, could not speak, could not do anything.

As the crowd quieted, the commander spoke. "His centurion?"

Lucius stepped forward.

The commander continued. "And the men whose quarters the traitor shared, the ones to whom he swore his loyalty?"

One came forward. Another. And another. Until all seven men stood with Lucius, facing Massina.

Slowly they circled him.

Calls from the crowd were hurled like stones.

"Blasphemer!"

"Traitor!"

And they began to chant.

"Kill! Kill! Kill!"

The eight appointed to do so, didn't.

The commander grew impatient. "Let the sentence be carried out!"

Massina looked up. "Father, forgive—"

Lucius threw the first punch, hard to the jaw, knocking him backwards.

The crowd cheered.

Ashuk turned and left his place in the crowd, unwilling to be a part of what was happening, if only the part of a spectator. Another slave followed him. Then another.

The other men, reluctant to join in, stood their place in the circle. Lucius looked at them, but they looked away, cutting their eyes to each other, waiting for someone to step forward.

Lucius hit him again.

As the crowd called out for more, the rest of the slaves slipped between the seams in the crowd and were gone.

Massina stumbled, regained his balance, and continued to pray.

"Do your duty," Lucius said to the seven.

But they just stood there.

The crowd booed.

More insistent now. "*Do your duty!*"

Flavius punched Massina in the stomach, doubling him over.

Silvanus slammed a knee into his head, standing him up.

Another hit him in the face.

Massina fell to the ground, and the men fell on him as one man, delivering a volley of fists, punching his face, kicking his ribs.

Until at last their duty was done.

Silvanus stood first, disgusted at the deed, blood on his hands, his forearms. Then stood Flavius. The others. Lucius was the last to stand, blood on his hands, a splattering on his face.

A final malediction from the commander.

"The history of the 14th Legion shall be a glorious one, remembered forever in story and in song. The man who lies before you, he *will not* share it in that glory; his name, stricken from the legion's records; his reward, given to another."

That night, Massina's comrades were all in their quarters, lying on their beds. Their eyes avoided the empty bed among them. No one spoke. Not of the deed they had done. Not of him. Ever again.

In another hut, the centurion sat alone at a small field table where an oil lamp enclosed him in a soft circle of light. He sat, staring at the wick, an almost empty wineskin in his hand. He raised it to his mouth, draining it, dropping it. He sat there, folded over, his eyes fixed, a great vacancy in them.

A flickering of the wick, and his eyes blinked. They fell on his hand. Its knuckles were swollen and cut; the blood on them, dried. He looked at the other, equally bruised, equally bloodied, equally indicting. The cuts would become scars. Though slight and almost imperceptible, they were the ones he would most remember. And most regret.

Early the next morning the legion marched over the bridge into the territory of the Hun. They marched to the open field at the edge of the forest, took their place on the field, in formation, where they waited for the enemy to appear.

The commander and his staff took a position on a hillside where they could take in the sweep of the landscape and signal strategy to the centurions on the field. There they waited for the enemy to appear. Forever, it seemed, until . . .

The enemy stretched from the forest like shadows at day's end, lengthening, darkening. Half-beast, they seemed; their hair, a tangle of filth, the color of rust. Charms and talismans hung around their necks. Their beards were abush, uncut and unkempt. There was no order to the teeming horde, no discipline. They lifted their weapons in the air, shaking them, beating primitive swords against primitive shields, as some called to their gods and others hurled taunts across the field.

A sudden silence.

Followed by a stillness.

Followed by a thunderous charge.

The front row of the first cohort crouched behind their shields, bracing for the collision; their swords drawn, ready to strike.

Watching all this from the hill, the commander could only see the broad strokes of the battle as it unfolded—the spill of the enemy onto the field, the two armies colliding; could only hear the muted sounds of the conflict—the battering of shields, the clashing of swords.

From a distance, the movements seemed slow and the noise sounded dull.

Within an hour, the battle had become a story.

The story, a page of history.

The page, already fading.

28

BRITAIN
AD 43

A different day. A different field. A different enemy.
Swords flashed in the morning sun, and it seemed as if time had slowed for the warriors on the field. The swinging of the blade. The shielding of the blow. The Roman swords, striking like adders. The enemy, falling in the field, one after another after another.

The field of battle, changing, one after another after another.

The enemy was no longer the Hun, clad in animal skins in the final stage of molt, but rather it was the Celt, naked from the waist up and marked in blue war paint. The form standing against them was no longer large and cumbersome, but rather it was tall and sleek. The skin was no longer ruddy and potmarked but rather was smooth and fair. The hair, no longer reddish and tangled but rather long and blonde; scruffy beards giving way to flowing mustaches.

But though the enemy was different, the tactics were the same. Fixed formations, each soldier given a space of three feet in which to maneuver. His movements, quick and efficient. He fought individually but also as a unit. He was part of a machine, a precise and powerful machine that had only one purpose—to kill as many of the enemy as quickly and efficiently as possible.

Four legions did the killing: the 2nd Legion Augusta, the 9th Legion Hispana, the 14th Legion Gemina, and the 20th Legion Valaria Victrix, all led by Aulus Plautius under the emperorship of Claudius.

The disorganized Celtic tribes in Britain fell to the disciplined ranks of the Roman legions. The battles were historic: Richborough, Medway, Caer Carodoc. And were punctuated by less historic ones—the pillaging of a village here, the burning of a wheat field there. Small victories, all tallied, they tipped the scales. In the seven years that followed, the southern half of Britain had been subdued, and every push northward brought a little more territory under Roman jurisdiction.

In all, Lucius spent seventeen years there, his rank rising with his reputation. Not all the life he lived there, though, was lived in fortresses or on battlefields. During those years, he helped bring about the transition from barbarism to civilization. The dream of Julius Caesar, which he had read about as a boy, was, in his manhood, becoming a reality. And he was helping to make it so.

Under Claudius, the reigning Caesar, Britain became a Roman province. Roman roads crisscrossed the countryside. Roman colonies flourished with retired veterans given plots of land for their service, taking wives from the Britons, raising families. The soldiers who had become civilians were now administrators, magistrates, governors, negotiating treaties with tribal leaders, establishing trade agreements, and collecting taxes.

Lucius had even thought of someday spending his retirement there.

But, when he thought about it, he realized he was not at home there.

He was not at home anywhere.

Even within himself.

Over the years, the centurion's skin had become a vellum map of scarring reminders, marking the battles he had fought, where he had fought them, when, and, most importantly, why. He recalled each and every one of them.

Each victory elevated him, yet, at the same time, diminished him. Years passed. And so much passed besides the years. He once thought himself a good man with noble ambitions. He thought that way no longer. Gone was the innocence of his childhood. Gone were the ideals of his manhood. All that remained were scars of battle, ravages of war, and memories of a love torn from his embrace so many years ago he could hardly remember what she looked like.

He drank more than he used to. It seemed the only thing he could rely on now, the only thing that delivered on its promises. They were small promises, admittedly, but they were kept promises.

Which was more than he could say of God.

More and more, he thought less and less of him.

Which is how God thought of him, he concluded, *less and less*. Or so he told himself in the conversations he had with himself in the hut where he drank by himself, the hut that was not home.

29

ROME
AD 60

A world away, Mary was in Rome, fighting different battles. She had fought long and hard over the years, so long and so hard that her body had worn itself out. Her hair had lost its sheen. Her skin had lost its suppleness. Her joints ached. Her hands were stiff. Her arms, weak. Her eyes, tired.

Still, she was beautiful. Perhaps more now than ever. Her face mapped the kingdom of God. In her eyes, mercy triumphed over judgment. In her smile, love cast out fear. Her words were like hands cupped around a dimly burning wick, held strong against the winds that threatened to extinguish it. Her neck was stately, quick to bow. Her feet, their movements so quiet and unpretentious in the way they came to the side of anyone in need. Her hands, so tender against the skin of everyone she touched. Her back, though bent by the weight of the world, was always stooping to serve, always seeking to lift someone up, whether it was someone's body that had given out, or someone's spirit.

She loved much because she had been forgiven much. The grace she had freely received, she freely gave. She was always giving herself away, even when she felt she had nothing more to give.

She had left John and Mary in Ephesus, feeling compelled to go to Rome. It was a rending farewell, for it was a final farewell. They all knew it. They all accepted it. The pain of the parting was made bearable because of the others who had accompanied her. And because of their mission. Rome was, after all, the heart of the Empire. If *it* could be changed, perhaps the Empire itself could be changed. Or so she thought, so she hoped, so she prayed. And so did those who traveled with her.

Most of the church in Rome came from the lower classes— the poor, the sick, those who were slaves. Outcasts, by and large. Here and there, though, a soldier was among them. Occasionally, an officer. Some of them even served in the household of the Emperor. That in itself was a miracle, or very close to one.

She had seen *such* miracles over the years. The blind given sight. The demons cast out. The dead raised. Things foretold by prophets, anticipated by angels. And she had witnessed them.

But it seemed to her now that the glory was that of a setting sun—a broad but brief flourish of color, turning gray and growing grayer. It especially seemed so on this day.

It was dusk, the light withdrawing from the windows of a house where Mary sat on the floor, cradling a sick child in her arms. The child's impoverished family sat with her.

"Please have mercy on her, Lord," Mary begged. "Please." As they were praying, Mary was wishing with all her heart that it was Jesus holding the child instead of her.

"You told us that where two or three are gathered in your name, you are in their midst. We are gathered in your name, Jesus, for your sake, your glory. Please be here. For her."

Mary had done everything she could for the little girl. She

had prayed for her, sung to her, cooled her feverish body with wet cloths.

But it was not enough. The girl was dead. Still, Mary refused to give up fighting for her. As the mother wept, the father took the child from Mary's arms. Others patted her shoulder, thanked her, tried to console her. In a moment of sheer exhaustion, Mary collapsed into herself and sobbed.

In Jerusalem, she had seen the shadow of Peter—a mere shadow—fall across a lame man, and he walked. She had seen a handkerchief from Paul—a plain handkerchief—placed on a blind woman's face, and she saw. But now, now it was all just bed rest, a little wine, some oil, fresh bandages, and her prayers. So many, many prayers.

She did not know when the wind started to change, when the temperature started to drop, when the leaves started to fall, but she was sure the season had changed. The kingdom of God had once come near, and wonderful things happened as a result. Now, it seemed so far away, that kingdom, that power, that glory.

30

BRITAIN
AD 60

S easons had changed in Lucius's life too. The general he
served was no longer Aulus Paulitos, it was Gaius Suetonius
Paulinus. The emperor, no longer Claudius but Nero.

Other things had also changed. His rank, for one.

He had left Jerusalem, a centurion. After his service on
the Frontier, he was promoted to *primus pilus*, a legion's most
senior centurion, overseeing all sixty of the centurions in the
legion. His cohort was the first in the legion's formation, first
to strike in battle, and he was at the front of it, leading the
charge. Now, after his years of distinguished service in Britain,
he held the position of *praefectus*, or camp prefect, a position
held by a former centurion who had been promoted to the legion's third in command. Commander of his own legion was
within reach. Possibly even general of his own army. After that,
a good retirement.

One more change was upon him. He was now sixty, entering the autumn of his life. Long past the age of a soldier in
the field. His mind was still quick, but his step was no longer.
Even so, he trained. Partly because he knew that the battle was

not to the slow of foot. And partly because he knew no other way to live.

The strategy for conquering Britain had been almost flawlessly executed. Hearing stories of Rome's victories, tribe after tribe signed treaties with the Empire, submitting to their rule and agreeing to their taxes.

Prasutarus, for example, king of the Iceni tribe. He had signed a treaty with Rome to be its ally, and for years Rome's relationship with the Iceni was amicable. Then he died. His will specified that half his estate be given to the emperor and the other half to his two daughters. The procurator of the region, a sly and self-serving man named Catus, declared the will illegal by Roman law and sent a group of soldiers to void the terms of the treaty and seize the dead king's possessions.

When the soldiers arrived at the king's village, Prasutarus's wife, Boudicca, protested angrily, opposing them tooth and nail. The soldiers dragged the deposed queen outside and, in a very public humiliation, stripped her and beat her with rods. They then raped her virgin daughters. And when they had finished with them, they ransacked their home and carted off their belongings. What should have been an orderly transition of a king's estate became a barbarous abuse of power. Tribal elders were robbed, not only of their authority but of their property, and the tribe sold into slavery.

Her daughters ravaged, her home pillaged, her dignity trampled, her authority stripped, her tribe subjugated, Boudicca was enraged. From the hatred that burned within her, she forged her revenge. She went from tribe to tribe, telling her story, inciting not only their outrage but soliciting their support. It was time to take back their land, and to teach the Romans a lesson so brutal they would leave and never return.

When Catus learned of this, he rode to deliver the news to the general personally. He feared the general's reaction and wanted to explain his actions, defending them if necessary.

General Paulinus oversaw all the legions in Britain, but presently he was with two of them on the northwest coast, building a fleet of flat-bottomed boats to carry his men across the shallow channel that separated the mainland from the Isle of Mona (Isle of Anglesey).

Paulinus hoped to strike a fatal blow by destroying the Druid altars that were there, along with their sacred groves. The Druids were the religious leaders of the Celts. All the tribes, in spite of their rivalries, revered them. Their prophets moved in and out of the various tribal encampments, spreading news of troop movements and how the other tribes were faring against the Romans. The kings of all the tribes looked to them for blessings of one kind or another. And they depended on them for prophetic guidance. Paulinus felt that if he destroyed the force that was unifying the tribes, they would become dispirited and surrender.

The invasion could not be launched until construction on the transports was completed, and it was during their construction that Catus arrived with his report. Lucius stood at the general's side as he gave it.

"You did *what?*" asked Paulinus, incredulous.

"As a condition of the treaty," explained Catus, "Prasutarus placed himself and his tribe under Roman law. The law is clear. Daughters can inherit property from their mother but not from their father."

"And beating his wife, the queen . . . in public. Where did you find *that* in the law?" snapped Paulinus.

"She resisted an order. Publicly. And so the lesson taught her was public."

"And her daughters?" Lucius asked. "What lesson were you trying—?"

"If we had killed them, *and* the shrew that bore them," Catus said, checking his tone, "we would not be having this conversation."

"*This conversation*, Catus," Paulinus said, speaking now in measured words, "while we are having it, Boudicca is rallying support to avenge those daughters, the shame she suffered, and whatever else that happened that day in that village. In the future, should you live to make such a blunder again—and I pray you do not—burn the village. Burn it to the ground. Leave no one to tell the story. If there is none to witness it, there is none to avenge it."

The transports were now ready and being loaded with siege engines and supplies. Final details of the assault were being discussed. The general and his officers stood in a large war room, gathered around a map of the island. As Paulinus spoke, Lucius touched the corresponding place on the map with his pointer. The general now made his final remarks.

"The Druids are a mysterious breed, half human; who knows about the other half? They are like the way of a mist before dawn, hovering between earth and sky." When he said this, it sent a chill through the room.

"If so, then Roman civilization is the sun," boasted one of the officers. "And when it rises the morrow upon their shores, it will burn that mist from the land!"

This brought laughter, lightening the mood of everyone.

Everyone, that is, except Lucius. "Yet how many ships have been wrecked not by superior navies but by mere mists? Mists that have thickened, blotting out the sun and blinding them from reefs that snapped their hulls"—and he snapped his pointer in two—"sent them to the bottom of the sea."

His point punctuated the conversation.

"He is right," Paulinus said. "Let us not think too little of our enemy."

"Nor too much," said another. "Our soldiers are superstitious enough as it is."

And this gained the other officers' approval.

In the tents of those very superstitious soldiers, the conversation turned to the Druids and the mysteries that surrounded their rituals.

"I, too, have heard the stories," said Sivanus. "And I am not afraid."

So full of their own stories, they were, that the remark went unnoticed, and instead it was their stories that were sloshed about, stories abrim with their fears.

"Y'know how augurs cut open birds to read their entrails," said Flavius. "*They* do the same, but with humans."

"Don't even kill 'em first," said another, "what I heard. Justs cuts 'em and reads 'em where they fall."

"Their secret places, in the woods," said Flavius. "It's where they offer sacrifices. *Alive.* Bleeding them first, then drinking their blood."

"How savage could they be?" asked a skeptical Silvanus. "They worship trees."

"Not trees," said one of the soldiers, "the spirits inside them."

"Trees with spirits," said Silvanus. "It's lunacy. And so is all this talk."

"Didn't you ever feel that way, sometimes at night, in a grove, walking," said Flavius, "feeling like you were being watched. And the only ones there were the trees."

⌁⌁⌁

It was a full moon on the night of the invasion. Under the cover of darkness, General Paulinus had sent his cavalry, made up of the best Batavian horsemen, to another landing so far down the beach he hoped it would go unnoticed. The crossing was shallow, and the horsemen walked beside their horses in water that was up to their necks.

The enemy, in the meantime, had massed on the beach where the flotilla of flatbed boats was to land. As they waited, waves washed upon the shore, a lonely sound in the night. But it was not lonely for long. As soon as the boats hit the beach, the Romans filled the night with sounds that, to the warriors waiting on the beach, were strange and foreign—the clattering of wood, metal, leather, officers' orders, soldiers' compliances. As the soldiers poured out of their transports, they were dressed for battle, ready to fight. When the battle-hardened Romans took their places in the formation, here is what they saw, staring back at them.

Ragged rows of wild-eyed warriors, raising their weapons in the air, shaking them defiantly.

Tempestuous women, robed in black, darting through the rows of men, brandishing torches.

Standing before this impending storm, as if holding it back, was a circle of Druid priests around a fire. They were robed in white; their hands reaching upward, as if grasping at the feet of their gods, pleading with them to curse the enemies that were gathered before them.

The enemies that were gathered before them were terrified. The sight so unnerved them that they stood as if in a trance. They could not move, could not speak, could not even think. Seeing his soldiers in such a state, General Paulinus cantered his horse before them, looked them in the eye, and spoke.

"Look at them," he said, and the men looked at them: so-called warriors half-clad in tatters, the other half in paint. "At their armor." And it was clear, as they looked, that they had none. "Their weapons." They looked, and saw that they were mostly crude and handcrafted. "Now look at yourselves." And they looked at one another. "At *your* armor, *your* weapons." Clearly superior. *Overwhelmingly* superior. "*You* are soldiers of the greatest army of the greatest empire the world has ever known." He paused as he maneuvered his restive horse. "Show them the greatness that is Rome!"

He signaled the trumpeter, who sounded the assault. The soldiers snapped their shields together, overlapping them. They marched into the wild fray that was their enemy, and they showed them the greatness of Rome. They showed them what it was like to face the soldiers of the greatest army of the greatest empire the world has ever known. They showed them the strength of their armor and the superiority of their weapons. And when the horsemen of Rome thundered from behind, they showed them the surprise of their tactics and the swiftness of their cavalry.

They showed it all.

All but mercy.

Lucius and the men of 14th fought their way to the center of the island, where they found priests standing inside a towering ring of sacred stones; their hands, raised; their voices, calling to their gods to rain down destruction. All that rained, though, were Roman javelins. The priests fell where they stood. The rest of their warriors defended the site in a furious but ultimately futile effort.

No one lived to tell the story.

The soldiers pulled down their sacred stones. They destroyed their sacrificial altars. They torched their sacred groves. The Druids, along with their writings, their rituals, and the magical spell they had cast over the tribes, were gone. Every trace, turned to ashes.

In spite of the fears of the soldiers, and in spite of the stories that fueled those fears, the island was taken without a single Roman casualty.

The groves burned like a pyre. A blaze of glory for Rome. And a cause of celebration. The soldiers razed their village. But before they razed it, they plundered it. Stores of wine fueled the festivities.

At the height of the celebration, three horsemen, worn from the race to get there, rode into their midst, and, with great urgency, approached the general.

31

The news was dire. On the opposite coast of Britain, Boudicca had massed a force of a hundred twenty thousand and stormed the city of Colchester, the current seat of the Roman government. The 9th Legion was wiped out, to the man.

With the taste of revenge in her mouth, Boudicca whipped her forces into a frenzy. First they tortured the retired men who had once been Roman soldiers, along with the Britons who had married them. Then they turned their wrath upon the citizenry—men, women, children—butchering them by the thousands.

The general was dumbstruck. He had expected the vanquished queen to retaliate. But nothing like this. Nothing even close to this. He dispatched riders to every town where retired Roman soldiers might live and pressed them into service. He then pulled Lucius into his tent to cobble together some kind of strategy.

Lucius encouraged him to learn the lessons of Julius Caesar when he had fought there a century earlier. Their siege engines were slow and cumbersome, and their soldiers were weighed down with far more equipment than they needed. The less encumbered Celts, half-naked and carrying only spears and shields, were more agile and used the weight of the soldiers' gear against them.

The general was persuaded. He sent the cavalry ahead with foot soldiers doing double time behind them. They traveled light because they wanted to strike fast to keep Boudicca's movement from gaining any more momentum.

When Paulinus's two legions arrived at Londinium (London), the docks were deserted, and the townspeople were terrified. After hearing firsthand accounts of the massacre at Colchester, Paulinus decided to retreat. With London unguarded, Boudicca's troops swooped down on the city, leaving it in flames and killing everyone.

From London, Paulinus retreated to Verulamium (Saint Albans), only to find it also in chaos. The citizens were panic-stricken, pleading with the general not to leave them. But he left there, too, retreating so that Lucius might find the army some place where they had a chance of making a stand.

After their retreat, Boudicca's insurgency fell on Saint Albans, burning it to the ground. Everyone who lived in that city, even everyone who lived nearby, were killed. The tally of Boudicca's revenge: eighty thousand dead; she left behind no wounded.

Lucius rode with a scout, searching out the most advantageous ground for a defense. They came to a broad plain near the Anker River in central England, almost halfway between Anglesey and Camulodunum (Colchester). That was the place, he decided. Thick forests were behind them and on either side of them. The broad plain, where the enemy would be coming from, narrowed to funnel the fight into this small pocket that was encircled on three sides by a garrison of trees. His soldiers would be slightly uphill of the enemy. Another advantage. The incline would tire the enemy and slow their advance.

With the three victories behind them, Boudicca's army swelled to two hundred thirty thousand. When the rest of the tribes learned of their success, they were eager to join the fight, each with grievances of their own to avenge. Their pursuit of the fleeing army was relentless.

The Roman soldiers were weary from flight. They had rushed to find Boudicca, and now they rushed to flee her. There was no time to write a last letter to tell a loved one their story, how it ended, what it was like knowing the ending would not be a good one. There was hardly time for a last prayer to air their regrets to the gods, to themselves, to the man to the right of them, or the one to the left, men who had fought side-by-side all of those years.

Lucius did consider such thoughts; his mind was full of other things. *What if they flank us somehow? What if some of them take to the forest and come at us from behind? What if the men lose heart? What if . . .*

It was then he thought of Ashuk. Lucius sat high in his saddle, looking for him. When he spotted him, he rode to him, extended his hand, and lifted him onto his horse. He rode to take his side next to the general and helped Ashuk down.

"I want you here," he said. "Beside me." Ashuk nodded. "You will need a sword." But there were no swords. Ashuk was scared. Lucius could see it in his eyes as they darted to the trees beside them, to the field in front of them, to the trees behind them. "I should have prepared you better."

"How does one prepare for such a day?"

Lucius could not answer that. Instead, he rode to the formation and asked a soldier for one of his javelins. He came back and gave it to Ashuk.

"Do not throw it. Jab it." And the slave made a jabbing motion. "Good."

Ashuk's hands were wrapped around the wooden shaft, and as he held it, the tip of the javelin trembled.

"On *this* side of me," Lucius said, pointing to the uphill side.

With a force of ten thousand, the odds against the Romans were twenty-three to one. They were all experienced, battle-hardened soldiers, but it looked, even to them, as if this would be their last stand. The cavalry stood on either side of the two legions, awaiting their directive from the general.

The Romans waited for the enemy to fill the field. And fill it they did. Lucius had never seen such vastness in a force mounted against him. In the distance, its movement was like an army of ants, a dark mass moving as one thing. Without a form. Without a face. Without a voice.

The closer it came, the more distinct it became, taking form, taking faces, taking voices. The first form Lucius recognized was Boudicca's. She rode a chariot drawn by two horses. Standing tall in that chariot, she shook her head, as if a recalcitrant mare shaking its mane, long and blonde and untrammeled in the wind. Her one hand was tight on the reins, the other directing the movements on the field. Before long, the field was set; her warriors, eager and restive.

Tens of thousands of noncombatants had followed in wagons. They formed a gallery in the shape of a half-circle behind them to watch the spectacle. The wagons were mostly full of women and children, there to watch their warrior on a day they were assured they would remember for the rest of their lives.

Boudicca's troops were a half-naked horde of heathens, painted in blue war paint, their long hair hanging limply in their faces. It was an army unlike any Lucius had faced, made up of both men *and* women. *Thousands* of women. And all of them angry. Some chanted to their gods, others taunted the Romans, berating them, cursing them, spitting in their direction. Their eyes seethed with hate. Soon the individual voices melded into one, and a chant arose.

"Boudicca! *Boudicca!* BOUDICCA!"

They beat their swords against their shields, the random individual beats becoming one, loud, defiant rhythm; accompanied by one, loud, defiant voice.

"BOUDICCA! BOUDICCA! *BOUDICCA!*"

The sound was deafening, and it filled the Romans with dread.

Boudicca signaled her horn blowers. She waved her chariots into action. The ground thundered as they raced toward the Romans. Horsemen rode beside them. And those on foot ran to keep pace with them, holding lightweight javelins above their heads.

The Romans on the frontline—Silvanus, Flavius, Antonius—looked at the storm about to overtake them . . . at the ground that was shaking beneath them . . . at one another. A look passed between them. They knew this was it, the end, for all of them. But none of them acknowledged it. A nod of resolve, then they braced themselves.

Lucius signaled his trumpeters, but the sound was drowned out by the advancing hoofbeats. The soldiers stood in formation, shields up, two javelins lying on the ground beside each soldier, ready to be launched.

The Britons sent a volley of their crude javelins flying, but they fell short of the frontline. The Romans held steady, waiting for the enemy to come within range.

When they did, Lucius called out. "Hurl javelins!"

The soldiers put to flight their longer, heavier javelins.

Thousands of them. The volley hit with such force and such accuracy, it stopped the enemy's advance. Horses went down. Chariots tumbled over them. Riders were thrown in the air and came crashing to the ground. Advancing Britons stopped in their tracks, impaled, and dropped to the ground. Or else their shields were impaled and too cumbersome to use, and they threw them aside.

"Again!"

Another volley was launched. Thousands of javelins filled the air. Thousands fell, finding their marks, bodies falling, a smothering amount of them, piling up, one after another after another. A chaos of warriors turned in retreat.

What happened next was beyond imagining.

Those who had been running behind the now-retreating warriors had been at their heels so fast that in the retreat the two forces collided. Thousands were trampled to death in the confusion. Thousands more lay crippled.

Seizing the moment, Paulinus gave the order to advance. The trumpet sounded, and the soldiers marched in lockstep, their shields held firm by their forearms, their swords ready to strike. They stepped over the bodies on the field, finishing the ones still alive, then met the enemy that had regrouped and rallied. Their war cries were unrelenting, but the Romans showed no response—no anger, no rage, no emotion at all.

What they did do, though, was to continue to march, continue to plow forward. The tactics were simple. They pushed back against the crush with their shield. Then they brought their sword underneath it, and thrust it through the enemy's stomach, pushing it into his heart or lungs.

Their opponents died instantly. Or else he fell to the ground with a punctured lung, gasping for air. As the line marched over him, the soldier put an end to him.

The soldier often never even saw his enemy's face.

That soldier on the frontline fought fiercely but briefly. When he tired, he fell back, moving down a lane in the formation where he would take his place at the rear. The soldier behind him then took his place on the frontline, fought fiercely, and then fell to the rear. Thus, there was always a fresh soldier fighting on the frontline, and always a chance for the weary one to catch his breath before returning to the fight.

Lucius saw Boudicca riding in her chariot across the field, rallying her warriors. Another offensive seemed to be massing. He called to Paulinus and pointed to the movement on the field. Ashuk craned his neck to see it. Paulinus nodded and signaled a change of formation. The trumpet sounded, and Lucius called to his men.

"Close ranks!" And the soldiers drew together. "Form wedge!" At his command, they formed three tight wedges that looked like the open jaw of some wild and ravenous animal. The Britons had never encountered anything like it. Caught in its teeth, they were gnawed to death, row after row of them.

The Britons ran helter-skelter, but the Roman cavalry had flanked them on either side. Tens of thousands were trapped in the churning chaos. The disciplined surge of the Roman soldiers routed the disorganized hordes. Panic set in. The legionary killing machine ripped through any remaining resistance, backing the enemy against the wall of wagons that had gathered behind them. The wagons' horses had all been downed by javelins, forming a barricade to the enemy's retreat.

In little more than an hour, the battle was over. Seventy thousand Britons lay dead, ten thousand of them women. The rest fled to the forests, where they were hunted down. Boudicca, fearing capture, fled to the forest. The defeat sealed her fate. She knew she would be captured, paraded about, humiliated in the basest of ways, raped, tortured, certain to die a slow and agonizing death. Her decision came quickly. Determined not to leave her fate in the hands of her enemy, she took a vial of poison from a pouch. Opened it. Drank it. Defiant to the end.

Ashuk watched as the Romans waded through the tangle of those strewn on the field, killing anyone still alive. He had seen the aftermath of battle before, but he had never seen carnage like this. And it shook him.

Lucius approached a wagon full of children who had come with their families not to participate in the battle but merely to watch it. Ashuk followed. The soldiers had already killed off the women in the wagons. Some of the children fell on the bodies of their mothers, wailing inconsolably. Others sat in the wagons, trembling. Still others had vacant looks on their faces, as if their souls had left them.

Battle-weary soldiers were all around them, standing to catch their breaths, sitting to inspect their wounds, lying on their backs, exhausted. Lucius looked at the children. He turned to the nearest soldier and gave the order.

"Kill them."

"But sir . . ."

Lucius shot him a look with such force it caused the soldier's head to bow.

Ashuk leaned into his master to intervene. "They are children," he said under his breath, and he said it in a tone as if trying to remind Lucius of something he had forgotten.

"They will not *always* be children. And they will remember what they have seen here."

Ashuk touched his arm, pleading. "Do not do this. Please." As Lucius turned away, Ashuk held on, gripping him. "I beg you, please. Please. Do not do this."

Lucius pulled Ashuk's hand away, then confirmed his order.

"Kill them all."

With those words, the killing of the children began. So did the screams, the weeping, the pleading of older children for the younger ones.

Wagon after wagon of them.

Until all the voices in all the wagons fell silent.

That night Lucius was in his tent, and three of his officers were leaving. He filled two goblets, handing one to Ashuk.

"A good day for Rome!"

Ashuk did not respond, either to the offer or to the ovation.

"A day of celebration," said Lucius, as if translating. He extended his arm, bringing the goblet to Ashuk's chin. "Drink with me." But Ashuk just stood there. "Why do you not speak?"

"Is it your command that I speak?"

"It is my command."

Ashuk's eyes searched the room for words. "When a barbarian does a barbaric thing," he said tentatively, "he is being true to his nature." He paused and took a breath, then continued.

"When a civilized man does something barbaric, he goes *against* his nature. And so he is the worse of the two, is he not?"

Lucius had trained Ashuk to think this way, drinking with his servant during so many of their late-evening Socratic dialogues.

Which made the words sting all the more.

Lucius did not answer, his face neither indicting him nor acquitting him. Ashuk dared once again to speak, knowing that this time it could cost him his life.

"I once served a civilized man. That man I no longer know. I will serve him to my dying day. I will cook for him, clean for him, carry for him. But I can no longer drink with him."

32

ROME
SUMMER AD 64

Mary lived with a family in Rome—Joshua and Anna, along with their three children, Lydia, Marcus, and Leah, the youngest, barely one. Anna was pregnant with their fourth. She tired quickly with this pregnancy, so Mary helped with many of the day-to-day responsibilities of running the household.

She loved being part of a family, a common grace that had not been granted her, until now. She loved the inquisitiveness of the children, plying her with questions about the *why* of things or the *how* of things. And she loved their playfulness, how spontaneous they were, dropping a conversation mid-sentence when a butterfly caught their eye and they suddenly left her side to run after it, or when an idea came to mind and they drew her into some whimsical moment of their imagination.

She loved their parents, too, delighted in the two of them together, how they spoke to each other, how they listened to each other. She savored the conversations around the dinner table. And she relished preparing dinner, most often with the children's help. Of all the things she loved, though, bedtimes were what she loved the most.

The children were in bed, which was a pallet of straw encased in ticking, and she was tucking them in. An oil lamp bathed everything in the room with soft, warm hues. Including the faces of Marcus and Lydia.

"It is late," Mary said, to counter their request.

"Just one?" asked Lydia.

"Please, Mary, please!" begged Marcus.

"The one where he walked on water," said Lydia.

"You have heard it four times."

The two nodded their heads enthusiastically, and Mary relented.

"Jesus was alone with his disciples on the shore of the Sea of Galilee. It had been a long day, the crowds had gone home, and he was tired. 'Row your boat to the other side,' he told them."

As she related the story, they hung on every word, interrupting now and then to ask a question, make a comment, have her elaborate on the details.

By the time she had finished, they begged for another.

Halfway into it, they were asleep.

Mary slipped out of their room into hers, where she sat in bed, and, under the soft glow of an oil lamp, penned a letter to Lucius. She had written him when he was stationed in Caesarea. But he never replied. Nor did he reply to the ones that followed. She never knew why. She didn't know if he had read them and dismissed them, or if he had discarded them, unread. She didn't know if they had even reached him. The Frontier was so far away, after all. And who knows how far away was his heart.

Eventually she stopped. But she never stopped thinking

about him, wondering how he was; never stopped praying for him, worried about his safety. Then one year, when she was feeling particularly and acutely alone, her thoughts found words and her prayers found paper on which to write them.

She never sent the letter. Nor did she send the ones that followed. She kept them in a box, until they outgrew it, and she had to get a bigger one to hold them. Over the years they became fewer. But once or twice a year, at least, she wrote, chronicling her life, her faith, how the church was going, how she was doing.

She did not write about her love for him, which now seemed a memory that faded a little more with each passing year. The love was still there, inside her, but it was very deep inside, and it was very still, very quiet.

A knock on the doorpost. Anna came in to find Mary finishing her letter. As she sat beside her, Mary signed it and put the stylus aside.

"How many is that?"

Mary shrugged her shoulders and handed her the letter, pointing to a large wooden box across the room.

Anna opened the top, revealing sheaves of them. She placed the letter onto the stack, almost reverently.

"You write letters you do not send."

Mary nodded, self-conscious at how strange it must have seemed.

"At some time or another, every woman has a letter she writes but does not send," Anna said.

The well from which those words were drawn was a deep one, Mary could tell, and the beginning of a smile softened her face.

Anna touched her thumb and forefinger to her mouth, wetting them, as she reached for the oil lamp.

"Shall I put out the wick?"

Mary shook her head.

"Thank you for your help today."

Mary nodded.

Anna left.

Once again she was alone; her only companion, a shadow on the wall.

208

33

ROME
JULY 19, AD 64

A full moon was making its descent in the early hours of a summer night when the first torch was tossed into a shop on the Palatine Hill outside the Circus Maximus. Another was thrown. And another. Before long the Circus was an inferno, sending flames into surrounding neighborhoods.

One of those neighborhoods was a sprawl of tumbledown housing, part of forty-seven thousand apartments that blighted the city, sending its shadows looming over the public sector and creeping uncomfortably close to neighborhoods where the aristocracy owned homes, of which there were only seventeen hundred in the entire city. The aristocrats, of course, loathed the run-down neighborhoods, along with the impoverished working class crowded into them. City planners loathed them, too. Most importantly, Nero loathed them. They kept him from building the magnificent public buildings that he felt would better reflect the glory that was Rome. They also kept him from building his palatial estate, which he named his *Domus Aurea*, or Golden House, which would better reflect his glory than the palace he had occupied.

The tenements were tinderboxes that caught fire quickly and, fanned by the wind, spread even more quickly. Their tenants spilled into the streets, yelling to their neighbors.

The fire raged, its acrid smoke stinging their eyes, their nostrils, their lungs. They covered faces as they ran, arms full of valuables, gathered in haste, dropping some of them in the jostling chaos of the streets.

The fire jumped from one street to another, falling upon unsuspecting houses as if a thief in the night, sacking one residence, razing another. Soon and without warning, it fell upon the house where Mary lived. Joshua and Anna woke first, yelling downstairs to Mary, who shot out of bed. Just as she did, though, a wall from the adjoining house collapsed, blocking the stairway and engulfing the home in flames.

"Anna!" she yelled. "Children! Marcus! Lydia!"

Anna at the top of the stairway, clutching Leah. "Go outside! We'll drop them to you from the window!"

The house crumbled around her, as if a great anger had been unleashed and ran amok, wild and ravenous. Mary escaped the inferno and stood beneath the window, where Joshua was lowering a terrified Leah, holding on to her arms until Mary was beneath her.

Joshua dropped her into Mary's outstretched arms. As Mary put the girl down, Anna handed Lydia to Joshua, and he immediately dropped her. Mary caught her and set her beside Leah.

"Stay with Leah!" Mary shouted, and Lydia took her and held her, shielding her eyes.

The structure was giving way, everything cracking and popping and crashing. Flames, closing in on the upstairs. Smoke pluming out the window, now empty. A scream from Anna, and Joshua calling to her.

"Anna!"

Marcus at the window, looking down at Mary, back to the bedroom. Marcus, torn. A crash, and the wall from another home fell.

"Jump!" yelled Mary, her arms reaching for him, desperately.

Marcus, terrified, unable to move. Flames now at his back. The girls, both crying.

Mary screamed at the top of her lungs. "Now!"

He jumped, hitting her hard and knocking her to the ground.

Nero, meanwhile, was at his palace in Antium, watching from his terrace. The city seemed a funeral pyre; the ascending smoke, underlit by flames.

The flames raced through the winding maze of narrow streets, devouring the stacks of crates that lined them, the vendors' carts, the storefront shelves, everything. A cohort of flames broke ranks and flanked the Palatine Hill, charging it; then the Caelian Hill, taking them both without resistance.

Mary was swept along in the torrent of people that flooded the streets, little Leah clutched to her chest, Marcus and Lydia clinging to her garment. As they ran, Lydia tripped and fell. Mary turned back to get her, but the girl had disappeared.

"Lydia!" she screamed. "Lydia!"

Mary grabbed Marcus's hand and fought her way back. "Lydia!"

She was bumped so hard she almost dropped the youngest, who was sobbing uncontrollably. She drew the girl to her chest and pulled her brother closer, all the while peering through gaps in the crowd.

"Lydia!" she yelled.

Her brother yelled, too. "Lydia!"

Pushing her way through the crush of people, she saw the

girl on the ground, her hands shielding her head as people ran over her, some of their feet hitting her as they passed. Mary picked her up. Spotting an empty alley, she pulled them to safety. There she sat, her back against a wall, where she drew all three children into her, hugging the fear out of them, or trying to. They closed their eyes and buried themselves into her strength. As she held them, she prayed for them. While she did, Leah, exhausted from all her crying, fell asleep.

The other two children opened their eyes, and as Mary struggled to her feet, they stood and helped her up. They looked down the street, where the people had fled. It was empty. They looked up the street, where the fire had raged. It had changed course.

She looked at the children, their faces smudged with soot. Gone was the terror in their eyes. Gone were the tears that had filled them.

The people that had fled the fire spread out to the outlying fields and orchards that surrounded the city. Mary wandered through the masses, looking for familiar faces. For a long time, nothing. Then, a group of friends, clustered around a tree. As she drew near, they saw her and stood.

"Thank God," said one of them, "you are safe."

"Lydia!" said a woman who scooped the girl into her arms.

"Marcus!" shouted one of the boys, as other children gathered around to welcome them.

One of the women drew near to Mary and whispered, "Their parents?"

Mary shook her head. She handed off the baby to the arms of an older woman, who rocked her. "And precious Leah! Sweet Leah. Sweet Leah."

The fire spread through the night and into the dawn, its smoke billowing into the sky. Many of the imperial buildings were made of marble and withstood the flames, but the private sectors were mostly made of wood and could not withstand them. Old walls of brick and mortar weakened under the oppressive heat and collapsed, one onto another onto another.

Thus fell the city. A house at a time. A wall at a time. Street by street. Neighborhood by neighborhood. Despite heroic attempts to save those trapped by the fire, many succumbed to the smoke, the heat, and finally to the flames. Others were crushed by falling walls. Still others, trampled to death. Animals also fell prey to the flames, pulling frantically at the tethers that bound them to their fate. Many of those that were able to break free lost their footing in the melee, and fell to the ground, their legs splayed and broken, unable to escape.

For six days and seven nights the fire burned. In all, ten of the fourteen districts were reduced to rubble. Everything people owned—furniture, clothes, heirlooms, jewelry, business wares—it had gone up in smoke and had come down in ashes.

The mournful sky, heavy with tears, slowly but steadily wept them.

When it was over, the strongest city in the world lay in ruin. People were overwhelmed by the enormity of it, reduced to tears at the sight of it, worn to the bone in fighting it. The smell of wet, charred wood was everywhere. Smoke rose from the rubble as if spirits of the dead leaving the earth. Here and there, smoldering embers burst into sudden flame, lived a moment, then died. The smell of things burnt filled the city. It was everywhere, thick and heavy, clinging to their hair, their clothes. They could even taste it in the water.

Efforts by the city's fire details had been futile. The fire, too big and too hot, exhausted their resources the first day. They soon gave up fighting it and turned their attention to rescuing those who were trapped in it.

Their wagons went through what neighborhoods they could and picked up those overcome by the fire, languishing from heat exhaustion, smoke inhalation, and those unable to flee due to their injuries. They were taken to places of refuge, designated by the emperor. Public buildings in the Field of Mars were opened, along with Nero's own gardens on Vatican Hill. The Garden of Agrippa and the Campus Martinus near the Pantheon were also designated as refugee camps.

Most took refuge, though, outside the city, congregating along the waterways, families finding loved ones in tearful reunions, or else in tearful realization of reunions that would never be.

34

The fire was not a respecter of persons or of religions: rich, poor, young, old, pagan, Christian, Jew: all were made equal by the fire.

When people returned to the city, they walked the streets half-dazed, as if their spirits had left them. Now and then could be heard the sounds of weeping. For the most part, though, everyone's tears had been spent.

Mary and several of her friends walked toward their neighborhood, stepping carefully around the broken bricks, the chunks of concrete, the fallen façades. She came to the remains of what was once her home, *their* home. She paused a moment to collect herself, bringing her hand to her face, covering her mouth.

She approached a neighbor who was sitting on a pile of stones, exhausted, his face sooty and streaked with tears. "Their bodies, have you seen them?"

The man looked up, confused. "What?"

"Joshua's, Anna's. Where are their bodies?"

He nodded. "Wagons. They're in wagons. Firemen came, carted off their bodies."

"Where did they take them?"

"A mass grave, outside the city."

Mary lowered herself onto the pile of stones and sat beside him, weeping. The other women came to her side and sat with her, just sat. When her tears had run their course, Mary stood. She walked slowly, mindlessly, and soon began stooping, rummaging through the layers of debris, finding bits of broken things, pieces of other things melded together by the heat. But nothing whole or intact. And certainly nothing salvageable.

Then she saw it.

The box of letters. Or what was left of it.

She bent down for a closer look. The only tangible evidence of her relationship with Lucius was reduced to black, brittle layers of . . . of what? She had no word to describe it. And she had no word to label the loss she felt. She picked up what little remained of her relationship with Lucius. As she did, the charred pages crumbled in her trembling hands.

It was for her a loss too many, and she ran from it, from all of it, bolting from the remains. Two of the women with her glanced at each other, puzzled, and ran after her.

She ran to another street where bodies of the dead had yet to be claimed, and there stumbled upon the body of a woman, a baby under her. The sight of them stopped her. She knelt with a dim hope and turned the body over, but the baby was dead. The moment felt like pressed fingers pinching her last flicker of hope. She sat on the ground beside them. Her heart sank, yet again. How much more could it take? How much further could it sink?

The women knelt beside her, neither speaking. Mary's eyes fell on the body of a man nearby, a rabbi from the looks of it. He, too, had something under him for which he had given his life to protect. She rolled him over. It was not a baby. It was a scroll. A large scroll of pale parchment, burned at its edges. A copy of the Torah.

"The synagogue," she said, pointing, "it is this way, isn't it?"

The women nodded. As she stood, the others lifted the scroll, and they walked to a synagogue in a neighborhood not far from theirs. When they reached it, they saw that it was in ruins. Mourners sitting in the ashes. Some silent, others sobbing, a few praying.

As the women drew near, one by one the mourners saw them, saw the scroll. And one by one they stood. At first, they were silent. Then a sudden spill of emotion that flowed into praises, hugs, and thanksgiving.

As they gathered around the women, one of the men asked, "Where did you find it?"

"Your rabbi," said Mary, her words careful, as she knew they would be painful. "We found him, a few streets away. *This*, under his body, shielded from the flames."

A great sadness came over them, and they fell silent.

The women handed them the scroll, slowly, reverently. And slowly, reverently, they received it.

"I know you," said one of the women, whose name was Sarah. Her husband, Jacob, stood next to her. "Some time ago you spoke with me. About Jesus, the Nazarene. The one you called the Christ." With the memory came a smile. "You are Mary."

The circle stood quiet and still.

Mary hesitated a moment, uncertain whether it was an indictment or simply a moment of recognition. "I am," she said. "I am Mary. The one who spoke to you about Jesus."

An awkward silence, which was filled by one of the men.

"You believe we're the ones who killed your king, don't you?"

Another silence, more awkward.

"The Romans killed our king," said Mary. "You did not take him from us; you gave him to us." Her face softened. "That is what his mother believed; what I too believe."

35

Early the next day, Seneca visited the apostle Paul. This was not his first visit. On his first visit, he came to talk philosophy. On subsequent visits, though, he talked only about the kingdom of God and the return of its King.

This visit, he brought a fresh roll of papyrus with him. He paused a moment outside, listening to singing on the inside. Seeing him standing there, a servant came to the door.

"I am here to see Paul."

When the servant opened the door, Seneca saw the apostle and a few others, lifting their hands in praise. His amanuensis sat next to him, also singing. Seneca stood there, patiently waiting. When he finished singing, Paul lowered his hands, opened his eyes.

"Socrates resigned himself to his fate, but sang no praises," said Seneca. "Your fate is as dire, yet you sing."

Seneca handed the papyrus to Paul's assistant.

"My fate is held by different hands," said Paul.

"You look well. Even sound well."

"A little out of tune," Paul said, looking up at the others, "but robustly so."

Taking advantage of the laughter that followed, Seneca bent down to put his mouth to Paul's ear, kissed it, then whispered, "A scapegoat is being sought."

36

Nero's own palace had been gutted by the fire, and he was commanding relief efforts from a government building on a nearby hill. He looked out the window to the wagons that were dropping off food, water, blankets, and medicine to the refugees. "Let them see their government as the teat of the wolf, suckling them through this, as the city's founders were once suckled." He turned to his advisors. "Open what storehouses we have. Send far and wide for supplies. Let there be no shortages."

The first thing the Romans did was to offer sacrifices and inquire of the gods. They pleaded for an answer. What had they done to incur their wrath? What, in the name of Jupiter, had they done?

The question went begging.

With no answer from the gods, the question reached the marble steps of the emperor, ascending them for an audience.

"The people are looking to you for an answer, your Excellence," said one of them.

"An answer?" Nero replied, indignant. "For what?"

"For the *why* of all this," he answered.

"The gods must be angry," suggested another. "Or else . . . ?"

The question hung in the air, no one wanting to say the word "arson," or speculate who could be capable of such a thing. The rumor circulating in hushed conversations was that the emperor was not only capable but culpable. His contempt for the poor was well-known, only surpassed by his revulsion for the dilapidated conditions in which they lived. His massive public works projects had been thwarted by the fact that so much of the city's land was in private hands—hands responsible for the squalor.

Nero paced the floor, pondering a reply. "Tell them," he said. "Tell them that I, vicar of the gods, will take their question to the gods myself. Until then," he said with resolve, "clear the streets, remove the rubble. Let the people know that their emperor is going to rebuild—bigger, grander, this time with marble. As the gods are my witness, the only blaze to touch this city again will be a blaze of glory."

City planners went to work, hiring displaced citizens to cart away the rubble, which was transferred to ships, ferried down the Tiber, and emptied into the sea. A continuous caravan of aid poured in from Ostia and surrounding cities. Sacks of corn and wheat were trundled to the four corners of the city, along with fruit, vegetables, wine, and olive oil.

Next, the negotiations.

If shop owners agreed to sell their property to the city, they were told they could rebuild in a new development in another part of the city . . . with the help of government aid. Out of the ashes, they were told, an even more glorious Rome would arise. And their willingness to relocate, they were told, would pave the way for the city's return.

One by one they agreed, though many were suspicious.

Work began only days after the fire had died out, which, to those many, seemed even more suspicious.

37

Lucius had distinguished himself not only in battle but also in strengthening Rome's foothold in Britain, and word of his accomplishments had reached the ears of the Emperor. Nero, a man not easily awed, yet was so impressed he sent orders to bring Lucius to Rome.

After Lucius's men loaded their ship with bounty from Britain, they set sail. Their ship navigated the craggy coastline, hugging the northern shores of Africa, offloading soldiers at designated ports, on-loading supplies at others.

With no scheduled stops for the week ahead, the ship was making good time. Lucius and the other men were asleep below, leaving a skeleton crew on deck to steer them safely into the next day. The moon was full and the sea was calm as Ashuk stood at the railing, studying the coastline for familiar landmarks. The ship hugged the shore so closely he could see the waves crashing against the rocks in bluish bursts of white. From his conversation with the steersman, he knew his homeland would soon be coming into view. The coast started looking familiar, and his anticipation swelled. One of the sailors approached him.

"That," the sailor said, pointing to the shore, "is Numidia."

Ashuk's whole face became a smile. "Thank you, sir! So

much! Thank you! A thousand times over!"

Each landmark brought a memory. Each memory brought a smile. Each smile receded as the landmark grew smaller in the ship's wake, disappearing into the darkness.

Ashuk knew that Numidia was not a scheduled stop. And though he longed for it, he did not speak of his longing. Not to the sailors, or the soldiers. And not to his master.

Ashuk knew nothing of the hierarchies of heaven, but he knew something of the hierarchies here on earth. Here, he was not master of his fate. Here, he was only a slave, standing on the deck of a ship not his, bound for the shore of a land not home.

He stood at that railing all night, watching those familiar shores slip away, the hope of going home slipping away with them, until, in the vast gray emptiness before dawn, the moon itself slipped away.

38

Days passed, each seeming colder than the one before. This day, the sea was rough, and the wind buffeted them. But the assault did not bother Lucius, who himself now stood at the ship's railing, his thoughts having left him. In wake of their leaving, he felt relieved of them and of the anxieties that attended them; relieved of the memories of war, of battles fought, of wounds received, of men lost.

A sudden swell lifted the bow of the ship and slapped it down hard, sending a spray into the air. As he wiped the water from his eyes, suddenly he was twelve again. His eyes opened to the misty past with a memory of him pushing a skiff into the surf as a wave crashed against it. He smiled as the boy steadied himself, taking hold of the oars and pulling against the sea, tentatively at first, then confidently, finally defiantly. The bow slapped against a wave, sending a cloven spray into the air that drenched him. He wiped his eyes with his forearm. Pulled at the oars. Harder. Harder again. Until he was past the curl of the waves and onto open water.

A gust of wind snapped the sail of his ship, jerking him back to the present. Again the sail snapped, catching a full breeze that caused the mast to creak. He squinted into the whitecapped sea. There, in the distance, a shoreline.

The shores of Alexandria. Home. At last. As they docked, Lucius asked Ashuk if he would like to accompany him to see the library where his father once worked.

"If it is your command."

Lucius paused. "My wish, not my command."

"I will stay."

Lucius threw a cape over his shoulders and went to the library alone, feeling the company of other officers an intrusion on this most sacred of places that occupied so much of his childhood. He had no siblings, growing up. What brothers he had, what sisters, he found waiting for him in sequestered places among the shelves.

As he entered, he took a deep breath. In that musty moment, his youth came back to him. How he loved the woody smell coming from the honeycomb of shelves that held the papyrus scrolls, loved the luxuriant feel of leather parchments, loved the cool sensation of clay tablets warming in his hands. He especially loved the codices, books of folded papyrus with holes bored in them and their wooden covers, held together by leather cords. The wood smelled of forest. The leather, of herded cattle. The papyrus, of marshes along the Nile.

It was like sniffing a goblet of aged wine, where he could smell the earth from which the grapes had been harvested, with all the fragrances in the loamy soil—the moldering leaves, the broken twigs, the darkness, the moistness, the sweetness. It was all there in one whiff. And he savored it.

Lucius touched an ancient scroll, moving his fingers from one to another. He missed the feel of Egyptian papyrus, something he had forgotten. The texture was smoother than what was available in Syria and Judea, because the process for making it was more painstaking and the materials more pure. It were as if the reeds along the Nile, from which the papyrus was made, grew up knowing the value of words in shaping ideas, the value of ideas in shaping citizens, the value of citizens in shaping cultures, and the value of cultures in shaping history.

These shelves were the safe harbors that launched his boyhood dreams, dreams that caught the winds of adventure and made chesty sails of his slackened years in Alexandria. How he loved the sea—the sight of it, the sound of it, the smell of it. It is what separated him from distant lands, and, at the same time, what joined him. He was always just a voyage away from anywhere. How many voyages had he stowed away on in his imagination so many years ago? So many he could not remember.

He saw a codex of *Gallic Wars*, written by Julius Caesar, a chronicle of his military campaigns, battling barbarians in the far reaches of the Empire. His hands moved across the numerous scrolls that made up Virgil's *Aeneid*, which extolled the greatness of Rome from the day of its fabled beginnings. His eyes fell on Livy's monumental work, *History of Rome*. How he loved Livy as a boy. Fragments of stories returned to him. He remembered one such story where Terminus, the god of boundaries, had refused to be present at Rome's birth. Its citizens interpreted this as an auspicious sign. So did Cicero, who concluded in *The Republic*, "The Empire of the Roman people shall be extended to the farthest ends of the earth."

Lucius suddenly realized that he had helped fulfill the prophecy, having returned from those far reaches and extending the Empire there.

It had seemed so noble. It had all seemed so noble. Once.

The man in him wondered. *Will a day ever come when men will clash with words rather than swords, and weaker ideas will fall in battle instead of fathers, sons, brothers, friends?*

Or was it the boy who wondered?

The boy he once was wandered through the library, stopping at the entrance of a lecture hall, where an orator was reading to his audience from *De Providentia,* one of Seneca's works. The man's voice was deep and full of passion; his gestures, dramatic and full of expression.

"'The creator and governor of the universe has indeed prescribed the course of events.... But why,' Seneca asks, 'why was God so unjust in the destinies he prescribed for mortals, as to send upon good men poverty, wounds, and cruel deaths?'"

The orator paused, looking up from his scroll.

Yes, why? Lucius asked himself. And as he did, it seemed the only question in all the world worth asking.

The orator continued. "'For the same reason that in the army the bravest men are assigned to the hazardous tasks; it is the picked soldier that a general sends to surprise the enemy by a night attack, or to patrol a road, or to dislodge a garrison. The raw recruit turns pale at the thought of a wound, but the veteran looks undaunted upon his own wounds, however serious, knowing that blood has often been the price of victory. In like manner God hardens, reviews, and disciplines those whom he approves, whom he loves.'"

The orator leaned over the lectern, enunciating each word with care. "You are art in the making." He paused. "But the making is never easy, neither for the sculptor, nor for the clay."

He returned to his text, quoting: "'To form a work of art worthy of the name Man, a heroic destiny is needed. His path will not be smooth; he must go uphill and downhill, be tossed on the waves, and guide his boat through raging waters; in spite of changing fortune, he must stay the course.'"

"Stay the course," he said, repeating it for emphasis. "Stay the course."

The students pondered the philosopher's words. So did Lucius.

"Which raises the question that Seneca anticipates we will raise," said the orator. "'What is the duty of a good man?'"

A nag of a question, Lucius thought, and one whose voice over the years had grown tiresome to him. No student ventured an answer. The orator rolled up the scroll and left the lectern. At the doorway, he stopped, turned, and answered it himself.

"'To resign himself to his destiny.'"

Not the answer Lucius was hoping to hear. He turned to walk away, out of the library, down the suddenly lonely streets of his childhood, down even lonelier lanes, until at last he arrived at the sea, hoping to find there some respite from Roman philosophy.

The wind had died, and the sun was out, warming the winter earth. He sat out on the shore, listening to the surf. Memories of his youth lapped at his feet, translucent moments curling in on themselves, washing over the shore, foaming away to nothingness.

After a while, he got up and walked along the shore, made jagged from the brittle shards of ice lining it. He stopped to pick up a smooth, flat stone and palmed it, moving it over and over in his hand as if it were a question he was mulling over in his mind. And, as if tiring of it, he sent it skipping across the water.

A second later, a *kerplunk* sounded in the water a few feet in front of him. He turned to see a boy, perhaps five, who had been watching him, a look of disappointment on his face.

"Here," said Lucius, picking up a flat rock. "Try this one."

The boy took it and threw it, but it met the same fate as his other rock.

"Like this," Lucius said, moving his arm in a sideways

motion and sending the rock skimming.

The boy tried again, picking up another rock, moving it in his hand until he got the right grip on it, then sidearmed it out to sea. To his amazement, it did not sink this time but skittered across the surface. He picked up another and did it again.

A smile spread over their faces, both the boy's and the man's.

Lucius's attention was captured by a passing warship as it plowed a furrow in the sea. The sight once filled him with confidence, a settled feeling that Rome would prevail over any waves of opposition. Now it gave him the unsettling feeling that the sea would swallow everything in the end, every ship, every sailor, even the empires for which they sailed. What once seemed mastery now seemed merely the skipping of carefully tossed stones across a vast and unconquerable sea.

A heaviness returned to him. And with it, the long-remembered words of Romulus, which every officer had drilled into him. They were the last words of the city's founder before he, too, was swallowed by that vast and unconquerable sea: "Go tell the Romans that the gods so will, that my Rome shall be the capital of the world. Therefore let them cultivate the art of war, and let them know and hand down to posterity, that no human power can withstand the Roman arms."

A low tide in Lucius's thoughts revealed other memories. Bodies. Thousands upon thousands of them, strewn on the battlefield, some butchered beyond recognition. A nightmare of images. And with the images, sounds that befit them. Moans of the dying. Screams of the tortured. Pleas of parents for their children.

Children.

The memory haunted him.

"The art of war." In Britain, Lucius had mastered that. And

in Britain, he had demonstrated "that no human power can withstand the Roman arms."

To what end? he now wondered. *To what end?*

A pain shot through him, deep and visceral. It felt as if something vital had been torn from him, the way a pack of wolves tears at the underbelly of a horse, exposing its insides until one of them plunges its jaws and pulls out part of the bowels. Then it is simply a matter of time. It does not make any difference how fast the horse runs, or how far. An essential part of him has been torn from him, and though the horse might elude the pack, he could not elude his destiny. He would tire, find a quiet place in some thicket and lie down, letting what life that remained in him ebb out of him.

It was like that for Lucius. Whether it was the war with Britain that had inflicted the wound, or the war within himself, he did not know. Perhaps it was the rending of his soul he experienced long ago when leaving Jerusalem. Who knows? All he knew was that it did not matter anymore. Whether he lived, whether he died, it did not matter. He was tired. And the sea had done nothing to revive him. Neither had Alexandria.

He stood on the shore, staring out to sea. He was never closer to home. At the same time, never farther away.

He turned to the boy beside him, but the boy was gone.

39

Nero was in a room with his most trusted advisors and military leaders.

"I have consulted with the gods," he announced, "as to the fire's cause. The fire was *not* their doing. It was done by those who decry our gods, dishonor our heritage, detest the very values that made Rome great. The fire, and all the destruction it wrought, came from the hands of those seditious Christians who live in our city like an infestation of vermin. The gods were not angry before, but now, now their anger waxes hot."

"I know of this sect," said a senator, "but I have never actually talked with anyone in it. Open the ledger and tally for me their offenses."

"They are haters of humanity, for one," said an aristocrat. "Malcontents, always finding fault, the whole carping lot of them."

"They refuse to take part in our sacrifices," said one. "Our fortunes in war and our prosperity at home depend on those sacrifices to appease the gods. It is vital to our—"

"They do not even acknowledge our gods," another chimed in.

"No different from the Jews," offered another.

A military man added, "They are secretive, congregating in

homes, caves, cursed places among the ruins outside the city."

"Bizarre rituals, too, from what I have heard."

"Cannibalism. It's part of it, part of the ritual," added another.

"*Cannibalism?*" asked Nero, his brows taking an arched interest.

"They eat human flesh and drink the blood. Hearsay and rumors, but there's a lot of 'em."

"But are there witnesses?" asked the senator.

"There *will* be witnesses," said Nero. "There *will* be a trial. And the gods *will* be avenged."

40

Seneca was alone with Nero in his chambers. The philosopher had been his childhood tutor, appointed by his mother, the same mother whose death Nero had finally succeeded in achieving. Since becoming emperor, he had grown tired of the old man, weary of his moral essays, his pithy advice that he proffered like a tray of delicacies. Though officially retired, Seneca felt compelled to intercede on behalf of the Christians. He handed the Emperor a scroll. Nero looked at it askance, opening it just far enough to see the title.

AD NERONEM CAESAREM
DE CLEMENTIA

"Do you remember it?" asked the philosopher, wistfully. "I gave it to you when you ascended the throne, at seventeen."

"Your lecture on 'mercy?'" he said dismissively, returning the scroll.

"A letter, not a lecture."

"You dare correct your emperor?"

"I dare not. But I do dare a word with him," Seneca said tentatively. "If I may." He turned his attention to the scroll, tracing words with his finger. "'Every house that mercy enters she will render peaceful and happy, but in the palace she is more wonderful, in that she is rarer.'"

"I am no longer your pupil, Seneca."

"And I, no longer your tutor."

"What then? My counselor? My conscience?"

"I beg your patience, your Excellence."

"I grant you a very little, and that is all."

"If indeed you are the soul of the state, and I believe you are, then the state is your body. If that is true, and I believe it is, mercy is essential. You see, you are merciful to yourself when you are merciful to another. And so even reprobate citizens, being the weaker members of the body, should be shown mercy. But if there should ever be need to let blood, the hand must be held under control to keep it from cutting deeper than may be necessary."

"Those *reprobate citizens*, which I assume you to mean those responsible for the fire, they are not the body's weaker members; they are its parasitic infection. The letting of blood *is* necessary. And the people of Rome will thank me for having such a quick and decisive hand."

"Again, I beg your Excellency's pardon for offering counsel, but it is my belief that, in the end, mercy will be a sharper instrument in your hands than judgment. And a surer one, in the end, to win the hearts of the people."

"Mercy is the gesture of a woman. And a weak woman at that. Would you have your emperor so portrayed? So viewed by the senate, the Praetorian Guard, the aristocracy, the very people of Rome, whose hearts you imply are up for grabs?"

"All of them hold you in the highest esteem."

"They esteem me because they fear me. They fear me because I am merciless."

41

The persecution began with soldiers going through the refugee camps, asking for Christians to identify themselves, or for others to point them out. One by one they were rounded up. Family by family. They went peacefully, most of them. But not all. As citizens of Rome, some insisted, they had their rights. According to law, they argued, they could appeal their case to Caesar.

According to law, those appeals were granted.

Which wearied Nero. They busied his schedule and tried his patience. One such appellant was being dragged off by two soldiers, when two others were brought before the emperor. The appellants were a man and a young boy. Nero skimmed a document that stated the charges. Both the man and his son fell on their faces, prostrate before him as he read their indictment.

"Rise," said Nero. "Make your case."

The two rose. "Your Eminence, most favored by the gods—"

With a dismissive wave of the hand, Nero stopped him. "It is the end of the day, and I have a party to attend."

"I am not a Christian, nor my son—"

"Who then?"

"I am a citizen of Rome—"

"—who *hid* a Christian family."

"What I did was—"

"*What you did* was *worse* than being a Christian," he said, with mounting emotion. "By protecting them, you defied an imperial order." So enraged now, the veins on his neck were protruding. "*My* order." He collected himself. "What you did was an act of treason." His voice now dismissive. "And you call yourself a citizen."

"Are there witnesses to the crime?"

A gaggle of them raised their hands.

The man dropped to his knees. "Please, do what you want to me, but let my son go. Have mercy on him, please, I *beg* you."

Nero stood. "The mercy I grant," he said, making a beneficent gesture, "is that your son will not live to see his father's slow, agonizing death."

He nodded to the soldiers, who took the two away, the man falling into hysterics.

42

The ridding of Christians from the city was systematic. Soon the prisons swelled with them—men, women, children—all awaiting their fate.

Which was carefully choreographed.

Rulers of Rome had long ago learned that providing entertainment for the masses was not only a way of gaining their affection but also of placating them in times of civil unrest, which was now brewing. Nero employed all his resources to present them with the most spectacular entertainment they had ever witnessed. He assembled architects and engineers, along with playwrights and directors, to consult with him. The event was to be staged at the Circus—not at the Circus Maximus, still in ruins from the fire, but at the smaller Circus Flaminius northwest of Capitoline Hill.

A model of the Circus stood on a table in the center of the room, and two of the planners were enthusiastically pointing to it.

"When the crowds are seated, they will look down on the arena and see a replica of the city before the fire," he said.

The other man broke in. "The seven hills," he said, pointing to them. "We cart in the dirt to make them. And these," he said, touching the buildings. "These façades represent some of the grand structures that were lost in the fire, your own palace among them."

"The crowd will be overwhelmed with emotion," interrupted the other.

"And these," he said, pointing to a veritable forest of miniature crosses, "they are crosses on which are impaled those responsible for the fire. Those crosses—and here is the beauty of it—represent the tenements that were destroyed. A torch will be touched to each one." He paused for effect. "And, as the flames fly upward, the audience will be on its feet, applauding you for bringing them to justice."

"To make sure the symbolism will be clear, the first cross torched will be here, at the Circus Maximus, where the fire started."

They took a step back as a dramatic finish to their presentation. Nero was impressed.

"A work of art!" he exclaimed. "A true work of art!"

"Exquisite," said another. The others echoed the sentiment, congratulating the two men. "Genius. Sheer, utter genius."

"What other ideas have you?" Nero asked, and another man stepped forward to explain *his* presentation.

Posters advertising the impending executions were plastered in public places in various parts of the city. Anticipation was high, both for the entertainment and for the food to be doled out on the day of the event. The news brought a collective sigh of relief—bread and circuses—the city was getting back to normal. It was also a relief to know that the fire was not the work of the gods.

The Christians slated for execution had been held in cages that honeycombed the structure of the Circus, most of which were underground. None of them were shown mercy. Regardless of age or gender all had been judged guilty of the same crime. All had been sentenced to the same fate.

That fate was meticulously planned and flawlessly executed. Models of the city's more prominent buildings consumed by the fire had been constructed to scale and placed in their respective locations in the arena. Holes were augured into the ground, and crosses were laid next to them. The crosses were slathered with tar that had been melted in cauldrons that seethed over fires. The victims were stretched out and impaled on crosses; the crosses then impaled in the earth.

One cross after another. One row after another. Until at last the arena was a forest of crosses. A black forest. The weepings, groanings, the sudden shrieks of pain of those awaiting the torch were interspersed prayers and last words to loved ones.

A man to his wife: "Soon we will be with him." His wife, too weak to reply, closed her eyes against the pain, waiting for the end to come, praying it would come quickly.

A father to his son: "Do not fear, my son. I am here, right here." The boy turned his head and fixed his eyes on his father's. The father strained as he reached for him. The boy moved his hand, his fingers extending as far as they could, even farther, until blood spilled from his wrist.

A mother, looking to her daughter's lifeless body. Now whispering, "Thank you, Jesus. Thank you."

Those last words, last gestures, last prayers rose from the arena like a dirge.

The grisly work took all morning and was finished shortly before the time came for the spectacle to begin. When the gates were opened, the crowds streamed into the magnificent structure and settled into their seats. Servants walked up and down the steps, distributing loaves of bread. The equestrians, senators, and members of the aristocracy were served wine with their loaves, along with an assortment of cheeses and smoked meats. On their way out, all received sacks of corn to take with them.

Mary and another woman stood in the shadow of the Circus, keeping vigil. They were horrified at what was about to happen, but they tried not to show it for fear of giving away their identity. They leaned into each other, and under their breath they prayed.

Cheers arose from the Circus, which meant that Nero must have given a short speech or made a pronouncement of some kind.

For a moment, all was quiet.

Then cheers so thunderous they shook the ground beneath their feet.

Their eyes caught a curl of smoke, weaving skyward. Shortly after, another. And another. As they watched, the wisps of smoke joined together to become a cloud, hovering above the Circus and spreading out over the city.

Tears streamed down the faces of the two women. Still they stood. Trembling, but they stood. Still they prayed. Whispering, but they prayed.

An hour passed, and smoke was everywhere, wending through the streets, mingled with the sulfurous stench of tar as it burned, the pungent smell of charred wood, and the trace of an odor foreign to them—the smell of seared flesh.

Nero rode his chariot among the crosses. Down burning streets of them. Through blazing neighborhoods. A city of crosses, up in smoke.

As the crowds cheered.

43

The night was chilly as Mary and a man named Benjamin, along with his wife Rebekah, met the Jewish couple, Jacob and Sarah, at a garden a little ways from the *Via Ostiensis*, the road that led to the port of Ostia. All were bundled against the cold. The couple led them to stairs that descended steeply from ground level, seven steps down, to a door leading to the Jewish catacombs.

Sarah cupped a small oil lamp in one hand, shielded from the breeze by a woven basket that she held in the other. Her husband put a key in the lock, turned it hard until it clicked. As he put his shoulder to the door, its hinges creaked but yielded.

Once inside, Sarah gave the lamp to her husband, who lit the wick of a small oil lamp ensconced in a shoulder-high alcove on the wall. It washed the entrance in a warm circle of light, revealing an arched corridor, several feet wide, that tunneled into the darkness.

The couple did not speak, only motioned with their hands. They walked slowly and quietly. Mary and Benjamin followed, noticing the inscriptions, the symbols, and the artwork along the way. Below the alcove had been painted a *menorah*, a candelabra with seven candles. On the opposite wall were pastoral images of green pastures, in which were lying a flock of sheep, a pool of water near to them, and a shepherd with his rod and staff, watching over them.

They followed the couple down the corridor, where Jacob stopped to light the wick of another lamp. Painted beams of light radiated from the alcove, as if a sun shining upon the next scene—the Garden of Eden, lush with vegetation, two trees standing prominently in the middle. Adam and Eve, their nakedness shielded by bushes, standing under one of the trees. She, with a piece of fruit in her hand, a bite having been taken, extending it to Adam. He, reaching for it, as a snake slithered away into the grass.

The next scene showing the two of them, cowering in the bushes, both clothed in fig leaves.

The following scene showing the two of them clothed in animal skins, walking away from the garden, looking over their shoulders at the two angels guarding its gate.

Another lamp was lit, illuminating tiers of graves on both sides of the corridor that had been carved from the limestone, each entombment covered with a flat stone and sealed with plaster. The light revealed an endless procession of the dead, going as far as the eye could see until the darkness shrouded them.

It was a long, slow walk down the corridor, Jacob stopping at each alcove to light a lamp that gave just enough light to take them to the next alcove. As she walked, Mary noticed the symbols on the walls: lambs, doves, peacocks, peacefully gathered beside the graves of their loved ones; palm branches, flowers, fruit, easily within reach of the interred; sun, moon, stars, shining down on the deceased from the heavens.

Jacob lit the final lamp in a circular room, where families gathered to cleanse the bodies and prepare them for burial.

"Not enough room for *all* your people to gather," said Sarah. "But for some. That will help, yes?"

They nodded.

"And enough light to read by," said Jacob, "should you need to."

"We will," said Benjamin.

They made the long walk back, one by one, extinguishing the lamps behind them.

"Our father was a wandering Aramean," said Jacob. "A stranger in a foreign land. This is not our people's home, this earth. I sense it is not your people's, either. In the meantime, while we are sojourners here, let us show hospitality, one stranger to another."

They arrived at the door, where one final lamp waited to be extinguished. Before Jacob touched his fingers to the wick, Sarah spoke.

" 'He is near to the brokenhearted.' It matters not to whom the heart belongs. It matters only that it is broken," she said with kindness in her voice. "When the eyes of the Beloved look from heaven, they are drawn to our tears, not looking to see if they are wept from eyes that are male or female, slave or free, Jew or Christian." And now the kindness pooled into her eyes. "This is what I believe, what my husband and I both believe."

When they came out of the catacombs, Jacob handed Benjamin the key.

"Today, the Roman sword comes for *your* people. In times past, it has come for ours. One day, a day not far off, I fear, it will come again."

A piercing gust of cold swirled in the stairwell, and they all cloaked themselves against it.

"Be discreet," Jacob warned. "Come in twos and threes, under cover of night, so as not to attract notice." He paused a beat, then bid them farewell. "Shalom."

"Shalom," said Benjamin.

44

Nero was in his royal box in the Circus, surrounded by his entourage. Seated next to him was Seneca, uncomfortable sitting there, his conscience abraded by the cruelties on display.

"The crowds are not what I had hoped for," remarked Nero as he surveyed the attendance. "Perhaps the people are bored."

Nero was fishing for an opinion, but Seneca withheld it.

"I was thinking about the executions in the Circus," mused Nero. "If I had it to do over again, I would stage the event at night. More dramatic."

Before Seneca could comment, cheers arose for a group of men and women who were being led to the middle of the arena, all of them wrapped in animal skins that had been cinched tight around them. The men who led them snapped whips across their backs, hurrying them along.

"What do you make of this apostle, the rabble-rouser . . . what is his name?" Nero asked, still fishing.

"Paul."

"You know him?"

"I know *of* him."

"So you have not seen him?" asked Nero, skeptical. "Visited him, perhaps? Consulted with him?"

"He is a learned man, I am told."

"I have Peter locked up. Also an apostle . . . *I am told.*"

Seneca let the remark pass, pretending to watch the drama unfolding in the arena. From the stands, the people grouped there looked like a herd of deer. Surrounding them on the periphery were wild dogs that had been starved for the event, crazed with hunger, baring their teeth, darting into the herd to clamp upon an unsuspecting leg or ankle. At each foray, the spectators cheered.

"Paul is a citizen, or so he claims, and requests an audience with the emperor." Nero looked at Seneca to see if what he said registered a reaction, but it did not. "I say, let him wait. Let him rot, for all I care."

One of the dogs lunged and sunk its teeth into one of the men's ankles, dragging him out of the herd and into the open, where the other dogs pounced on him, making quick work of him. It was a furious competition for the carcass, each dog vying for it, one pulling it his way, then another making a run at it, pulling it another way.

The crowd loved it. So did Nero.

One of the men ran from the herd, provoking the dogs to leave the others and chase him down.

"Coward!" yelled Nero. Then turning to Seneca, "Trying to save his own skin. See how they chase him. Listen to the crowd. They love it." Nero turned to his standard bearer. "Send them more bread."

The standard bearer waved a golden pole with a brown flag as servants scurried to resupply the crowds.

The dogs caught up with the fleeing man, tearing off the animal skin that clothed him, then tearing off his own skin.

Inside the huddle of those who were about to die, one of the men told the others. "This time, I will be the one to go. If they eat their fill, perhaps they will be done with us. Or perhaps the crowd will have mercy. Or God."

"Do not go, Servus. Please."

"Stay with us."

"We are stronger together."

The man bolted from the herd, running around it to lure the dogs away from it. "Catch me if you can, you filthy—"

"Look, Seneca! Over there! One of them trying to get away again."

In an instant, they were upon the man, tearing at him savagely, lunging for his neck, his arms, his legs, anything they could sink their teeth into.

"They are such cowards, don't you think?"

"I think you are mad," he said, and stood to leave.

As soon as he left, Nero waved over one of the Praetorian Guard and whispered something in his ear.

The action in the arena was at a standstill, the pack of Christians in the center of the arena, drawing tight, like a cinched purse. And then Nero heard something. A sound, coming from the arena. He cupped his ear. A song of some sort, growing stronger, bolder, almost defiant.

"They are singing," he said, incredulous. But now he was no longer incredulous. Now he was angry. "Those mangy curs are singing!"

The melody went into the stands, where the people sat and could hear the small group of Christians as they sang a hymn before dying. The crowd listened, sympathetically. They talked among themselves, then started to chant.

"Mer-cy! Mer-cy! Mer-cy!"

Nero was appalled. He could not believe these despicable Christians had won the hearts of his people with such a manipulative move.

"Fools! All of you! Can you not see what they are doing? Bewitching you with their spells. Seductresses! All of them!"

"Mer-cy! Mer-cy! Mer-cy!"

"You want mercy? I will give you mercy," he said in a sinister tone. "Send in the elephants," he said to his standard bearer. With a furious wave of a gray flag, massive doors in the arena were pulled open.

The people saw the elephants waiting to be summoned, and they knew what was about to happen. One of the spectators called to those in the stands. As he walked down the steps, row after row followed him.

The chants grew louder. "Mer-cy! Mer-cy! Mer-cy!"

So many people followed the man to the exit that it caught Nero's attention.

"You will miss the best part of the show, you weak-stomached old women!"

He nodded to the standard bearer, who gave the signal to unleash the elephants. They stepped into the arena, tentative at first, pawing their massive feet at the dirt, bellowing through their trunks.

The chants now came from the entire crowd, more insistent; now they were standing, facing the Emperor. "MER-CY! MER-CY! MER-CY!"

Nero sat, stewing in his anger. At Seneca who left. At the Christians who sang. At the crowd who chanted . . .

"MER-CY! MER-CY! MER-CY!"

Driven from behind by trainers with whips, the elephants stampeded directly into the tight circle of men who were singing in the middle of the arena.

Trampling them in a cloud of dust.

Silencing their voices.

And the voice of the crowd.

45

The prison was dark, stuffy with fetid smells and the oil burnt from lamps that lined the walls. The lamps released shadows to roam the prison, creeping warily down the floors, up the walls, across the ceilings, as if seeking some crevice of escape.

Two soldiers guarded the entrance, their spears upright, quick to lower and cross them, forming a sudden gate to the presence of anyone whose presence was unauthorized. Mary had passed the first sentry and was now here at the second. Their spears lowered and crossed.

"Your name?"

"Mary," she said as she handed him a note that granted her permission. "Here to see Peter."

"The Galilean Peter?" he asked.

She nodded. The spears uncrossed, and one of the soldiers escorted her to his cell. Along the walls were hung instruments of torture: rods, chains, straps of leather, a cat-o-nine-tails to which had been embedded shards of pottery to flay skin, bits of metal to gouge muscle, balls of iron to splinter bones. Mary looked at them as she passed, to the blood that had dried on them, to the floor where more blood had fallen, staining the stone, some of it fresh.

When she reached Peter's cell, he stood. His eyes were sunken; his body, gaunt. For a while, neither spoke. Their years with Jesus, so full of wonder. Now this. He had said it would come to this, preparing them, so neither of them was surprised. Still, hearing it was different from living it.

Peter finally spoke. "How fare the others?"

"So many. So very, very many," she said, and the words stuck in her throat. "Gone. In a day."

"The end cannot be far." When he said this, he surreptitiously slipped her a folded piece of papyrus. "One of the guards is sympathetic, supplying me with writing materials. Not so, the others."

Tears filled her eyes. She searched the walls for words, then turned to face him. "I, I have so much . . . to thank you for." Her face, full of gratitude, glistening. "This is not how I thought it would—"

"The Master told me it would end like this. For me, anyway. It need not end like this for the others, or for you. Leave the city. By night, in small numbers, so as not to attract attention."

"Why?"

"It is not important I survive. It *is* important the message survives. Take the hope of it with you."

"Where?"

"North. There are cities to the north that will welcome the message and those who bring it." He clutched the iron bars. "If it does not survive here, it must survive elsewhere."

"And you?"

"If he comes, I will be here to welcome him. If he tarries, I will be the one to go, and he, the one to welcome *me*. Either way, I will be with him. Soon, I hope." He reached his hand through the cell to touch her arm.

"You have a destiny to fulfill," he said. "But it is not here."

46

The small group of Christians sat in a circular room within the Jewish catacombs. Benjamin stood, reading from the papyrus Mary had smuggled out of prison, the last portion of Peter's letter to the Christians who had been dispersed to foreign countries in the east, where they lived as strangers. Before sending the letter on to them, though, he wanted it read to the church in Rome, some of whom were now gathered to hear it.

Mary sat with Marcus and Lydia by her side, holding Leah in her arms.

"'The end of all things is at hand,'" read Benjamin. "'So use sound judgment and be sober-minded for the sake of prayer. Above all, maintain a fervent love among yourselves, for love covers a multitude of sins.'"

As Benjamin read Peter's words, an offering of images from Mary's past came back to her, as if smooth, wave-washed gifts from the Sea of Galilee were being pitched upon the shores of her consciousness.

A memory of Peter. So different now, quicker to hear, slower to speak. And when he did speak, his words were kinder, more patient. He no longer felt the surge of anger that compelled him to call judgment down from heaven on some unreceptive city. Now, on those same unreceptive cities, his only compulsion was to call down mercy.

A memory of Jesus. She remembered when he and his disciples first came to Galilee and the stir it created. Everyone talking about him, the things he said, things he did. It was all they talked about. People from all around the lake traveled to see for themselves what the fuss was all about, and she could not help but to be drawn into the stories, the speculation, the controversy.

Another memory of Jesus. When he stilled the storm within her by delivering her from her demons, she fell at his feet. It was there, at his feet, that everything changed. She would follow him anywhere, she told herself. And she did. She would do anything, give up anything. And she did. Her life forever changed the day he came to Magdala, the moment he first looked into her eyes, first spoke her name, first set her free. Never had a man spoken to her so kindly, treated her so tenderly, changed her so completely.

How could she *not* leave everything to follow such a man?

He spoke words too incredible to believe, did things too incredible to believe. Yet she had heard them with her own ears, seen them with her own eyes. For her, it would have been too incredible *not* to believe.

Still another memory of Jesus. Different words now, coming from his lips. Sobering words. He had told them after he left them that difficult days would come. He told them about the persecution they would go through, the hatred, the rejection. She remembered those words, remembered trying to imagine what it would be like. But she never imagined it would be like this. Never like this.

They had been torn from their homes, their families. Their property confiscated. Imprisoned. Beaten. Slandered. Spit upon. Burned alive. Fed to wild animals. And now. Now they were hiding under the ground, among the dead.

She did not know how much worse it could get. Or how much more she could take. Her heart broke daily, hourly. It was too much to bear, this brokenness. It was just too much.

And yet, whenever she was at her most despondent, God brought someone into her life who looked at her with Jesus' eyes, spoke to her with his words, touched her with his hands. Someone who stooped to pick her up, to lift her, to carry her. Someone who shouldered her burdens, who bound up her wounds, palmed the pieces of her broken heart with such a sense of the sacredness of what they were holding that it reminded her that she had not been forsaken.

Never would she have imagined that the someone God would bring into her life would be a child, let alone three of them. But since she saved those three children from the fire, everything changed. Now she had to take *them* into consideration, their needs, their care, their safety. She had never had children, but because of that one fateful moment, she now had three of them. Hers to love, to teach, to raise, to protect. They were the ones who gave her a reason to carry on, who gave her the strength to fight another day. The strength to believe again, to hope again, love again.

The words Benjamin read interrupted the memories.

"'Dear friends, do not be surprised that a trial by fire is taking place among you, as though something strange was happening to you. But rejoice insofar as you now share the sufferings of Christ, so that when his glory is revealed, you may also rejoice and be glad. If you are insulted in the name of Christ, you are blessed, because the Spirit of glory, that is, the Spirit of God, is resting on you.'"

As he spoke, the words of Peter fell on their parched souls

like a life-giving rain. You could see it in their bodies, slumped with weariness, now straightening. On their faces, etched with worry, now softening. In their eyes, sunken with sorrow, now glistening.

Benjamin continued. "'But not one of you should suffer as a murderer or a thief or a criminal or as a meddler in the affairs of another; but if someone suffers as a Christian, he should not be disgraced, but should glorify God by this name. Because the time has come to begin judgment with the house of God, and if first with us, what will be the outcome for those who do not obey the gospel of God? And if the righteous person is barely saved, what will become of the ungodly and the sinner.'"

The children vied for space on Mary's lap, and somehow she accommodated them, all three of them. They settled into her, comfortably. And it felt comfortable, them on her lap and loving to be there. The final words that Benjamin read helped her soul to crawl upon the lap of her heavenly Father and find that same comfort.

"'So then, let those who are suffering according to the will of God by doing good, entrust their souls to a faithful Creator.'"

If the children could trust *her* so completely, frail as she was, she thought, surely she could entrust herself *and* her children to someone who had proven to be so faithful a friend and so powerful a guardian.

47

The tattered remains of church's leadership in Rome had designated twenty of them to leave the city to go north. They left at night. Most were men, who walked beside their wagon and behind it. Mary and a few of the women came along, riding in the wagon, along with the orphans—Marcus, Lydia, and little Leah.

The wagon was filled with supplies and padded with straw where the women and children sat. It was drawn by two horses, Benjamin at the reins, keeping a steady pace. One of the women held Leah. The other two children were nestled into Mary.

The cold, night sky was ashiver with stars, and all in the wagon were covered up and nestled together. Maybe it was the cold that caused the feeling that felt so much like anxiety, the trembly feeling that ran through them, raising goose bumps. Maybe it was the darkness. Maybe it was uncertainty of the journey. Whatever caused it, the children were unusually talkative and especially inquisitive.

"Is it far, where we are going?" asked Lydia.

"Yes," said Mary.

"Will you be with us?" asked Marcus.

"Yes."

"The whole way?" Lydia asked.

"The whole way," Mary said, smiling at them.

"And stay with us when we get there?" Marcus asked, somewhat fearful that she wouldn't.

"Forever and always."

One of the wheels hit a hole, and the wagon flounced everyone in it. When they settled back into the hay, Lydia changed the subject, taking the conversation down a more somber road.

"Will we see Abba and Mama when we get there?"

"You will see them someday, but not then."

"When?" she asked.

A moment of hesitation, then she answered. "When you die."

The children fell silent.

"What is it like to die?" asked Marcus.

"It is like going away."

"Can you come back?" asked Lydia.

"No."

"Does it hurt?" she asked.

"Sometimes."

"How do you know?" asked Marcus.

"I have been with people who have died. For some, it hurt. For others, it did not."

"It hurts to die in a fire," he said.

"It does."

Which put a pause in the conversation. Then a tear, wending its way down Marcus's cheek.

"I don't want to die," said Lydia.

"I don't want you to die, either."

"But someday I will," the girl said.

"Someday we *all* will."

"Even baby Leah?" she asked.

Mary nodded, but it pained her to do so.

"I don't want to die by myself," said Marcus.

"I don't either," said his sister.

"Will you go with us?" asked Marcus.

"Please?" asked Lydia.

"If I can, I will. Certainly."

"What is it like," asked Marcus, "this 'going away'?"

Mary thought a moment. "Have you ever stood on a dock and waved goodbye to someone who was going away on a ship, someone you loved?"

Both nodded.

"You say goodbye, you wave, you cry. And you stand there, watching the ship for a long time, getting smaller and smaller, until you can no longer see it. But even if you cannot see it, the people you love are still on it, aren't they?"

Again, they nodded.

"They sail and they sail and they sail, until they come to other people they love who are waiting for them on another dock, on a faraway shore. When someone we love dies, it is sad because we have to wave goodbye and not see them for a long time. But at the same time we are saying goodbye, others, who have been waiting a very long time for them to get there, are jumping up and down, shouting to each other, 'They're here! They are finally here!' And when their loved ones—like your abba and mama—get off the ship, they throw their arms around them and say, 'Welcome home!'"

The children were less afraid now.

"Your abba and mama are on that faraway shore, standing on the dock with Jesus, waiting for you to get there, waiting for all of us to get there."

"Even baby Leah?" asked Lydia.

"Yes, even Leah."

The children thought a moment about what Mary had said, weighing the alternatives.

"I don't want to get on the ship," said Marcus.

"I don't either. Not now anyway," said Lydia. "Does that upset Jesus?"

"He understands."

"It makes him sad, though, doesn't it—that we don't want to be with him right away?"

"When he was here, and it was his time to leave, it was hard for him to go, right away."

"Did he cry?"

"Yes."

"Hard?"

"Yes."

"How do you know?"

Mary hesitated. "Some of my friends, they were with him. When he died. And the night before. They told me that he was sad, and that he was afraid. But he prayed. And he prayed some more. And then, when he finished praying, he was ready to go."

"Was he still sad?" asked Lydia.

She paused a beat before answering. "I think so, yes."

"Still afraid?" asked Marcus.

"Not as much, I don't think." She looked into Marcus's eyes, which were fixed on hers. "Are *you* still afraid?"

"Not as much."

She turned to look into Lydia's eyes. "And you?"

"I am less afraid," she said, "but I am still sad."

"I am less afraid," said Mary, "now that I have talked with the two of you."

"Are you still sad?" asked Marcus.

"Yes."

"We will be with you; you know that, don't you? Marcus and I will both be with you."

She smiled.

"The whole way," added Lydia, smiling back.

"Leah, too," added Marcus.

She drew them close and held them.

Held them for a long time.

Until the three of them fell asleep in one another's arms.

PART III

AD 65

ROME

NORTH OF ROME

48

FEBRUARY, AD 65

Lucius's ship finally docked in Ostia, the port city that led to Rome. From there, the cargo was loaded onto a transport that sailed up the Tiber River. It sat low in the water, covered by a gray dome of sky, a light snow falling along the way. The river was fringed with ice along its banks, and the frigid air frosted everyone's breath.

It was very much an inward voyage for the old soldier, for Antonius and Sylvanus, too, who also had been summoned by the emperor. They were all older now, grayer, heavier. Their bodies were badged with scars, proudly worn for the battles they had fought and the valor they had shown in fighting them.

At long last, Lucius arrived in Rome, which he had never seen, for an audience with the emperor, whom he had never met.

He and the other officers were greeted at the dock by an impressive entourage. While the cargo was being removed, the officers were invited into ornate chariots, drawn by two horses, and manned by one driver. Ashuk stood in the chariot behind Lucius as they rode to Rome.

When the procession reached the city, the scale of its

destruction overwhelmed all the soldiers who were seeing the ruins for the first time. The seven hills that once boasted the greatest city in the world were now humbled by the great vacancy that stood in its place. They had heard the stories. They had imagined the destruction. But none of them had imagined this. Lucius could not believe his eyes.

"I was told, in Ostia, that the city had been laid siege by fire," he said to his driver. "But *this* . . . the breadth of it . . . eh . . . I cannot. . . ."

"There are no words," said the driver.

The city was a fretwork of scaffolding, ladders everywhere and laborers climbing up and down them at a brisk pace. Their chariots rode through streets that were congested with supply wagons, carts carrying rubbish to the dumps, and slaves shouldering building materials to construction sites. It was a hive of activity, abuzz with architects consulting with builders, builders giving directions to workers, workers giving orders to slaves. Among them all were vendors of every kind, catering to the labor force, selling everything from food to tools to work clothes.

Craftsmen were everywhere—stonemasons, bricklayers, carpenters, iron workers, sculptors, and artisans of every kind. The sawing, the hammering, the chiseling, the clanging of metal, the setting of stones, it was all so loud a person could hardly keep a thought in place.

The chariots arrived at one of the imperial buildings where Nero was meeting with the planning commission to revise building codes. They had banned wood buildings at a previous meeting. Now they banned the use of wood for structural supports. Going forward, all load-bearing beams had to be made of brick, stone, or marble.

The meeting was interrupted by the entrance of the soldiers, who had been brought there by several of the Praetorian Guard.

It was Lucius's first glimpse of the emperor.

He was shorter than Lucius imagined, and younger—only twenty-nine. Young enough to be his son, should he have had one. He could hardly believe his eyes. *This* was the man who embodied the greatness of Rome? Disappointment passed over his face, a sullen cloud passing over the rolling landscape that had been his life, his dream, his career.

As Nero approached, the soldiers bowed. The emperor raised his hand.

"Soldiers of Rome, a grateful Empire salutes you. I have business to attend to, but tonight you will have my full attention at a banquet in your honor. In the meantime, the city is yours, and every pleasure it has to offer. *Whatever* your pleasure."

Nero approached Lucius. "Lucius Alexander Titus. I recognize you from the description given by your superiors. Tonight you and your officers dine with me. Until then, what is *your* pleasure?"

"To see Rome."

"Come back in a year," he said, amusing himself. "A jest, at least, half so. There is not much to see, but if that is your pleasure, see it you shall." He waved over a nearby guard. "Assign him an escort." Nero touched Lucius's arm. "I will summon you before dinner. I have something to show you."

Lucius and Ashuk accompanied the escort on horseback through the city. They traveled the road that ran parallel to the Tiber River, passing the amphitheater of Statillius Taurus, then moving on to the theater of Balbus. Both structures had survived the fire and were breathtaking.

When they came to the outskirts of the city, they passed

workers who stood on scaffolds, boring holes in charred bricks and cleaning out crumbling mortar before they attached marble façades to cover the decay.

"This way," Lucius told the escort, pointing.

"I would not recommend it."

"You can lead the way, or *I* will."

The escort tacitly consented, guiding his horse down a side street, Lucius and Ashuk following closely behind. The structures were still in ruins from the fire. The deeper into the neighborhood they went, the more desperate the conditions.

"Nothing to see here," said the escort.

"I fought for it all," Lucius replied. "I want to see it all."

Garbage was strewn over the street, haggard dogs nosing through it. The poor were picking through it, too. As the men drew near, beggars retreated to the shadows, fearful of reproach. The sick were lying in the recesses of the ruins, left to die. The stench was overpowering. A cart carrying two bodies was in front of one of the tenements.

"The Christian part of the city," the escort explained. "They're the ones started the fire. A blight, they were. It's the last of them, what you see. Close to it, anyway."

When the tour of the city ended, the escort led them to their quarters. Lucius and Ashuk dismounted, and they were led up the white marble steps by one of the Praetorian Guard. At the entrance, servants awaited them, opening massive doors under a colonnade. The hallway was lined with impressive sculptures and decorated with priceless works of art. A house servant greeted him.

"Your reputation precedes you. We are honored." The servant bowed. "I will take you to your room."

And to Ashuk he said, "Servants' quarters are downstairs."

"He comes with me," said Lucius firmly.

"As you wish," the servant replied, bowing as he did.

He ushered them down the hall and opened a door, leading them inside. As Lucius surveyed the exquisite room, the servant pulled Ashuk aside, whispering, "Is it true your master was the centurion who oversaw the crucifixion of Jesus of Nazareth?"

"A lifetime ago," Ashuk whispered back. "A very *long* lifetime."

A well-dressed house servant ushered Lucius into Nero's chamber, a cavernous room with vaulted ceilings that was dedicated to city planning. The room was filled with tables that held scaled models of proposed projects. A detailed map of the city hung framed on one wall. A hive of compartments on another wall held scrolls of blueprints. Some of the prints had been unscrolled on a long, rectangular table, their corners held down by busts of the Emperor.

"Greetings!" said Nero.

Lucius bowed. "It is my honor."

"Let your eyes feast on the glory of . . . *Neropolis*." Nero said this with emphasis as he made a sweeping gesture that took in the entire room. Lucius so feasted, going from table to table, examining the plans for the city's renaissance. "When I am finished, all previous glory will be eclipsed." Lucius came to the model of an expansive estate. "And the jewel in this imperial crown—my Domus Aurea! Takes your breath away, does it not?"

"Indeed."

"Here," said Nero, pointing to the grounds. "Here is the lake with its myriad of fountains, and the park, the menagerie where exotic animals will be free to roam. And free to be hunted by my guests." He smiled. "A dense forest here, and there vineyards." He moved from one end of the table to the other with mounting enthusiasm. "A city unto itself. But that is not the best part. The best part is my house. My golden house." He pointed to the palatial complex.

"The baths themselves will be one of the great wonders of the world, a flow of hot or cold water, whatever the desire. Of salt or fresh. Even scented. Here. Look." He moved to a cross-section of the model. "The music room. With the largest hydraulic organ ever built. And the stage, where I will perform both classic plays and those of my own writing. It will have the best art in the Empire, best sculptures, best music, best plays, and . . ." He took the top off of one of the models, revealing a huge circular room. "This amazes even me." He motioned Lucius to look. "Enter the banquet hall. The floor, it revolves. And the ceiling, it sends perfumed mists over the guests." He replaced the dome, then touched a statue of himself that stood at the front of the palace. "Gold. A hundred feet of it." Nero stood back, and with a grand, histrionic gesture, he solicited Lucius's praise: "Well, what do you think?"

Lucius stammered at the extravagance. It seemed spun from the mind of an egomaniac, and the only thing more egomaniacal was the way Nero gloated over it.

"There could be a place for you here. A place to grow old and fat and fill your cup with desires denied you on the Frontier," said Nero.

"I am already old," said Lucius, "and my desires are few."

Lucius remained a puzzle to Nero.

"You could have retired years ago, in the vigor of youth. Why didn't you?"

"I did not want to retire until the work Julius had started in Britannia was finished. Took a long time, longer than I thought. But I wanted to help fulfill his vision."

The remark gave Nero pause. "How did a king manage

to wield such influence over a soldier so long after the king's death?"

And that gave Lucius pause. "The story he left behind." Which a opened a door that led him wistfully back to his childhood. "I grew up in a library, where my father worked. My days were spent with my nose to the pages of Caesar's *Gallic Wars*; my nights, dreaming of the glory of Rome. Had no brothers, no sisters. My mother died, too young. Stories were the family that raised me. Raised me to be a soldier. All I ever wanted to be was a centurion, fighting for something noble. And so securing the island for the good of Rome seemed the noble thing to do."

"And Rome is the richer because you did."

Lucius's words spilled out without forethought or measurement of consequence. "Richer, or better?"

"Richer *is* better."

49

As Lucius descended the stairway for the evening's festivities, he caught a glimpse of the emperor, who was dressed in the gold-embroidered purple toga of the *triumphator*, marking him as the triumphant military leader of the Empire. Since this evening was to celebrate the conquest of Britain, Nero made sure that every guest realized where the credit for such a victory belonged.

Lucius was met by a cadre of officers who joined the flow of guests on their way to the dining room. The archway was plastered white and frescoed with a bacchanalian romp that extended from one end of the looming hall to the other. The artwork depicted scantily clad young men and women with loose-fitting togas, frolicking through the woods in various stages of undress. A faun piped the steps of their dance as a rotund Bacchus reigned over the celebration with a goblet in one hand and a leg of lamb in the other. Tendrils of vines wove their way through the tableau, lush with leaves and plump with clusters of grapes, creating a sense of rhythm to the walkway.

Potted palms lined the mosaic floor at evenly spaced intervals. Golden lamps, their wicks burning scented oil, sat on bronze stands, plump and still, like frogs on lily pads. The lamps hued the hallway the way the sun hues the high arch of sky just after sunset.

Soft-sandaled aristocrats walked by bended fronds, and it seemed the fronds were servants fanning them as they passed. They talked of politics, always of politics, as if it were all that mattered. The needed passage of new laws. The tedious demands of public office. Hushed offers of reciprocated favors. Fawning praise of the emperor. Self-deprecating remarks about themselves. Revered silence as the emperor spoke. Hearty agreement when he finished. Or forced laughter, depending how jovial a mood the emperor was in.

Politics bored Nero. Spectacle was what intrigued him. Feasts at his palace. Recitals at the theater. Races at the Circus. He was able to get through the evening with these politicians only by virtue of the distractions he had arranged to entertain them.

The laureled conclave spilled into the dining room. The cavernous room caught Lucius's eye. He craned his neck, taking it all in. Others, who were used to the emperor's flair for ostentation, were eyeing the massive table, maneuvering for seats nearest him.

Two servants carried out a rectangular table and placed it in the room. Lying on the table was a full-length skeleton. Other servants brought oaken vats of wine and placed them on either side of the table, along with a dazzling array of goblets, which the servants filled and distributed to the guests. All waited to drink until Nero made the opening toast.

He stood, raising his goblet: "Let us live while it is allowed us to enjoy life. Drink and be merry." Then he extended his arm in the direction of the skeleton. "For thus shall you be after death."

He toasted his guests, and they him.

The emperor clinked his goblet against Lucius's. "Your name has been spoken of, several times today." He paused to gauge Lucius's response, but there was none. "You are lauded by your superiors," he said, "which causes me to favor you."

Lucius lowered his head, acknowledging the compliment.

"And by your subordinates, which causes me to fear you." An uncomfortable pause lingered between them. "*Should* I fear you?"

"Fear only what I fear—that I somehow prove unworthy of serving you."

The words were not fawning, but there was no fervor in them either.

"Your strategy in Britannia was the brilliance of a general." The emperor looked for a trace of treachery in the man's eyes, but there was not so much as a glimmer that he could detect, and he was a master of detection. "Do you covet such a position?"

"I covet only to do the emperor's will."

Nero paused, still studying him. "It is my will that you sit."

He motioned Lucius to the seat next to him. The burnished soldier took his place next to the royal chair, ornately carved and gilded.

Nero asked Lucius about the campaign in Britain as barefoot slaves padded about, standing behind guests, filling their goblets and toweling their hands from the grease of the wild boar they picked at as it passed, or of the succulent game birds: pheasant, quail, and dove.

"I was hoping to meet Seneca while I was here," said Lucius at a lull in the conversation.

Nero cut his eyes to one of the senators, who wiped his mouth with a napkin to conceal a snicker. "You know him?"

"Only through his writings. I have read them all. Unless he has written something new."

"He tutored me, you know," said Nero. "Or did you? He

served me well in my youth, reasonably well thereafter, but then, then his loyalties came into question. He conspired with Paul, that weevil of a man. 'Consulted with him,' is the way Seneca put it. Imagine that. A confidant of the emperor consulting with an enemy of the Empire. Well, he consults no longer."

Again, those around them cleared their throats, dabbed their mouths with their napkins, and took sips from their goblets to avoid laughing.

"He's dead?" asked Lucius. "Executed for consul—"

"No, no," interrupted Nero. "What do you take me for? I did not kill him. I retired him. Relieved him of his duties. He was becoming such a bore. The only thing worse than a bore is a bore who cannot stop talking, a wearisome trait he passes off as 'advising.' And his philosophy, with all its shoulds and oughts. I found it all—what is the word?—*confining*. In the end, it was not philosophy that set me free, it was the arts. Later in the evening, I will play something, sing something. You'll see."

"So Seneca is alive?"

"He is alive and well, shunned to my country estate, where there is no risk of him boring anyone."

Their conversation was drowned out by a claustrophobic crowd of dancers, musicians, and jesters.

Nero stood. "Walk with me," he said, pointing to the hallway that led to his gardens. "I need air."

Once outside, Lucius saw a line of wooden crosses, where enflamed bodies illumined the gardens. Shadows hid among the trees as if grotesque spirits of the dead, shielding themselves from the horrific sight.

The victims had been tied to wooden beams that crisscrossed at diagonals. To fuel the flames they had been dressed in clothes soaked with tar and oil. Their chins, what remained of them, had been lashed to the Vs in the crosses. All that was left of them curled wraithlike into the night sky.

The two walked side by side at a leisurely pace, Nero waiting for Lucius to speak, as if hoping to measure him by the first words that came from his mouth. But Lucius did not speak, did not stop. He kept stride with the emperor. And he kept quiet. Which apparently troubled Nero all the more.

"What say you of all this?" the emperor asked.

Lucius, distracted by all that surrounded him, did not hear the question. He stopped at one of the crosses, where a woman burned beyond recognition hung dead. A memory flamed before him, of Mary. And he studied the remains on the cross to see if it could be her.

"I am whispered rumors of your past." Nero watched as the light played over Lucius's face, a face worn from the weariness of war. "Did you know him, this Jesus, the one they call the Christ?"

"I never knew him," he said. "I only saw him die."

"And afterward? Did you see him *after* he died?"

Lucius shook his head. "I just heard stories."

"He claimed to be a king, I am told."

"If so, his kingdom was not of *this* world."

"If so, we have nothing to fear."

"If so, we have *everything* to fear, you and I."

Nero was suddenly suspicious. "Where lie your loyalties?"

Lucius brought a fisted arm across his chest, a rote gesture. "Caesar is my only king; the glory of Rome, my only ambition."

The words were not said with conviction, as a younger soldier obsessed with ambition might say them, but calmly, as an older soldier whose ambitions had grown tired from the years of obsessing.

Relieved, Nero made broad, sweeping gestures as if to gather Lucius into the dramatic center of his being. "Celts to the west. Barbarians to the north. The hordes of Asia to the east. We are surrounded by the forces of darkness. But *here,*" he said, balling his hand into a fist, "here within these city walls, the glory of Rome burns eternal, does it not?"

Lucius surveyed the human torches. "It does tonight."

Nero raised his voice, pushing his finger into the night air. "Tonight and tomorrow night and for as many nights as it takes to rid the Empire of these vermin."

He turned to face the soldier, now pushing his finger into his chest. "It matters not whether the vermin are Christians or Jews. Rats or mice, they still eat through the sacks of Roman grain. In time, we will rout them all." He paused dramatically, to make his point. "Today, Christians gnaw the greater hole." Nero's face lightened. "So today, they light my gardens. Tomorrow it will be the Jews. I have received word of unrest—in Jerusalem, Caesarea." He paused again. "Already my word has gone out." He smiled wickedly, maniacally, as shadows of the dead flickered across his face. "So it is written," he said under his breath, as if it were a kept secret, "so it shall be done."

The spell that Nero had spun over himself was broken by a servant. "Your gifts are ready and awaiting you, your Excellency."

As the servant left, Nero put a paternal arm around Lucius, an incongruous gesture because of the difference in their ages. "The bellies of Roman ships arrived abloat with bounty. And tonight, tonight a grateful emperor is sharing them. Come. Come and receive your reward for a lifetime of service to the greatest empire the world has ever known."

50

It was a few hours before dawn, and the festivities were over. At least, for Lucius. He entered his royal suite, carrying a heavy, exquisitely crafted box. He put it on the table, wearily. It was the end of a long evening that had come at the end of a long journey that had come at the end of a long life.

A lamp burned beside a box of stationery. It was the finest papyrus, smooth and without imperfection. A stylus. Ink. A seal, with wax. And in the waning hours before dawn, he penned a letter.

When he finished, he signed it and sealed it. He had had too much wine, too much food, too much of everything, especially of Nero. He felt nauseated. He stood at the window, where he saw a corner of Nero's gardens. The crosses were now so much smoldering charcoal.

So this is it, he told himself. *This is what I have been fighting for all these years. This is why I went to the Frontier, to defend these borders? This is why I went to Britannia, to expand them? This is why I sent my soldiers into battle, why lives were lost, and the losses deemed not only acceptable but laudable? This is it, Rome, the heart of the Empire. The dark heart. Filled with egomania, paranoia, treachery, and every manner of lust, each of them insatiable.*

This.

It was not so much that his heart had sunk at the realization, but it was as if the very ground beneath him had sunk, and all that he once thought solid, all that he had built his life upon, all of it in one cataclysmic moment of clarity had fallen into an abyss of awareness that he had been fighting the wrong wars all of these years, losing territory within himself with every territory he had gained for Rome.

It was those thoughts he took with him to bed.

The next day, Lucius woke to find Ashuk bringing a tray from the emperor's kitchen, but he waved off the food. He got out of bed, went to the table, where he picked up the letter he had written only hours before. Ashuk followed, thinking his master had some errand for him to run.

"I served a lifetime for a kingdom I had never seen, until now," he said to Ashuk. "I can no longer call myself a soldier of that kingdom. Nor a citizen." He looked at the ornately carved wooden box. "I am a man who has traded his life for a box of gold." Lucius opened it, revealing its contents. Gold coins, freshly minted, with the bust of Nero glinting from each one.

He handed Ashuk the letter, who looked at it quizzically. "A letter of emancipation," Lucius explained. "And the gold," he said, putting the box in Ashuk's hands. "I mentioned it in the letter so no one could accuse you of stealing it. It cannot atone for my sins, which are many, but it can allow you to go home, to your people . . . a free man."

An unexpectedly awkward moment for Ashuk, who stood silent, and troubled. His eyes turned away.

"Why the sadness? You are free."

Ashuk's eyes made a slow return. "And you are not. That is my sadness." He measured his words carefully. "You were a different man after you met her. And different still after you left her. Perhaps it is not too late to find her. Perhaps, even now, it is not too late."

"I would not know where to look, even where to begin to look." And it seemed the admission took what little life that remained in him.

"She was here," said Ashuk.

"What?"

"Three days ago."

Lucius's eyes sparked to life. "Who told you?"

"A servant in Caesar's household, a woman."

"How did she know?"

"She was Mary's friend. Good friend. She sought me out when she learned you were here. Told me that Mary came to Rome years ago. But after the fire, when persecution broke out, Peter sent her away."

"Where?"

Lucius met Caesar's servant in a storeroom while Ashuk kept watch while they are on the floor, studying a map.

"Twenty, counting the children," she said.

"Children?"

"Mary's."

"She has children?"

"Their parents died in the fire. She cares for them like her own."

"Someone's coming," said Ashuk.

She hurriedly pointed out the route, her voice lowered. "This road here, going north. But they won't be on it. They'll be to the left of it, far enough away to be out of sight."

At the sound of servants talking, they got up. He stuffed the map in his coat, and she busied herself at a shelf.

Back in their lavish quarters, Ashuk helped Lucius get ready for his journey. He placed the armor and weapons on the bed, then picked up the metal breastplate.

"It no longer serves me," said Lucius, "nor I, it."

Over his undergarments Lucius put on his boots, a woolen garment, a plaited leather jacket, a belt, and his cape. He took his dagger but left his sword. Ashuk picked it up.

"Your sword?"

Lucius patted the sheath that holds his dagger. "This is enough."

Ashuk extended it to him. "You should take it."

"I should have left it a long time ago."

There was a knock on the door, and Ashuk cracked it open, revealing the Numidian servant who showed them to their room.

"The horse is ready," he said.

"Your fastest?" asked Lucius.

The servant nodded.

At the stables the Numidian servant held the reins to a spirited mare. Ashuk handed Lucius a saddlebag and a blanket.

"May your god be with you," he told Lucius.

"My god?" And he paused. "My god has forsaken me."

He clasped Ashuk's forearm.

Lucius mounted his horse. "A good destiny to you, my friend."

"And to you . . ."

He kicked the horse's flanks and galloped away.

As he did, the words he had never imagined hearing nor speaking fell from Ashuk's lips.

. . . "my friend."

51

Lucius rode through the day, into the night, and on toward the dawn. The farther north he rode, the colder the weather was, the snowier the landscape. His steed's hooves bit the hard earth as the wind whipped across his face, numbing his ears, his nose, his lips. His eyes stung, and ice ledged the brows above them.

He slowed when he saw what looked like a confrontation of some kind. All he could make out was a small band of soldiers and a disorganized huddle of peasants milling around in an adjacent field. He rode to the soldiers, reining in his mare. They were mercenaries, and that alone disgusted him. Rome increasingly had hired foreigners to do some of its fighting, enticing them with the lure of fortune that awaited them in plundering enemy homes, stealing livestock, and pilfering whatever they could from the pockets of the dead. These warriors had little respect, either for rank or for protocol. They had little discipline while they were on duty, and none while they were off. And they had no sense of loyalty, as they were always shifting allegiances, depending on the pay. And no sense of honor, save whatever honor existed among thieves.

"I am looking for a woman."

"Who isn't?" smirked an officer, inciting a riot of laughter around him.

Lucius did not laugh. He surveyed the people who had been rounded up. He called out, "Mary! Is a Mary Magdalene among you?"

No one answered.

He turned to the officer in charge. "Who are they?"

"Enemies of the Empire."

"*They?*" He was incredulous, for they were merely farmers and their families.

"Following orders, that's all," explained the officer.

He showed Lucius Nero's letter with its imperial seal. Lucius skimmed it, returned it. "That is the charge, *being Jews?*"

"Jews, Christians, Huns. What difference? An enemy's an enemy."

Like a nervous ball of sheep, the Jewish families drew together. Mothers pressed their babies to their bosoms. Older children shielded the younger ones, putting arms around their shoulders and hands over their eyes. Fathers stood on the outside facing the soldiers, forming a barrier between their families and the soldiers.

The officer ordered his archers. "Fill your bows!" Each pulled an arrow from his quiver, set the notch in the bowstring, drew it back.

Lucius protested. "They are peasants, of no consequence. Save your arrows for the Huns."

"Let fly!"

The *twang* of bowstrings was followed by the *thip* of arrows finding their marks on the chests of the older men, who fell backward from the impact. The archers fired randomly now, the arrows piercing through the backs of women and into the infants they held in their arms. As the mothers fell, screams of the younger girls rent the air. With a final volley, the screams were silenced.

The soldiers were quick to the business of plundering the houses. "First gets, first keeps," as the saying went. Turning from the thievery, Lucius led his horse to water, letting her drink her fill for the journey ahead.

From the scene of the massacre came the sound of a woman crying. Lucius heard it and turned his head. The officer heard it, too.

"Quiet the cur," he told the soldier next to him.

The soldier unsheathed a dagger. Instead of killing her, though, he returned with her, his hand clutching the shock of hair that fell past her shoulders. The others stopped their looting and fixed their lecherous eyes on her.

"The spoils of war!" shouted one of them.

"Pass her around."

The men roared, and a few of them groped her.

"Stand your turn," snapped the soldier who found her.

The officer pushed him away. "Officers first." He pulled her head back with one hand, kissing her roughly.

Lucius was taking it all in, knowing where it would all lead, how it would all end. He pulled a bow from the nearby supply wagon and filled it with an arrow. He drew back the string, searching for his target. It was a clear shot to the officer's chest. He drew the string back farther.

He shot.

The sound of a *thip* as the arrow found its mark.

The officer's face freezing, his eyes widening.

He turned his face to the side where the young woman clutched the arrow in her chest. She looked at Lucius, and a moment passed between them. Of gratitude, perhaps. Or forgiveness. And she fell to the ground.

Lucius returned the bow to the cart and mounted his horse.

The officer accosted him. "Whaddya think you're doin'?"

"Following orders, that's all. Orders *you* seem to have forgotten."

The officer was enraged. *"She was the spoils of war!"*

Lucius cantered his horse around him, speaking calmly. "She was an enemy of the Empire." He pulled back the reins. "And you, a sorry excuse for a soldier."

Lucius kicked his horse's flanks and rode away. As he rode, he felt something of himself coming back, something of the life he had lost so many years ago.

52

He pushed his knees into the horse's ribs, and it lengthened its strides. The sun was to the left, throwing the striding shadow onto the snow beside him. It seemed a race between two horses, equally matched, equally driven. For the better part of an hour, they did not let up, pushing each other, stride for stride.

A frozen pond came into view, and Lucius pulled lightly at the reins, steering his horse to water. He stopped at the pond and dismounted. He unsheathed his dagger, and with hilt fisted in hand, punched a hole through the ice so his horse could drink. When she finished, he cupped his hand and drew water for himself. After a few swallows, he splashed a handful into the burn of his reddened eyes, rubbed them, then brushed away the remaining droplets before they froze to the stubble on his face.

He took a flattened map from his satchel, rolled it out, and compared it to the terrain. Turning it slightly to align it with the setting sun, he got his bearings. His route was over a range of rugged hills directly in front of him.

It would take a day to ride around them. At least. He picked the lowest hill, which was also the steepest. Once at the base, his horse picked its way up the incline. Here and there she faltered. Each time she did, Lucius let her get her footing, then continued the climb. She stopped, her great bulk shivering. Gathering strength, she lurched forward. As she did, a branch slapped across its face, sending a tree full of snow cascading around them. The horse shook its head and snorted to clear its nose. Lucius brushed his head, his shoulders, his arms. Bending forward, he patted the horse's neck.

"Easy, girl. Easy."

Almost to the top. One more push. He summoned all of his strength and kicked against her. In response, she summoned all of hers and charged the hill. One thunderous bolt, hooves skittering against the slick surface. Her legs flew out from under her, throwing Lucius as she landed sideways in the snow, whinnying.

Lucius gathered himself to his knees to survey the damage. Nostrils flared, pluming out frost. Chest heaving erratically. Eyes bloodshot and bulging with terror. Her coat, sheened with sweat, all twitchy and trembling. The only sound was its labored breathing.

Lucius patted her coat, speaking to her. "Steady. Stay. Stay."

He ran his hands down her legs to check for broken bones, but there were none. He patted her neck to calm her, her jaw, her muzzle. It helped. He took a rope out of his saddlebag and looped it around an uphill tree. The other end he tied to her reins. After cinching it tight, he took the loose end of the rope and wrapped it around his forearm. He then got behind the horse and dug his feet into the ground for a foothold. Once he had one, he pushed, all the while taking up the slack in the rope.

"Come on, girl. Go!"

He pushed against the massive mound of coarse hair that was her rump. She struggled to right herself, frantically, but she could not. He pushed again.

"Up! Get up! Come on!"

She struggled to her front knees, steadied herself on one front foot, now the other, now her back feet, and then she was up.

"Good, girl! Good, good!"

Instead of going over the hill, he traversed it with her while she got her confidence back. Once on the crest, he saw that a smaller hill still faced them. He walked his horse down the hill, again traversing it in switchbacks until they arrived at the bottom.

Flecks of snow were falling, thick and heavy, and he felt it best to assault the hill tomorrow. His mare was exhausted. So was he. He bedded down for the night under a stand of evergreens, their branches forming a canopy above them. He got his horse to kneel, then to lie down. He stretched out beside her, sidling next to her warmth. He did not know how much farther he could push her, how much farther he could push himself.

He rubbed his face to take away the numbness. Then, more gently, he rubbed his eyes, which were tired and dry and bloodshot. They seemed to be searching for something. But he was weary of the search and for a moment closed them. When he opened them, he wiped the snow from his arms, which were a stitch work of scars, all shapes and sizes, each telling the story of a different battle.

He looked at them, realizing he had forgotten which battles had inflicted which wounds. The stories of the battles themselves were crumbling, like scrolls of ancient papyrus, fragments breaking off, creating gaps in the story. Gaps of recalling what happened and when. Gaps of understanding why this battle was so important. Gaps of accounting where its price was balanced somehow against the cost of his soldiers' lives. A hundred for one; a thousand for another.

Who even remembers their names? he wondered. *Who they were, where they came from, who they loved . . . let alone the stories they left behind?*

His thoughts moved stiffly but resolutely. *Tell me, Seneca. This life, this fleeting life filled with so much heartache . . . so many hopes, dreams, prayers . . . dashed against . . . what? . . . the indifferent shores of Nature? Chance? After all you have said, it is my turn to speak. I say . . . let not the dying deceive themselves with talk of God. There is no providential hand guiding us. And assuredly not guiding me.*

There is only the life I have lived.

And what was the point of that? Speak, Seneca, if you dare. The good of the Empire? The glory of Rome? And when it is the Empire's turn to die, what is the point of the life it has lived? When it is buried and its bones ground to dust, of what value is the dust? And Rome? When it is one day trodden underfoot by some barbarian horde, where goes its glory? It will slip beneath the horizon like the setting sun, taking its glory with it, never to dawn again.

Do not talk to me of destiny.

Sleep came quickly, but it was fitful.

He stirred the next morning, late, a sudden numbness waking him. His horse's chest was cold and hard. He sat up, and a layer of snow fell from his blanket. For a moment he just sat there, staring. He brushed the layer of flakes from its shoulders, then from its neck, its face.

He was too tired to think, to feel, to move. His shoulders grew heavy, their weight pulling him forward. His eyes fell on his hands. His skin, once thick and smooth, was now thin and slack and splotched with age.

He pushed his hand toward his dagger. His fingers, mottled from the cold, could barely bend around the hilt.

Together, like a group of assassins, they slowly pulled the dagger from its sheath.

Brought it to his chest.

Pushed.

But their strength had left them, and the dagger fell to the ground. He stared at it, without expression. His eyes blinked, once, twice, then closed. For a long time he sat in darkness. Finally he opened them. He took his hand and pushed away the snow on the ground, as if smoothing the wrinkles in a sheet before climbing into bed.

And there he lay himself down to die.

53

Lucius slept through the next day and into the late afternoon, which had been warmed by the sun that had broken through the low covering of clouds. Its sudden heat had softened patches of snow held by the branches. Handfuls fell to the ground in plops . . . one . . . then another . . . and another.

Finally, one fell on Lucius, hitting his shoulder . . . and another, hitting his head.

His eyes fluttered. The branch above him came into focus, still shaking. His nose twitched at a scent in the air. He sniffed. The scent of burning wood.

His eyes shot open.

He moved. His joints were stiff and swollen and wracked with pain. But he moved. Again, a little more. With great effort, he pushed himself up.

Then he saw it.

Curls of smoke just beyond the hill.

He hefted himself to his knees, to his feet, to his hope.

One step, then another. And another still. He trudged up the steep incline, slowly at first, slipping, stumbling, but all the while ascending.

Upon reaching the crest, he caught his breath and peered

down at a large frozen pond cupped in the palm of the sur-rounding hills. Campfires dotted the circumference at evenly spaced intervals. *Roman* campfires. From that circumference, a group of people who had been stripped of their clothes were being led to the center of the lake.

With the blood pumping through him in his ascent, Lucius thawed. His legs grew stronger, his footing more sure. He started his descent; his face slapped by branches; his feet, tripped by roots. He stopped at a tree to steady himself, and from there he looked to the middle of the pond where the people now sat, bunched together.

He ran, and, gaining speed, tumbled headlong. But he picked himself up, pushed himself down the hill, never letting up.

He reached the encampment, out of breath, and grabbed his knees for a moment's reprieve. Two soldiers, warming themselves at a fire, saw he was a soldier, and assisted him.

"Take me . . . to the officer in charge."

One of the soldiers took him to a tent, where a young offi-cer rose to greet him.

"Request permission to question your prisoners."

Taken aback by the request, the officer looked leery. "To what end?"

"To find someone. A woman."

His tone was now insistent. "*To what end?*"

"To mine, if I don't find her."

The officer studied Lucius, his eyes, his wrinkles, his scars.

"I once sat where you are sitting, a soldier of Rome, a centurion."

The younger man weighed the merits of his elder. "Rank has its privileges," the officer said. "*And* its privacies. Be quick."

The sun had slipped beneath the horizon, filling the sky

with a flush of color. Lucius stepped onto the frozen pond, cleating the ice as he walked toward the center of the lake, where sat a shivering mass of nakedness, twenty or so.

He stopped a few feet away while his eyes swept from person to person. The people looked up, wondering if he had been sent to negotiate with them or simply to put an end to them.

Then he saw her.

Her face was down-turned, her hair covering it in stiff strands. Her arms cradled a child, and her body was buttressed by a boy on one side, a girl on another.

"Mary!" His voice wakened her. She lifted her head, straining to recognize him. He knelt beside her. "It's you! Oh, dear God, it's you!" He covered her shoulders with his cape. "I can talk to the centurion in charge, reason with him, I am sure." His voice trembled with hope. "Come."

Her words came slowly. "I can't." Her eyes turned to her children, her hands moving over them lovingly.

"If you stay, you will die."

"I died before I came."

A hard moment for Lucius. He turned, and all that followed him was the hollow sound of ice crunching beneath his boots.

Coming to the centurion's tent, Lucius drew back the flap. The blood in him was at a boil, and its heat enlivened him.

"The woman, her being here, it is a mistake."

"Then bring her. Let her warm herself by *Roman* fires, fill herself with *Roman* food, clothe herself with *Roman* clothes. She has only to recant."

Lucius left the tent, flustered. Color had left the sky, taking with it the colors of the earth, leaving behind a muted collection of grays. As he approached the middle of the pond, he saw that his cape was no longer around her shoulders but draped over her three children, who were snuggled next to her on one side. He bent a knee squarely in front of Mary, cradled her head in his hands, and looked into her eyes.

"Do not do this."

"I am not doing this," she said. "Rome is."

"Will you hear no reason?"

"Will reason be *all* you hear?"

He rose to his feet, slowly. Reason had left him. So had words. He left to make another appeal. By the time he reached the tent, reason had returned to him. He entered to see the centurion sitting at his table, poring over a map. This time, he did not stand.

"Why not take a sword and make quick work of them?" Lucius asked.

"I would rather make an example of them."

"For *whom?*"

"For anyone who passes by. A monument to the futility of resisting Rome."

"You call *that* resisting?"

"I call it foolishness, but my thoughts are not important. The emperor calls it a resistance movement."

"What are they resisting?"

"The emperor's divinity."

"I have met the emperor. Dined at his table. Walked with him, talked with him. He has no divinity. And precious little humanity."

The young centurion weighed the worth of arguing the point and found no merit in engaging him.

"I am a soldier. With orders. They, out there," he said, pointing in the direction of the captives. "*They* are my duty."

Lucius looked at him, seeing an image of his former self,

an image that now repulsed him. "You say it as if you thought it noble."

The centurion paused at the affront but did not take offense. He drew his dagger, laid it flat on the table, and pushed it toward Lucius. "Show them mercy if you like, if you think that more noble."

Lucius took the dagger.

54

Lucius walked out of the tent, into the darkness.
A low moon rising over the hills sent his shadow ahead of
him.

The only sound was hobnails on the ice.

He clutched the dagger in his hand, squeezing it tighter
with each step.

Halfway to the shivering mass in the middle of the pond,
his steps slowed, his fingers relaxed.

The dagger fell clinking onto the ice.

A few steps farther, and he dropped his helmet.

He continued walking, then let fall his breastplate.

As he walked, he unfastened his belt, letting it fall, too,
along with his sheath.

A few steps farther he took off one boot, then the other.

Finally, his undergarments.

He took his place among them and sat beside Mary.

He looked into her eyes, and she into his. Her face had
lost its feeling, and her lips could only form the beginning of a
smile. "You returned for me."

A lifetime of longing pooled in his eyes. "I have loved you
for so long. And I have never even held your hand."

Mary took his hand in hers, drawing it to her face, and touched the back of it to her lips.

"I remember a man," came a voice, and it was a voice from the past. Lucius looked up. It was Cassio, the soldier who was at Jesus' tomb, surrounded now not by his fellow soldiers but by his wife, his children, his grandchildren. "A long time ago, in Jerusalem . . . a noble man, though he did not know it then and perhaps does not know it now, heard my story . . . a story too incredible to believe . . . yet he believed it. I prayed I could find him someday. To thank him"—the words came hard—"for a family I would have never had . . . were it not for him."

They were losing the battle with the cold, all of them. Their eyes were heavy, their faces were numb, and their lips were slow to form words. Marcus, who was huddled next to Mary, did the best he could to form these.

"Do you have a story?"

Lucius looked at him, puzzled.

"Of Jesus," the boy said.

"Did you see him do a miracle?" asked Lydia, and it took all the strength she had to ask it.

He paused a moment before answering. "I only saw him die."

A hush fell over them.

"Of all stories," said Benjamin, "that is the one we need to hear most."

Their eyes, weak as they were, fixed on him in anticipation. As the stars trembled above them, the small company of believers huddled closer as if to warm themselves by the fire of his story. When its telling was over, no one spoke.

Mary rested her head against the strength of his chest, the cold rim of her ear warming against his skin. The cold had battled her body until only a torso of warmth remained. Her teeth no longer chattered, her lips no longer trembled. His heat spread from her ear to her neck, her head, her face. She no longer felt cold. She felt only the cushion of his chest against her head, the comfort of his skin against her skin. Her lungs breathed in time with his, as if the rhythm of her existence had been reset, and it lulled her to sleep.

He longed for nothing else. Nothing of Rome. Nothing of Alexandria. Nothing of the sea. It was enough to have her in his arms. Forever and always in his arms.

The night deepened.

As it did, the pale marble sculpture glistened in the moonlight; their bodies melded together, their heads leaning against one another.

Mary, her head at rest on Lucius's chest.

And Lucius, his cheek at rest upon her head.

The night softened.

The landscape was a nested gray silence. The first color came to a covering of low clouds, vaguely pink, tinting the brooding stillness in the middle of that frozen, windless sea.

The only sound, birdsong in the distance.

Then came the dawn.

THE END

SOURCES

T*he Centurion* is a work of historical fiction. The text of Scripture was the inspiration for the story. That text, along with the testimony of history, provided the parameters of my work. Literary license was taken only when those sources were either sketchy or silent. The following sources were consulted to make sure the historical and cultural backgrounds of the story were accurate. The entries are sequentially arranged in the order of their appearance in the book.

I have included these notes to give readers the opportunity to go a little deeper into the history of the era and into the lives of the characters. Over the years I have taught writing and mentored a number of writers, but because I am no longer able to do that, I have included this section to give those who are interested in writing a look into the creative process and an understanding of how I arrived at some of my decisions.

Regarding the Aramaic phrase "Eli, Eli, lama sabachthani?" See Matthew 27:46 (rsv)—"And about the ninth hour Jesus cried with a loud voice, saying, 'Eli, Eli, lama sabach-thani?' that is, 'My God, my God, why hast thou forsaken me?'" The quote expresses the pain of abandonment that Jesus felt during the three hours of darkness on the cross. It finds an echo in the centurion's feelings of abandonment that led to the erosion of his faith. And it is intended to give readers an emotional place where they can identify with the main character, for at some time or another we have all experienced similar feelings.

Regarding Ovid. Ovid was a poet who wrote under the reign of Augustus. Born in 43 BC, Ovid traveled to Rome as a teenager, where he studied Greek and Latin literature, along with rhetoric. He later went to Athens to study philosophy. Among his writings are *Metamorphoses* ("Transformations"), *Amores* ("Love Poems"), *Ars Amartoria* ("The Art of Love"), *Fasti* ("Holidays"), along with some lesser works. The *Metamorphoses* is his greatest work, written at the height of his creative powers. It is a series of 250 stories, woven into an unbroken narrative that chronicles the entire span of Greek and Roman mythology. Beginning with the initial transformation of the primeval chaos into the creation, it ends with the transformation of Julius Caesar into a star. Ovid's works were quoted widely during his lifetime. He died around AD 18. For a fascinating study on his colorful life, see the chapter "The Poet" in *Romans and Barbarians* by Derek Williams (New York: St. Martin's Press, 1998), 116–65.

My use of Ovid's story is meant to do two things. One, to foreshadow the love story. And two, to help establish the point of view from which the story is told. The story is told not from a Jewish perspective or a Christian perspective but rather from a Roman perspective, seen through the centurion's eyes. Because of this decision, I do not quote from Christian or Jewish sources but from Roman ones, such as Ovid, Virgil, and Seneca.

Regarding the use of BC and AD. The terms BC (Before Christ) and AD (*anno Domini*, Latin for "in the year of the Lord") are ways of reckoning time that date from centuries after my story takes place. Although the Roman calendar, or Julian Calendar, began to see changes within two hundred years after Christianity was legalized, the present Gregorian Calendar was not formalized by Pope Gregory XIII until AD 1882. It remains the most common way of reckoning time today.

Since I decided to write my story from a Roman perspective, I realized that this way of reckoning time was an anachronism. If I were to be rigorously consistent, I would have used the Roman way of reckoning time, which started not with the birth of Christ but rather with the birth of Rome. The founding of Rome was believed to be 753 BC, which, from a Roman perspective, would be 1 AUC (*ab urbe condita*, Latin for "from the founding of the city"). Consequently, AD 33, where I begin my story, would be 786 AUC. At the end of the day I decided that to be rigidly consistent regarding the method of dating would come at the expense of distracting my readers. And that is why I opted for AD instead of AUC. It is less consistent, but it is more clear.

Regarding the Passover moon. "The three great annual festivals, the Passover with the Feast of Unleavened Bread at the vernal full moon, the Harvest Feast, or Feast of Weeks, in midsummer, and the Feast of the Ingathering, or of Booths, at the time of the vintage, marked in ancient Palestine are the three great seasons of the agricultural year." George Foot Moore, *Judaism in the First Centuries of the Christian Era*, vol. 2 (New York: Schocken Books, 1971), 23. "The Passover was to be celebrated at the full moon in the first month of a year beginning in spring." Roland deVaux, "Religious Institutions," in *Ancient Israel*, vol. 2 (New York: McGraw-Hill, 1961), 485.

This seemingly inconsequential piece of historical information allowed me to use the moon in a number of ways in the story.

Sometimes the moon is used to tell time, as in this case:

> The moon was low and almost transparent
> against the pale gray sky.

Sometimes it is used to give unity to a spatial transition, as in this instance:

> The fullness of the Passover moon ladled
> its whiteness onto the quarried limestone of
> Jerusalem, spilling over the straightness of its
> gap-toothed walls . . . over the unevenness of
> the structures within them . . . over the nar-
> rowness of its streets that connected the urban
> sprawl of shops and homes, along with the
> secular encroachments of Roman occupation.

Other times, the moon is used to enhance the drama, as in this example:

> From the shadows came a voice. "What
> has become of us?" Mary Magdalene stepped
> into a shunt of moonlight.

Regarding Passover. For Old Testament references to Pass-over, see Exodus 12:1–13:16; Deuteronomy 16:1–8. For New Testament references, see John 1:29, 36; 19:36; 1 Corinthians 5:7; 1 Peter 1:18–19; Revelation 5:12. For background to Pass-over, especially at the time of Christ, see Anthony J. Saldarini, *Jesus and Passover* (New York: Paulist Press, 1984). For back-ground to Passover rituals of the Temple at the time of Christ, see Alfred Edersheim, *The Temple: Its Ministry and Services* (Grand Rapids: Eerdmans, 1972), 208–48.

Theologically, the juxtaposition of the Jewish holiday to Good Friday makes the comparison between the sacrifice of the Passover lamb and the sacrifice of the Lamb of God impossible to miss. John the Baptist made sure we wouldn't miss it when he saw Jesus and proclaimed: "Behold, the Lamb of God who takes away the sin of the world" (John 1:29 RSV). And Paul, looking back on the crucifixion, made sure we wouldn't miss it when he said, "Christ, our Passover Lamb, has been sacrificed" (1 Cor. 5:7 NIV).

Regarding the geography of Jerusalem. For background to the geography of Jerusalem, particularly the Kidron, Hinnom, and Tyropean valleys, see I. W. J. Hopkins, *Jerusalem: A Study in Urban Geography* (Grand Rapids: Baker Book House, 1970), 28–44. Regarding the infamy of the Valley of Hinnom, Joachim Jeremias writes, "*Road sweepers* may be referred to in b. B. M. 26a (cf. b. Pes. 7a): 'According to R. Shemaiah b. Zeira the streets of Jerusalem were swept every day', evidently to secure the levitical purity of the city. The fact that the Valley of Hinnom was a dump for filth and rubbish agrees with this statement. The upper end of the valley, between the tower of Hippicus and the Gate of the Essenes in the south, was called . . . a 'place of filth'. The gate called the Dung Gate M. Eduy, i.3 (cf. p. 5), the quarter of the despised weavers, gave immediately on to the Valley of Hinnom at its debouchment into the Kidron Valley. This accords with the fact that the Valley of Hinnom was a place of abomination from ancient times, since it was connected with the worship of Moloch (II Kings 23:10; Jer. 2:23 and elsewhere), and was supposed to be the same as Gehenna (Hell), which took its name from it. It was still in modern times the place for rubbish, carrion and all kinds of refuse." Joachim Jeremias, *Jerusalem in the Time of Jesus* (Philadelphia: Fortress Press, 1969), 16–17.

There are a few reasons why I used the Valley of Hinnom in the story. Geographically, it is a low place. Historically, it is a low place. And emotionally, it is a low place. The three come together when Peter's spirits are at a low point, introduced by this sentence: "Peter looked out over the Valley of Hinnom, which cut through the side of the city like a gaping wound."

Regarding the Temple in Jerusalem. For background to the Temple in Jerusalem in the first century AD, several sources were helpful, including Alfred Edersheim's *The Temple: Its Ministry and Services* (Grand Rapids: Eerdmans, 1972). For an archaeological study of the Temple mount, see Jack Finegan, *The Archaeology of the New Testament* (Princeton: Princeton University Press, 1969), 116–33. For a visual layout of the Temple mount, with all its structures, see Ian Wilson, *Jesus: The Evidence* (San Francisco: HarperSanFrancisco, 1996), 110–11.

One of the functions of the Temple in the story is to show the contrast between the holiest place in the city, where atonement for the nation's sins was made, and the unholiest place, where Jesus was executed. Since Jesus was the King of the Jews, the Temple would have been the rightful place of honor for him. Instead, the place he was sentenced to was a place of shame outside the city walls; his only crown, one of thorns; his only throne, a cross.

Regarding the Fortress of Antonia. The Fortress was divided into two sections: one for utility, the other for luxury. The larger section on the northern part of the Fortress housed troops in adequate but austere barracks. The smaller section on the southern part contained lavish residences for officers, visiting dignitaries, and for Pilate and his entourage when he visited the city. Pilate was the Roman Procurator of Judea, headquartered in Caesarea, and visited Jerusalem often. Relations with the Jews were tenuous and frequent visits necessary both as a show of force and as a gesture, however feigned, of conciliation.

For archaeological remains of the Fortress of Antonia, see Jack Finegan, *The Archaeology of the New Testament* (Princeton: Princeton University Press, 1992), 156–61. See also page 196: "This tower or fortress probably became the citadel which Josephus (*Ant.* xv 11, 4 § 403) says the Hasmoneans built and called Baris . . . a name perhaps derived from the Hebrew word for 'fortress' seen in Neh. 2:8. Herod, in turn, made the Baris stronger for the safety and protection of the temple and, to please his friend Mark Antony, called it Antonia (*Ant.* xv 11, 4 § 409). Josephus (*War* v 5, 8 §§ 238ff.) says the Antonia, the work of King Herod, was built upon a rock 50 cubits high, precipitous on all sides, and covered with smooth flagstones to make it unclimbable. The edifice itself rose to a height of 40 cubits and had towers at its four corners, three of these 50 cubits high, the one at the southeast angle 70 cubits high to command a view of the whole area of the temple. Inside the Antonia resembled a palace in spaciousness and appointments. Broad courtyards provided accommodation for troops, and a Roman cohort was quartered there permanently. Particularly at festivals the soldiers kept watch on the people in the temple area to repress any insurrectionary movement. Stairs led down at the point where the fortress impinged on the temple area porticoes, so that the soldiers could descend rapidly. The tribune and his soldiers and centurions ran down these steps to apprehend Paul (Ac 21:32). Also there was a secret underground passage from the Antonia to the eastern gate of the inner sacred court (*Ant.* xv 11, 7 § 424)."

Regarding Greek and Roman deities. A helpful introduction to the deities of the Greeks and Romans can be found in the illustrative volume of *Titans and Olympians: Greek & Roman Myth* by Tony Allan and Sara Maitland (London: Duncan Baird Publishers, 1997). A glossary of gods, their responsibilities, and how the names changed when the Romans adopted the Greek gods, can be found on page 138. The gods were divided into two major groups: the great celestial deities, of which there were twelve, including Jupiter and Neptune; and the choice deities, of which there were eight, including Saturnus and Janus. Behind them was a minor group of inferior deities, including Hercules and Pan. See also, Alexander Adam, *Adam's Roman Antiquities* (Philadelphia: J. B. Lippincott & Co., 1872), 181–91. For a more exhaustive reference, see N. G. L. Hammond and H. H. Scullard, eds., *The Oxford Classical Dictionary* (Oxford: The Clarendon Press, 1970).

The pantheon of Roman deities was helpful in telling the story in a number of ways. For example, it helped to set this scene by giving me ideas how to decorate the centurion's quarters:

> He traced his hand over the shoreline of
> the map, then rested it on a sculpture of Nep-
> tune. Of all the Roman deities, Neptune was
> the centurion's favorite. The brother of Jupiter,
> Neptune ruled the sea. A sculpture of him
> stood on a pedestal, one foot resting on part of
> a ship with a trident in his right hand, a dol-
> phin in his left. He was an imposing figure the
> way the sculptor had portrayed him, caught in
> a tension between great fury and great calm.

The sculpture of Neptune introduces the theme of the centurion's childhood dream of going off to sea, which is fulfilled later in the story when he travels to Britain.

The Roman gods are also used in adding drama to some of the scenes, such as this one:

> As the darkness crept toward the hill,
> those huddled in the crowd filled the eerie
> silence with nervous chatter. "What is
> happening?"
> "What could it mean?"
> "What if we angered the gods?" Valassio
> asked. "You believe in the gods, don't you?"
> "Roman ones."
> "What if there's others," remarked Massina, "and you Romans, by giving homage to
> your own, make the others jealous? Ever think
> of that?"

Regarding the Romans as architects. "The Romans might be called the greatest architects of antiquity. They borrowed almost all their architectural forms and building techniques, but wrought such changes on them that by the first century A. D. they had created a daring and unique style that was profoundly to influence the western world. The style was based on the arch and its extensions, the vault and the dome, hitherto little used, and it was made possible by a Roman innovation—concrete that did not buckle under the stresses of huge structures." Robert Payne, *The Horizon Book of Ancient Rome*, ed. in charge, William Harlan Hale (New York: Doubleday & Company, 1966), 247.

Roman architecture is used in the story to visualize the

glory of Rome, which was a driving ambition for everyone from emperors to soldiers to the citizenry. This idea comes to a climax in Part III when Lucius comes to Rome for the first time, where the diminutive stature of the 29-year-old Nero is dwarfed by the grandeur of the city's architecture.

Regarding the Romans as road builders. "Roads were mainly for official use, but private citizens were granted passports to use them. They found posthouses about every ten miles, and every thirty, inns sold food, lodging, and carnal pleasure. Thus encouraged, many set out to see the world, doing much to unify the empire's disparate peoples. But the system's greatest importance was the speed with which troops could be deployed and information relayed over the roads. Julius Caesar once went 800 miles in eight days, and postriders could move twice as fast." Robert Payne, *The Horizon Book of Ancient Rome,* ed. in charge, William Harlan Hale (New York: Doubleday & Company, 1966), 251.

The Roman road leading away from Jerusalem is a symbol for the beginning of the centurion's journey away from God. Throughout the story there are other roads, paved and unpaved, over which the centurion travels, each taking him farther away.

Regarding the *Pax Romana*. See the chapter titled "The Roman Peace" in Robert Payne, *The Horizon Book of Ancient Rome,* ed. in charge, William Harlan Hale (New York: Doubleday & Company, 1966), 262–81. "For some two hundred years following the accession of Augustus, the Mediterranean world was virtually at peace. War, when it was waged at all, was confined almost entirely to frontier areas. Never in human history had there been so long a span of general tranquility, and never again was peace maintained so steadily among so many people. One mighty state seemed almost to embrace the world, with only the savage tribes of northern Europe and of central Africa and the mysterious nations of the Orient living beyond the pale. The *Pax Romana*, the Roman Peace, extended from Scotland to the vast Sahara Desert, and from Portugal to the borders of Persia. Throughout much of the empire, men lived out their lives in quiet contentment, safe from marauding armies, going about their affairs in the knowledge that they were sheltered by Rome, a stern but generous master that demanded unyielding obedience to laws, at the same time granting to each community the right to adapt those laws to local circumstances. Under Roman protection trade flourished, cultivation was extended, and prosperity was brought to regions that had never before progressed beyond mere subsistence" (p. 262).

The Roman Peace stands in contrast to the lack of peace that the centurion has within him. He is filled with conflict, which grows more intense the farther he travels away from his faith.

Regarding the extent of the Roman Empire in the first century AD. For a map showing the extent of the Roman Empire from the death of Augustus (AD 14) to the death of Trajan (AD 117), see Robert Payne, *The Horizon Book of Ancient Rome*, ed. in charge, William Harlan Hale (New York: Doubleday & Company, 1966), 8–9.

The Roman Empire in the first century included all the coastal countries of the Mediterranean Sea. It encompassed what is now Britain, Northern Africa, Spain, France, Italy, Greece, Asia Minor, and the Middle Eastern countries at the eastern edge of the Mediterranean.

The lust for world dominance eventually became the Empire's undoing, as it became unable to provide the vast amounts of money and manpower to satisfy that lust. It became the centurion's undoing as well. His dream of being a part of the Empire's dream came crashing in on him as he stood on the shores of his boyhood home in Alexandria.

> Lucius's attention was captured by a
> passing warship as it plowed a furrow in the
> sea. The sight once filled him with confidence,
> a settled feeling that Rome would prevail over
> any waves of opposition. Now it gave him the
> unsettling feeling that the sea would swallow
> everything in the end, every ship, every sailor,
> even the empires for which they sailed. What
> once seemed mastery now seemed merely the
> skipping of carefully tossed stones across a
> vast and unconquerable sea.
> A heaviness returned to him. And with
> it, the long-remembered words of Romulus,
> which every officer had drilled into him. They
> were the last words of the city's founder before
> he too was swallowed by that vast and uncon-
> querable sea: "Go tell the Romans that the
> gods so will, that my Rome shall be the capital
> of the world. Therefore let them cultivate the
> art of war, and let them know and hand down
> to posterity, that no human power can with-
> stand the Roman arms.

Regarding Roman interest in books. For background on methods of writing, including instruments of writing and compilations of writings, see Alexander Adam, *Adam's Roman Antiquities* (Philadelphia: J. B. Lippincott & Co., 1872), 359–67. Themes are the values that matter to us. Truth. Love. Justice.

Mercy. Honor. Loyalty. Goodness. Family. Community. Beauty. Honesty. They are what we live for and what we are willing, if necessary, to die for. We all have them, even though we may not be aware of them. Look at the books in your library, and they will likely form a collection of the themes that make up the story that is your life.

We live from the themes that are most dear to us. And we create from the themes that are most dear to us, regardless if that creation is a family or a painting or a book.

This particular theme in the story came from my childhood love of books. Two places my parents dropped me off when I was growing up were the River Oaks Theater and the River Oaks Public Library. Both fed my imagination and led to my vocation.

Regarding the library at Alexandria. "The first famous library was collected by Ptolemy Philadelphus at Alexandria, in Egypt, B. C. 284, containing 700,000 volumes. . . . Adjoining the Alexandrian library was a building called MUSEUM, for the accommodation of a college or society of learned men, who were supported there at public expense, with a covered walk and seats where they might dispute. . . .

"A great part of the Alexandrian library was burnt by the flames of Caesar's fleet, when he set fire to save himself, but neither Caesar himself nor Hirtius mentions this circumstance. It was again restored by Cleopatra, who, for that purpose, received from Antony the library of Pergamus, then consisting of 200,000 volumes. It was totally destroyed by the Saracens, A. D. 642.

"A keeper of the library was called a BIBLIOTHECA." Alexander Adam, *Adam's Roman Antiquities* (Philadelphia: J. B. Lippincott & Co., 1872), 366–67.

Regarding the rank and responsibility of a centurion. "'Centurion'.... The commander of a 'century'—one hundred soldiers —the smallest unit of the Roman army. (In New Testament times there were ten centuries in a cohort and sixty centuries in a legion, making about six thousand soldiers per legion.) The centurions, often called the backbone of the army, were responsible for keeping discipline, for inspection of arms, for commanding the century in both camp and field, and for the command of the auxiliaries." Allen C. Meyers, ed., *The Eerdmans Bible Dictionary* (Grand Rapids: Eerdmans, 1987), 198–99.

"In battle a centurion could only retreat with honour intact if the general sounded the recall or if the enemy fell back before him. The stress of being the focus of heroic leadership must have weighed heavily on these men. A centurion could not show fear and in every battle he was expected to be the first man to charge and the last to break off fighting, or to die covering the retreat of his men.

"When a centurion did show fear in battle—and almost every centurion was marked out by decorations because proven valour was one of the requirements for promotion to the rank—he was subject to the most terrible of punishments. In 38 BC a *primus pilus* named Vibillius panicked and fled from a battlefield in Spain. He must have been a brave man to have reached such an exalted rank but clearly this was one battle too many. The governor of the province decided to make an example of him and had the centurion beaten to death by his comrades (*fustuarium*), because his flight from the battlefield had put their lives in danger." Ross Cowan, *For the Glory of Rome: A History of Warriors and Warfare* (St. Paul, MN: MBI Publishing Company, 2007), 133–34.

Regarding the dress of the Roman soldier. See Alexander

Adam, *Adam's Roman Antiquities* (Philadelphia: J. B. Lippincott & Co., 1872), 248-253. See also Albert Harkness, *Caesar's Commentaries on the Gallic War*, with introduction, notes, and vocabulary (New York: American Book Company, 1901), 32-35.

As I am jotting down this fairly insignificant bit of bibliographical information, it came to me that at least part of my love for words and stories came from the two Latin teachers I had, one in ninth grade, the other in tenth. I took the courses only because my father urged me to, because he thought it would be good for me to learn, somehow better prepare me for the future. Being a compliant kid, I took the class without even a thought of resistance. Both teachers were lovely women, committed teachers, and convinced of the importance of what they were teaching and that it would enrich the lives of their students both personally and professionally.

I still remember the opening lines to *Caesar's Gallic Wars*— *Gallis est omnis divisa in partes tres.* "All Gaul is divided in three parts." That was my introduction to the lineage of words that make up our language. And it was my introduction to the legacy of Rome, which has been left behind in a language long dead.

It was a public school where I learned this. In that educational system I had the experience of making art with my hands, making music with my voice, and making the past come alive with the words and stories I learned in Latin class.

Many of those subjects are gone from the curriculum, like some extinct species we know about only because of the bones they left behind in the fossil record. And that makes me sad, not only for the species that have gone extinct . . . but for the ones that have survived and now live without them.

Regarding the dress of the Roman citizen. The toga was the primary garment of the Roman citizen. For a description of it and other articles of clothing, see Jerome Caropino, *Daily Life in Ancient Rome,* edited with bibliography and notes by Henry T. Rowell, translated from the French by E. O. Lormer (New Haven: Yale University Press, 1940), 154–55. See also, Alexander Adam, *Adam's Roman Antiquities* (Philadelphia: J. B. Lippincott & Co., 1872), 286–91.

Regarding slaves in the Empire. Slaves were "the backbone of Roman society and a major source of income for Caesar. A vigorous slave trade flourished all over the Mediterranean world, and thousands of captives were transported to Rome every year to satisfy the growing demand by newly wealthy and even middle-class households. Estimates are that slaves made up 35 to 40 percent of the population of Republican Rome, a higher percentage than in the American South before the Civil War." Ramon L. Jimenéz, *Caesar Against the Celts* (New York: Barnes & Noble Books, 1996), 101.

For more information, see Jerome Caropino, *Daily Life in Ancient Rome,* edited with bibliography and notes by Henry T. Rowell, translated from the French by E. O. Lormer (New Haven: Yale University Press, 1940), 57–75. Although earlier treatment was sometimes harsh, laws were progressively passed to ensure more humane treatment of slaves. For Roman legislation regarding slaves, see Alexander Adam, *Adam's Roman Antiquities* (Philadelphia: J. B. Lippincott & Co., 1872), 23–29.

Regarding the importance of Roman law. See Will Durant, *Caesar and Christ* (New York: Simon & Schuster, 1944), 391–406, especially page 391: "Law was the most characteristic and lasting expression of the Roman spirit. As Greece stands in history for freedom, so Rome stands for order; as Greece bequeathed democracy and philosophy as the foundations of individual liberty, so Rome has left us its laws, and its traditions of administration, as the bases of social order." For a thorough examination of citizens' rights, the senate, public forums, the rule of magistrates, specific laws, and judicial proceedings, see Alexander Adam, *Adam's Roman Antiquities* (Philadelphia: J. B. Lippincott & Co., 1872), an excellent compendium of research distilled from primary Latin sources.

Regarding the ritual of sacrificing Passover lambs at the Temple. See Alfred Edersheim, *The Temple: Its Ministry and Services* (Grand Rapids: Eerdmans, 1972), 208–28. For information on sacrifices from a Jewish perspective, see the Internet site, "Come and Hear" (www.come-and-hear.com/editor/br_2.html). For a discussion on how the Passover sacrifice relates to the sacrifice of Jesus, see "The Temple Sacrifices: Transition and Triumph" by Mark D. Kaplan (www.kubik.org/vcm/temple.htm).

Regarding the quote from Virgil. The quote comes from Virgil's work, *The Georgics* (Bk1: 461–497, "The Portents at Julius Caesar's Death"), translated by A. S. Kline, 2001. The full reference is:

> So, the sun will give you signs of what late evening brings,
> and from where a fair-weather wind blows the clouds.
> or what the rain-filled southerly intends. Who dares say,
> the sun tricks us? He often warns us that hidden troubles
> threaten, that treachery and secret wars are breeding,
> He pitied Rome when Caesar was killed,
> and hid his shining face in gloomy darkness.

Regarding Mary Magdalene. "'Mary Magdalene,' from Magdala of the Sea of Galilee. . . . She was one of the women who 'ministered' to Jesus and contributed financially to him and his disciples (Matt. 27:55–56 par.; Luke 8:3). Mary Magdalene was present at the crucifixion and burial of Jesus (Matt. 27:56, 61 par.), and was among the women who went to visit the tomb on Easter morning (28:1 par.). It was she who reported his resurrection to the apostles (Luke 24:10; John 20:18). Identified as one 'from whom seven demons had gone out' (Luke 8:2, see also Mark 16:9)." Allen C. Meyers, ed., *The Eerdmans Bible Dictionary* (Grand Rapids: Eerdmans, 1987), 696.

There are a number of traditions relating to Mary Magdalene and what became of her. None are attested by historical documentation, only stories, legends, and traditions. Both Eastern and Western traditions in church history believe she left Jerusalem sometime after Jesus' death, along with other believers who left to escape persecution (cf. Acts 8:1). The tradition of the Eastern Orthodox Church is that she was a virtuous woman all her life and not to be identified with the sinful woman of Luke 7:36–50 or with Mary of Bethany.

Gregory of Tours, writing in the sixth century, believed she went to Ephesus, where she served alongside John until she died.

One tradition says she went to Rome with Peter, but she left when the persecution of Christians became intense.

French legends indentify her as Mary of Bethany, the sister of Martha and brother of Lazarus. They suggest she was put in a boat without oars, rudders, or sails, and sent adrift on the Mediterrean, her boat eventually landing in southern France. She and others who were in the boat with her engaged in evangelistic work there, it is said. Eventually, though, she became a recluse, living a contemplative life in a cave for the next thirty years until her death.

See Susan Haskins, *Mary Magdalene: Myth and Metaphor* (New York: Harcourt, 1994). Also, there is a substantive paper that won the Hines Award in the Humanities/Social Science Division in 2003. You can find the PDF online at www.la-grange.edu/resources/pdf/citations/religion/magdalene.pdf.

One tradition held that Mary Magdalene was a sinful woman, likely promiscuous, conjecturing that she was the un-named prostitute in Luke 7:36–50. To me this is unlikely since in the very next chapter (8:2) she is introduced as a new char-acter. My decision was not based on historical tradition but rather on the logical conclusion that at least one of the demons that possessed her would have likely led her into a life of sexual excess.

Regarding the centurion's response to the earthquake and Jesus' death. New Testament references to the faith of the centurion who oversaw the crucifixion of Christ are Matthew 27:54: "Now the centurion, and those who were with him keep-ing guard over Jesus, when they saw the earthquake and the things that were happening, became very frightened and said, "Truly this was the Son of God!"; Mark 15:39: "When the centurion, who was standing right in front of Him, saw the way He breathed His last, he said, 'Truly this man was the Son of God!"; Luke 23:44–47: "It was now about the sixth hour, and darkness fell over the whole land until the ninth hour, because the sun was obscured; and the veil of the temple was torn in two. And Jesus, crying out with a loud voice, said, 'Father, into Your hands I commit My spirit.' Having said this, He breathed His last. Now when the centurion saw what had happened, he began praising God, saying, 'Certainly this man was innocent.'" (Above quoted from NASB).

Regarding the sluicing of blood from the Temple mount.

Speaking of how the vast amounts of blood were removed from the Temple at such times as Passover, Alfred Edersheim explains: "The system of drainage into chambers below and canal, all of which could be flushed at will, was perfect; the blood and refuse being swept down into Kedron and towards the royal gardens." Alfred Edersheim, *The Temple: Its Ministry and Services* (Grand Rapids: Eerdmans, 1972), 55.

"Admittedly the Kidron valley is a *wadi*, with water flowing only in winter (*Ant.* 8:17; John 18:1), but an artificial supply which made the valley so extraordinarily fruitful was the blood of the Temple sacrifices. . . . The Temple floor was paved and sloped in particular directions, so that the blood from sacrifices could easily be rinsed away (Pseudo-Aristeas 88, 90). . . . The channel which drained it away began by the altar. . . . This drainage channel led underground into the Kidron valley." Joachim Jeremias, *Jerusalem in the Time of Jesus* (Philadelphia: Fortress Press, 1969), 44.

Instead of showing the blood mingled with water flowing from Jesus' side, I show the soldier below him thrusting the spear. I then cut to the scene at the Temple where the water begins to flow out the side of the city's wall.

When the soldiers came to Jesus, it was clear he was already dead. To make sure, though, Antonius took a spear and placed it on Jesus' chest , feeling for a fleshy spot between the ribs. Finding it, he thrust the spear into his heart.

At the Temple, the high priest signaled the other priests, and they lifted several amphorae of water to wash down the altar. Drains at the altar's base led to an underground pipe that shunted blood out the side of the city wall into the Kidron Valley. The water mingled with the blood as it flowed out the shunt until it became mostly water with only a trace of blood. With the cleansing of the altar, the work within the walls of the Temple was finished.

I made this choice for the same reason that I showed the sacrifice of the lamb at the Temple instead of the brutality of the cross. We had seen the violence of that day graphically portrayed in *The Passion of the Christ*, and I did not want to duplicate it. Instead I opted to use a figurative representation of the violence, something that conveyed the same truth but with images that were less familiar.

Regarding the roasting of the Passover lamb. "According to Jewish ordinance, the Paschal lamb was roasted on a spit made of pomegranate wood, the spit passing right through from mouth to vent." Alfred Edersheim, *The Temple: Its Ministry and Services* (Grand Rapids: Eerdmans, 1972), 232.

I thought this a small but theologically significant scene when Ashuk picked up his roasted lamb from a street vendor, the lamb being trussed with a wooden spit, reminiscent of the cross to which Jesus had been trussed.

Regarding the importance of Livy. Titus Livius came to Rome, where he studied rhetoric and philosophy, dedicating the last forty years of his life, from 23 BC to AD 17, to writing a seven-hundred-year history of Rome. For the influence of Livy's writings on the imaginations of his readers, see Will Durant, *Caesar and Christ* (New York: Simon & Schuster, 1944), 250–52.

Durant notes that Livy "set forth, through history, the virtues that had made Rome great—the unity and holiness of family life, the *pietàs* of children, the sacred relation of men with the gods at every step, the sanctity of the solemnly pledged word, the stoic self-control and *gravitas*. He would make that stoic Rome so noble that its conquest of the Mediterranean would appear as a moral imperative, a divine order and law cast over the chaos of the East and the barbarism of the West. Polybius had ascribed Rome's triumph to its form of government; Livy would make it a corollary of the Roman character" (p. 251).

Regarding Roman soldiers. For background on the Roman soldier, see Michael Grant, *The Army of the Caesars* (New York: Charles Scribner's Sons, 1974). See also Derek Williams, *Romans and Barbarians* (New York: St. Martin's Press, 1998), 116–65 and Alexander Adam, *Adam's Roman Antiquities* (Philadelphia: J. B. Lippincott & Co., 1872), 244–86.

In the course of fleshing out the characters in my story, I made a lot of decisions regarding the influences in their lives. One of those influences in the centurion's life was the stories he had read, both as a boy and as a man. The classics inspired many boys to become soldiers, and many soldiers to become heroes. Russ Cowan explains how:

"Exposure to literature did not lessen the warlike nature of the Roman soldier. In many ways it reinforced it. The soldier was most likely to read (or hear being recited) passages from the classics of Ennius and Virgil. Their epic poems took the reader into the very heart of battle, with its dust and heat, blood and gore; Ennius wrote of decapitated heads with eyelids still twitching. As well as imitating Homeric models, Ennius may have drawn on his personal experience as a centurion and described the torture of enduring bombardments of javelins and sling bullets, of shields being punctured and helmets dented, of clothing soaked with sweat, and of aching limbs and burning lungs. Yet he also emphasized the personal and national glory to be won in war, that the battlefield was where a man proved his true worth and overcame fear. Virgil reminded the soldier not only of the need to defend the fatherland but his duty to extend it. Reading assured the *bellator* that he was involved in a just fight." Ross Cowan, *For the Glory of Rome: A History of Warriors and Warfare* (St. Paul, MN: MBI Publishing Company, 2007), 248.

Regarding the divisions of the Roman army. "Each legion was divided into ten cohorts, each cohort into three *maniples,* and each *maniple* into two centuries. So that there were thirty maniples, and sixty centuries in a legion; and if there had always been 100 men in each century, as its name imports, the legion would have consisted of 6000 men. But this was not the case.

The number of men in a legion was different at different times. In the time of Polybius it was 4200.

There were usually 300 cavalry joined to each legion, called JUSTUS EQUITATUS, or ALA. They were divided into ten *turmae* or troops; and each *turma* into three *decuriae*, or bodies of ten men.

The different kinds of infantry which composed the legion were three, the *hastati, principes,* and *triarii.*

The HASTATI were so called, because they first fought with long spears, which were afterwards laid aside as inconvenient. They consisted of young men in the flower of life, and formed the first line of battle.

The PRINCIPES were men of middle age in the vigour of life: they occupied the second line. Anciently they seem to have been posted first; whence their name.

The TRIARII were old soldiers of approved valour, who

formed the third line; whence the name. They were also called
PILANI from the *pilum* or javelin which they used; and the
hastati and *principes,* who stood before them, ANTEPILANI.

There was a fourth kind of troops called VELITES, from
their swiftness and agility, the light-armed soldiers, first ins-
tituted in the second Punic war. These did not form a part of
the legion, and had no certain post assigned them; but fought
in scattered parties where occasion required, usually before the
lines. To them were joined the slingers and archers."

From Alexander Adam, *Adam's Roman Antiquities* (Philadelphia: J. B. Lippincott & Co., 1872), 248–49.

Regarding the crosses used in crucifixion. Three main types of
crosses were used for crucifixions at the time of Christ. There
was what was later termed St. Andrew's Cross, where the beams
were diagonally crossed in an X. There was the Tau cross in the
form of a T. And there was the traditional cross, known as the
Latin cross, †. Alfred Edersheim believed the cross of Christ
was the Latin cross. He argues, "This would also most readily
admit of affixing the board with the threefold inscription, which
we know His Cross bore. Besides, the universal testimony
of those who lived nearest the time (Justin Martyr, Irenaeus,
and others), and who, alas! had only too much occasion to learn
what crucifixion meant, is in favour of this view." Alfred Edersheim, *The Life and Times of Jesus the Messiah* (Grand Rapids:
Eerdmans, 1971), bk, V, chap. XV, 584–85.

Regarding crucifixion. Although literary evidence for crucifixion is plentiful (Josephus, *Ant.* XIV: 380–81, Cicero, Livy,
among others), archaeological evidence for crucifixion is not.
"In 1968, archaeologists discovered the skeleton of a man,
younger than Jesus, named Yehohanan, who was crucified about

2,000 years ago. His bones were found in a burial cave at Giv'at ha-Mivtar in northeastern Jerusalem, more than a mile north of the Damascus Gate. This is the first physical evidence ever found of an actual crucifixion." Wendell Phillips, *An Explorer's Life of Jesus* (New York: Two Continents Publishing Group/ Morgan Press, 1975), 395.

The archaeologist who made the discovery was Vassilios Tzaferis. He published his findings in the article "Crucifixion— The Archaeological Evidence," in *Biblical Archaeology Review* 11, no. 1 (January–February 1985). From his study of the body, he concluded: "From the way in which the bones were attached, we can infer the man's position on the cross. The two heel bones were attached on their adjacent inside (medial) surfaces. The nail went through the right heel bone and then the left. Since the same nail went through both heels, the legs were together, not apart, on the cross.

"A study of the two heel bones and the nail that penetrated them at an oblique angle pointing downward and sideways indicates that the feet of the victim were not fastened tightly to the cross. A small seat, or *sedile,* must have been fastened to the upright of the cross. The evidence as to the position of the body on the cross convinced the investigators that the *sedile* supported only the man's left buttock. This seat both prevented the collapse of the body and prolonged the agony.

"Given this position on the cross and given the way in which the heel bones were attached to the cross, it seems likely that the knees were bent, or semi-flexed, as in the drawing [shown in the article]. This position of the legs was dramatically confirmed by a study of the long bones below the knees, the tibia or shinbone and the fibula behind it.

"Only the tibia of the crucified man's right leg was available for study. The bone had been brutally fractured into large, sharp slivers. This fracture was clearly produced by a single, strong blow. The left calf bones were lying across the sharp edge of the wooden cross, and the percussion from the blow on the right calf bones passed into the left calf bones, producing a harsh and severing blow to them as well. The left calf bones broken in a straight, sharp-toothed line on the edge of the cross, a line characteristic of a fresh bone fracture. This fracture resulted from the pressure on both sides of the bone—on one side from the direct blow on the right leg and on the other from the re-sistance of the edge of the cross.

"The angle of the line of fracture on these left calf bones provides proof that the victim's legs were in a semi-flexed po-sition on the cross. The angle of the fracture indicates that the bones formed an angle of 60° to 65° as they crossed the upright of the cross. This compels the interpretation that the legs were semi-flexed.

"When we add this evidence to that of the nail and the way in which the heel bones were attached to the cross, we must conclude that this position into which the victim's body was forced was both difficult and unnatural" (p. 52).

Regarding the scene of Peter at the crucifixion. The only dis-ciple the gospel writers identify as witnessing the crucifixion is John (see John 19:26–27 and John 13:23, the qualifier, "the disciple whom he loved," is universally recognized as John). The other disciples had fled the night he was betrayed (Matthew 26:56). Peter, we are told, followed Jesus as far as the Temple courtyard before denying him there (Matthew 26:58, 69–75). It is assumed from these accounts that Peter was not at the crucifixion. However, the disciple writes in 1 Peter 5:1 (NASB) —"Therefore, I exhort the elders among you, as your fellow elder and witness of the sufferings of Christ. . . ." From that last phrase I inferred that he was referring to being an eyewitness of the crucifixion. Since the gospel writers do not mention him, though, I concluded that he must have circled back to the site of the execution, likely during the three hours of darkness, and stood on the periphery of the crowd, possibly cloaking his identity.

Regarding the earthquake and the soldiers who were guarding Christ's tomb. Matthew 27:62–66 tells of the guard whom Pilate stationed to secure Christ's tomb. See also 28:2–4 (NASB): "And behold, a severe earthquake had occurred, for an angel of the Lord descended from heaven and came and rolled away the stone and sat upon it. And his appearance was like lightning, and his clothing as white as snow. The guards shook for fear of him, and became like dead men."

Regarding the centurion reporting to Pilate after Christ's death. See Mark 15:42–45 (NASB): "When evening had already come, because it was the preparation day, that is, the day before the Sabbath, Joseph of Arimathea came, a prominent member of the Council, who himself was waiting for the kingdom of God; and he gathered up courage and went in before Pilate, and asked for the body of Jesus. Pilate wondered if He was dead by this time, and summoning the centurion, he questioned him as to whether He was already dead. And ascertaining this from the centurion, he granted the body to Joseph."

Regarding the quote from Seneca. Seneca was a stoic philosopher of Spanish descent, who was raised and educated in Rome. He lived from 4 BC to AD 65. He was also Nero's tutor in his childhood and one of his counselors in his adulthood. He is credited with writing twelve philosophical essays, 124 letters dealing with moral issues, nine tragedies, and one satire. The quote that Lucius reads to Ashuk is from Seneca's *Moral Letters to Lucilius,* written toward the end of his life in AD 64. Seneca was accused as being part of an assassination plot to kill Nero and was sentenced to commit suicide in AD 65.

Regarding stylistic decisions. One of the decisions I had to wrestle with in writing the story from a Roman perspective was whether or not to use contemporary names for certain geographical settings, which would be familiar to the reader, or to use the ancient Latin names, which would not be. I went back and forth a lot on this, and what I finally decided was to use the Latin names in dialogue and their contemporary counterpart in the narration. In narration, though, I used the Latin name when it was first introduced, putting the contemporary name after it in parenthesis. Thereafter, I used the contemporary name in the narration. For example, when I first referred to London, I used the ancient Latin word that the characters in the story would have used—Londinium—followed by its contemporary counterpart in parenthesis (London). After that initial citing, however, I used the contemporary name.

Because the point of view in the story is Roman, I tried to use as many Latin references as possible but not so many as to be distracting to the reader. The decision to tell the story from primarily a Roman point of view affected a lot of particulars in the story. For instance, in an earlier draft I went into a lot of historic detail on the Passover, citing not only Old Testament passages but also traditions that would have been practiced by the Jewish community in first-century Jerusalem. It seemed out of place when I stood back and looked at it, but I wasn't sure why. I felt the information was helpful, historically, but finally I concluded that it did not serve the story being told, which was about a Roman soldier.

Another thing affecting the style of the writing was that I wanted the narrative to *feel* old. Because of that, I used what I felt sounded like a more ancient way of talking, using vocabulary, syntax, and colloquialisms that sounded a little foreign to our ear but not so foreign that they would be distracting.

For example, I used the prefix *a* in a number of my descriptions, such as *awash, abrim, athaw,* and *adrip.* You see this style of expression more in poetry than in prose, but the further back you go in time the more you see that style used in prose as well. *Awash* is a familiar word to most of us. *Abrim,* less so. *Athaw* and *adrip,* probably not at all. The last two may have been used in times past, I'm not sure. I didn't look them up. I simply came up with them because I liked how they sounded, which was old.

I also used a few older words such as *save,* meaning "except." For example, the sentence: "But the Empire, save the far reaches, is at peace." I did this because I wanted not just the dialogue of the characters to sound ancient, but also the narration. Here is an example where I did that with the dialogue. It is the scene where the commander tells his soldiers what to do with Massina's dead body. He says: "And trouble not the ground to welcome it." That means, of course, do not dig a grave for him, just leave him outside the camp to rot.

It is a tricky balance for a writer. If you don't use older-sounding expressions, you run the risk of the storytelling sounding too contemporary, thus breaking the spell of the "willing suspension of disbelief." But reading dialect is difficult and distracting. And so what I have tried to do in my story was to use prose that evokes the era without being so slavishly devoted to the era that it distracts the reader.

Regarding the appearance of Caesarea. The beginning of Part II has the centurion seeing Caesarea in the distance. Caesarea was the imperial capital of the Roman province of Judea and its architecture reflected the grandeur that was Rome.

The description was inspired by a trip to the Holy Land. When we came to Caesarea, our guide told us that all the buildings of the city were once covered in a white marble façade about a half inch to three-quarters of an inch thick. When the barbarians sacked the city, they removed the façades and threw the marble into the Mediterranean Sea not far from the shore. Well, while a lecture was being given in the amphitheater, I wandered off to see what I could find. I waded out a ways, a ways farther, and then, sure enough, I came across some wave-washed fragments of those façades. I imagined what the city looked like in the daytime, when Lucius saw it, and how it looked later at night in the moonlight, and that is how I came up with the following description.

> Caesarea lay in the distance as if a great
> white shell had washed up on the beach; a
> seamless slate of sea to the west, a great brown
> barrenness to the east. Every structure in the
> city had been overlaid with a white marble
> façade that made the city gleam during the
> day and at night seemed hewn from slabs of
> moon. It shone in stark contrast to Jerusa-
> lem with its drably weathered, coarsely cut
> limestone.

Regarding the Roman defeat in the Teutoburg Forest. The account of the Roman defeat in the Teutoburg Forest is known as "The Varus Disaster," Lieutenant General Publius Quintilius Varus being the commander of the three legions that were destroyed in an ambush by the Huns in September of AD 9. The essential content of Lucius's description of the disaster came from the excellent historical chronicle of the 14th Legion, mostly from the chapter "The Varus Disaster," in the book by Stephen Dando-Collins, *Nero's Killing Machine* (Hoboken, NJ: John Wiley & Sons, 2005), 113–29.

After the defeat, the Romans never again attempted to cross the Rhine and invade the Germans. This was a stunning victory for the Huns at the time, but it postponed civilization coming to Germanic tribes for centuries.

Regarding writing in the Roman Empire. "The materials first used in common for writing, were the leaves, or inner bark *(liber)* of trees; whence leaves of paper *(chartae, folia, vel plagulae),* and LIBER, a book. The leaves of trees are still used for writing by several nations of India. Afterwards linen, and tables covered with wax were used. About the time of Alexander the Great, paper first was manufactured from an Egyptian plant or reed, called PAPYRUS, *vel-um,* whence our word paper . . .

"Paper was smoothed with a shell, or the tooth of a board or some other animal. . . . The finest paper was called at Rome, after Augustus, AUGUSTA *regia;* the next LIVIANA; the third HIERATICA, which used anciently to be the name of the finest kind, being appropriated to the sacred volumes. . . .

"The skins of sheep are properly called parchment; of calves, VELLUM. Most of the ancient manuscripts which remain today are written on parchment, few on the papyrus. . . .

"The instrument used for writing on waxen tables, the leaves or bark of trees, plates of brass or lead, etc., was an iron pencil with a sharp point, called STYLUS, or GRAPHIUM. . . . On paper or parchment, a reed sharpened and split in the point, like our pens, called, CALAMUS ARUNDO, *fistula vel canna*, which they dipped in ink, as we do our pens.

"SEPIA, the cuttle-fish, is put for ink; because when afraid of being caught, it emits a black matter to conceal itself, which the Romans sometimes used for ink." Alexander Adam, *Adam's Roman Antiquities* (Philadelphia: J. B. Lippincott & Co., 1872), 359–67.

Regarding the sending of letters. "When a book was sent anywhere, the roll was tied with a thread, and wax put on the knot, and sealed; hence, *signata volumina*. The same was done with letters. . . .

"Letters were sent by a messenger, commonly a slave, called TABELLARIUS, for the Romans had no established post. There sometimes was an inscription on the outside of the letter, sometimes not. . . .

"The Romans had slaves or freedmen who wrote their letters, called AB EPISTOLIS, (A MAN vel AMANUENSES,) and accounts (A RATIONIBUS, *vel ratiocinatores*), also who wrote short-hand, (ACTUARII vel NOTARII,) as quickly as one could speak." Alexander Adam, *Adam's Roman Antiquities* (Philadelphia: J. B. Lippincott & Co., 1872), 364–65.

Regarding the *Sacramentum*. In doing research on the Roman soldier, I came across a number of interesting articles. One, in particular, was the inspiration for what I wrote on the oath that the soldiers took to each other and to the Emperor. Later in the article he tells how the word was adapted by the early Church. And this is where I got the idea of juxtaposing the *sacramentum* taken by the soldiers with the sacrament of communion that Peter administers.

Daniel G. Van Sylke analyzed over 150 occurrences of the word by ancient non-Christian authors. He concluded the word was used in primarily three contexts: military, legal, and what he terms as "analogous military." Here is what he writes concerning the military context in which the word was found.

It is well known that both as a republic and later as an empire, Rome was an emphatically military culture. Roman ideals were exported, defended, and imposed by the might of Rome's army. Moreover, the histories of Rome written by the ancient Romans are largely histories of warfare. If the extant records of ancient Roman historians are an accurate indication of typical Roman culture, among the institutions of ancient Roman society the military loomed largest in the minds of the Romans themselves. It is not surprising, then, that the vast majority of instances in which ancient Latin authors employ the word *sacramentum* occur within military contexts. . . . Livy mentions the military sacrament thirty times. . . . He never uses the plural: for Livy, there is only one sacrament, and it is that of the Roman military. In utilizing the verbs *dicere* and *iurare* with the ablative, Livy reveals that he is designating a verbal formula with which soldiers swear military obedience to the consuls. . . . The following passage provides an example:

In any case, this was the year in which the Gauls encamped at the third milestone on the Salarian road, across the bridge over the Anio. The dictator, after he had proclaimed a cessation of public business because of the Gallic disturbance, bound all those of military age by the sacrament, and going out of the City with a great army, set the camp on the nearer bank of the Anio.

Livy, then, understands the sacrament as the verbal formula of an oath by which or with which young men are bound to military service in obedience to a consul. The following passage, concerning events that took place while Hannibal was ravaging Italy in 216 BC, witness to the content of the sacrament:

Then the soldiers were bound with an oath [*iure iurando*] by the military tribunes, which had never been done before; for until that day there had been nothing other than the sacrament, that they would assemble at the order of the consuls and not depart without the order, and where they had gathered into companies or centuries, by their own will they swore among themselves, the cavalry having been divided into companies and the infantry having been divided into centuries, that they would not abandon one another for flight or fear, and they would not withdraw except for the sake of picking up or seeking a spear, or of striking an enemy or saving a citizen. The voluntary covenant amonst themselves was transferred to a formally administered oath to the tribunes. Daniel G. Van Sylke, "*Sacramentum* in Ancient Non-Christian Authors." *Antiphon* 9.2 (2005): 167–70, *passim.*

Then, after Slyke establishes the usage of the word in military contexts, he examines how, by extension, the way the word was adapted to fit the context of the early Church.

The moral and relational aspects of the military sacrament as it was understood in the first Christian centuries made it most apt for developing Latin Christian modes of self-understanding. The military sacrament put one into a new set of responsibilities occasioned by a new set of relationships: with the emperor, with one's fellow soldiers, with the citizens of Rome, and even with Rome's enemies. It obliged soldiers to serve exclusively the emperor in whose name they swore. The emperor in turn rewarded them for their service with land and money. The sacrament also entailed mutual obligations among the soldiers themselves. It was a more or less fixed verbal formula periodically renewed and recited by the troops communally. Above all, fidelity to it, which entailed fidelity to the emperor and to one's fellow soldiers, was required even in the face of death; the soldier who preserved fidelity unto death was rewarded with glorious renown.

The military sacrament's rich set of implications was converted readily to a Latin Christian self-understanding. Through
the Christian sacrament, one enters upon a new set of relations
and responsibilities with Christ, with one's fellow Christians,
and with the enemies of Christ. The very concept of sacrament
provided a means of Romanizing or Latinizing the covenantal
relationship that Christians perceived between themselves and
their God, and likewise amongst themselves, enabling them
to express it in the discourse of Roman culture. Entering into
a sacrament with God entailed responsibilities on the part of
the Christian, but it also entailed promises on the part of God,
which are manifest in the typology of scripture and the rites of
early Christian communities. This may explain why, from an
early point in the history of Latin Christian literature, so many
dimensions of the faith came to be called sacraments. Daniel G.
Van Sylke, "*Sacramentum* in Ancient Non-Christian Authors."
Antiphon 9.2 (2005): 205–206.

Regarding Roman baths. Baths in the Roman Empire were
public places where people gathered not just to bathe but to
exercise, socialize, get massages, eat, drink, read, and listen to
readings. It was also a place where business was conducted.
Both men and women frequented the baths on a daily basis, the
women usually visiting in the morning hours and the men more
at the end of the workday. The baths were of all sizes, ranging
from small, exclusive ones to the Baths of Diocletion that could
accommodate up to three thousand.

It was under Augustus that baths first began to assume an
air of grandeur, and were called THERMAE, *bagnios* or hot
baths, although they also contained cold baths. An incredible
number of these were built up and down the city [of Rome].

Authors reckon up above 800, many of them built by the emperors with amazing magnificence. The chief were those of Agrippa near the Pantheon, of Nero, of Titus, of Domitian, of Caracalla, Antoninus, Dioclesean, &c. Of these splendid vestiges remain. . . .

The person who had the charge of the bath was called BALNEATOR. He had slaves under him, called CAPSARII, who took care of the clothes of those who bathed.

The slaves who anointed those who bathed were called AL-IPTAE, or UNCTORES. The instruments of an alipes were a currycomb scraper (STRIGILS, v. – *il*) to rub off the sweat and filth from the body, made of horn or brass, sometimes of silver or gold . . . . The slave who had the care of the ointments was called UNGUENTARIOUS.

As there was a great concourse of people to the baths, poets sometimes read their compositions there, as they also did in the porticoes and other places, chiefly in the months of July and August. Studious men used to compose, hear, or dictate something while they were rubbed and wiped. . . .

Under the emperors, not only places of exercise, but also libraries were annexed to the public baths. Alexander Adam, *Adam's Roman Antiquities* (Philadelphia: J. B. Lippincott & Co., 1872), 308, 311.

Regarding the port of Massilia. The port to which Lucius and his men sailed was Massilia, which is modern-day Marseilles in the south of France. At the time, Massilia was under the provincial jurisdiction of Rome.

Regarding marches in the military, from *Adam's Roman Antiquities*:

The form of the army on march, however, varied, according

to circumstances and the nature of the ground. It was sometimes disposed into a square (AGMEN QUADRATUM), with the baggage in the middle.

Scouts (*speculators*) were always sent before to reconnoitre the ground. A certain kind of soldiers under the emperors were called SPECULATORES.

The soldiers were trained with great care to observe the military pace, and to follow the standards. For that purpose, when encamped, they were led out thrice a month, sometimes ten, sometimes twenty miles, less or more, as the general inclined. They usually marched at the rate of twenty miles in five hours, sometimes with a quickened pace twenty-four miles in that time.

The load which a Roman soldier carried is almost incredible: victuals for fifteen days, sometimes more, usually corn, as being lighter, sometimes dressed food, utensils, a saw, a basket, a mattock, an axe, a hook, a leathern thong, a chain, a pot &c., stakes usually three or four, sometimes twelve, the whole amounting to sixty pounds weight, besides arms; for a Roman soldier considered these not as a burden, but as part of himself. Under this load they commonly marched twenty miles a day, sometimes more. There were beasts of burden for carrying tents, mills, baggage, &c. Alexander Adam, *Adam's Roman Antiquities* (Philadelphia: J. B. Lippincott & Co., 1872), 257–58.

Regarding the setting up of camps, from *Adam's Roman Antiquities*:

The discipline of the Romans was chiefly conspicuous in their marches and encampments. They never passed a night, even in the longest marches, without pitching a camp, and fortifying it with a rampart and ditch. Persons were always sent before to choose and mark out a place for this purpose. . . .

When the army staid but one night in the same camp, or even two or three nights, it was simply called *castra*, and in later ages MANSIO; which word is also put for the journey of one day. . . .

When an army remained for a considerable time in the same place, it was called a *castra* STATIVA, a standing camp, AESTIVA, a summer camp; and HIBERNA, a winter camp. . . .

The winter quarters of the Romans were strongly fortified, and furnished, particularly under the emperors, with every accommodation like a city, as storehouses, workshops, an infirmary, &c. Hence from them many towns in Europe are supposed to have had their origin; in England particularly, those whose names end in *cester* or *chester*.

The form of the Roman camp was a square, and always of the same figure. In later ages, in imitation of the Greeks, they sometimes made it circular, or adapted it to the nature of the ground. It was surrounded with a ditch, usually nine feet deep and twelve feet broad, and a rampart, composed of the earth dug from the ditch, and sharp stakes stuck into it. . . .

The camp had four gates, one on each side. . . .

The camp was divided into two parts, called the upper and lower. . . .

The tents (*tentoria*) were covered with leather or skins extended with ropes. . . .

In each tent were usually ten soldiers, with their decanus or petty officer who commanded them. . . . The centurions and standard-bearers were posted at the head of the companies. . . .

In pitching the camp, different divisions of the army were appointed to execute different parts of the work, under the inspection of the tribunes or centurions, as they likewise were during the encampment to perform different services, to procure water, forage, wood, &c. . . . Alexander Adam, *Adam's Roman Antiquities* (Philadelphia: J. B. Lippincott & Co., 1872), 252–56.

Regarding watches for the camp, from *Adam's Roman Antiquities:*

A certain number of maniples was appointed to keep guard at the gates, on the rampart, and in other places of the camp, before the praetorium, the tents of the legati, quaestor, and tribunes, both by day and by night, who were changed every three hours.

EXCUBLAE denotes watches either by day or night; VIGILLE, only by night. Guards placed before the gates were properly called STATIONES, on the ramparts CUSTODLAE. . . . Whoever deserted his station was punished with death.

Every evening before the watches were set, the watch-word (symbolum) or private signal, by which they might distinguish friends from foes, was distributed through the army by means of a square tablet of wood in the form of a die, called a TESSERA from its four corners. On it was inscribed whatever word or words the general chose, which he seems to have varied every night.

A frequent watch-word of Marius was LARS DEUS; of Sylla, APOLLO DELPHICUS; and of Caesar, VENUS GENITRIX, &c; of Brutus, LIBERTAS. It was given by the general to the tribunes and praefects of the allies, by them to the centurions, and by them to the soldiers. The person who carried the tesserae from the tribunes to the centurions was called TESSERARIUS. Alexander Adam, Adam's Roman Antiquities (Philadelphia: J. B. Lippincott & Co., 1872), 256.

Regarding scars as badges of honor. "Scars were a symbol of valour and much flaunted and often used to elicit sympathy or support. Catiline's centurions and *evocati* (veterans who had completed the standard term of service but were asked to re-enlist on account of their quality) died to a man at Pistoria, all with their wounds to the front, something that clearly impressed their opponents (62 BC)." Ross Cowan, *For the Glory of Rome: A History of Warriors and Warfare* (St. Paul, MN: MBI Publishing Company, 2007), 134.

This is illustrated in the valor of one of Rome's greatest soldiers, Lucius Siccius Denatus. During his forty years of military service Denatus fought heroically in 120 battles. In Pliny's *Natural History* (7.101), the historian makes this remark at the death of Denatus: "He had forty-five scars at the front of his body, but none on the back."

And finally, this comment from Seneca: "Warriors glory in their wounds and rejoice to display the blood spilled with luckier fortune. Those who return from the battle unhurt may have fought as well, but the man who returns with a wound wins the greater regard." *Seneca: Moral Essays*, Vol. 1, "On Providence," translated by John W. Basore (Cambridge: Harvard University Press, 1928), 27.

Regarding the 14th Legion. The best book I found that chronicles the history of the 14th Legion was Stephen Dando-Collins, *Nero's Killing Machine* (Hoboken, NJ: John Wiley & Sons, 2005). I heartily recommend it for further reading on the subject.

Regarding the stationing of the 14th Legion. Lucius and his men were assigned to shore up the 14th Legion, which was stationed along the Danube. The camp was named *Carnuntum*, and its remains are located in Lower Austria, halfway between Vienna and Bratislava. It became the permanent headquarters of the legion until Nero recalled them in AD 64. Source: *Carnuntum,* Wikipedia.

Regarding Rome's conquest of Britain. See Ramon L. Jimenéz, *Caesar Against the Celts* (Edison, New Jersey: Castle Books, 2001), especially pages 67–176 for the Roman campaigns in Britain. See also Albert Harkness, *Caesar's Commentaries on the Gallic War,* with introduction, notes, and vocabulary (New York: American Book Company, 1901). Also, Stephen Dando-Collins, *Nero's Killing Machine* (Hoboken, NJ: John Wiley & Sons, 2005).

Regarding the Roman victory over Boudicca. For a well-written, well-researched book about the Roman victory of Boudicca, see Stephen Dando-Collins, *Nero's Killing Machine* (Hoboken, NJ: John Wiley & Sons, 2005), 1–7, 198–232.

Regarding the lecture on Seneca at Alexandria. The lecture that Lucius hears in the library at Alexandria is taken from Seneca's essay *On Providence.* It can be found in *Seneca: Moral Essays,* Vol. 1, translated by John W. Basore (Cambridge: Harvard University Press, 1928), *passim.*

Regarding Nero. For background on the Caesars, see Gaius Suetonius Tranquillus, *The Twelve Caesars,* trans. Robert Graves (New York: Penguin Books, 1957). See also Will Durant, *Caesar and Christ* (New York: Simon & Schuster, 1944). For Nero, specifically, see Carlo Maria Fanzero, *The Life and Times of Nero* (New York: Philosophical Library, 1956); and Stephen

Dando-Collins *Nero's Killing Machine* (Hoboken, NJ: John Wiley & Sons, 2005).

A helpful family tree is in the front of the next book, showing Nero to have descended from the lineage of Claudius, Tiberius, Augustus, and Julius Caesar. Miriam T. Griffin, *Nero: The End of a Dynasty* (New Haven: Yale University Press, 1985).

A chronology of Nero's life can be found in Michael Grant's book, *Nero: Emperor in Revolt* (New York: American Heritage Press, 1970), 1–14, which I have reproduced following for ease of reference:

TABLE OF DATES

AD

37 (December 13)	Birth of Nero (as Lucius Domitius Ahenobarus).
39	Nero's mother Agrippina exiled.
	Nero taken to the house of his aunt Domitia Lepida.
40	Death of Nero's father Gnaeus Domitius Ahenobarus.
41	Claudius succeeds Caligula.
	Agrippina recalled from exile.
48	Death of Claudius' wife Messalina.
49	Claudius marries Agrippina.
	Seneca becomes Nero's tutor.
	Nero betrothed to Claudius' daughter Octavia.
50	Nero adopted as Claudius' son.
51	Nero assumes *toga virilis* of adulthood.
53	Nero marries Octavia.
	His first public speeches.

54 (October 12)	Nero succeeds Claudius.
55	Death of Claudius' son Britannicus.
	Agrippina ousted from power.
	Corbulo assumes eastern command.
59	Death of Agrippina.
	Youth games.
60	British revolt. Neronian Games.
62	Death of Burrus, commander of the Praetorian Guard;
	Tigellinus and Faenius Rufus succeed him.
	Octavia divorced and killed. Nero marries Poppaea.
63	Birth and death of Nero's daughter Claudia.
64	Great Fire of Rome. Persecutions of the Christians.
	Work begins on the Golden House.
65	Conspiracy of Piso. Deaths of Seneca and Lucan.
	Nymphidius Savinus becomes joint guard commander with Tigellinus.
	Death of Poppaea.
66	Deaths of Petronius, Thrasea Paetus and Barea Soranus.
	Nero marries Statilia Messalina.
	Jewish revolt begins.
	Visit of Tiridates of Armenia to Rome.
	Conspiracy of Vinicianus.
	Nero leaves for Greece.

67	Death of Corbulo.
	Nero takes part in Greek Games and declares Liberation of Greece.
68	Galba declares himself representative of the Senate and Roman People in Spain.
	Verginius Rufus defeats Vindex at Vesontio. Death of Vindex.
(June 9)	Death of Nero.

Regarding the fire at Rome. The date the fire started was July 19, AD 64. Michael Grant, *Nero: Emperor in Revolt* (New York: American Heritage Press, 1970), 151. It happened on a full moon. Grant, 154.

Account of the fire can be found in Tacitus, *Annals,* XV, 2–42, esp. 38. "It began in the Circus, where it adjoins the Palatine and Caelian hills. Breaking out in shops selling inflammable goods, and fanned by the wind, the conflagration instantly grew and swept the whole length of the Circus. There were no walled mansions or temples, or any other obstructions which could arrest it. First, the fire swept violently over the level spaces. Then it climbed the hills—but returned to ravage the lower ground again. It outstripped every counter-measure. The ancient city's narrow winding streets and irregular blocks encouraged its progress.

"Terrified, shrieking women, helpless old and young, people intent on their own safety, people unselfishly supporting invalids or waiting for them, fugitives and lingerers alike—all heightened the confusion. When people looked back, menacing flames sprang up before them or outflanked them. When they escaped to a neighbouring quarter, the fire followed: even districts believed remote proved to be involved. Finally, with no idea where or what to flee, they crowded on to the country roads, or lay in the fields. Some who had lost everything—even their food for the day—could have escaped, but preferred to die. So did others, who had failed to rescue their loved ones. . . .

"By the sixth day enormous demolitions had confronted the raging flames with bare ground and open sky, and the fire was finally stamped out. But before panic had subsided, or hope revived, flames broke out again in the more open regions of the city. Here there were fewer casualties; but the destruction of temples and pleasure arcades was even worse. . . ." Tacitus, *Annals* XV, 38, 2–41, 2, *passim*.

For other information on the fire, see Miriam T. Griffin, *Nero: The End of a Dynasty* (New Haven: Yale University Press, 1985), 125–42.

Regarding the cause of the fire. The historical record is unclear, as F. F. Bruce explains.

"We need not inquire into the cause of the fire; most probably it arose by accident, like the Great Fire of London in 1666. Once such a fire started, it would find plenty of fodder in the congested buildings of the city. But rumour was not content to ascribe the fire to accident, and some curious reports began to circulate. Some men who ought to have been checking the conflagration were seen (it was said) actively helping it on, and when challenged they said they had their orders. The Emperor himself was suspected of starting the conflagration. There is no proof of this; even if he 'fiddled while Rome burned,' that does not make him an incendiary. In fact, he threw himself actively into the organization of relief for those who had suffered in consequence of the fire. But when he found that the finger of rumour pointed to him as the instigator of the fire, he did not like it. The people would not cherish kindly feelings toward one who was believed to have destroyed their homes and their living, too. So Nero looked about for scapegoats, and he had no difficulty in finding some. The sequel may be told in the words of Tacitus, who obviously had no sympathy with the scape-goats, but knew that there was no evidence to connect them with the fire.

> Therefore, to scotch the rumour, Nero substituted as culprits, and punished with the utmost refinements of cruelty, a class of men loathed for their vices, whom the crowd styled Christians (Tacitus, *Annals XV,* 44.)."

The entire quote is from F. F. Bruce, *The Spreading Flame: The Rise and Progress of Christianity from its first Beginnings to the Conversion of the English* (Grand Rapids, MI: Wm. B. Eerdmans Publishing Company, 1958), 141–42.

However, in his book *The Life of Nero,* Suetonius explicitly states that Nero was the one responsible for the fire. Other historians also point a finger in his direction. Michael Grant, for one.

"First of all, efforts to fight the fire were seen to meet with obstruction. 'Nobody dared fight the flames. Attempts to do so were prevented by menacing gangs. Torches, too, were openly thrown in, by men calling out that they were acting under orders.' And Tacitus, who mentions this curious report, adds that, although these mysterious figures *may* just have been loot-ers wanting to get on with their looting unhampered, it was also possible that they were acting upon instructions. If so, who had given them? Who else but the emperor? Another sinister happening was a *second* outbreak of the fire, after it had seemed to be at an end. The fact that this new conflagration started on an estate belonging to the guard commander Tigellinus makes people think that he himself had started this new fire—in order to finish off a job which had been well begun (by the emperor) but not completed." Michael Grant, *Nero: Emperor in Revolt* (New York: American Heritage Press, 1970), 152.

After studying some of the horrendous things Nero did—such as having his own mother put to death and roving the streets at night in disguise, where he committed vicious crimes against his own people—the conclusion I came to before I started the novel was that it was highly likely that Nero gave the orders to torch parts of the city. He had extensive blueprints for the city's renaissance, including extravagant plans for his own palace, whose grounds spanned an area of some 125 acres. One historian notes: "The Fire destroyed shops, tenements, large private homes and temples in the heart of the city, and thus gave the artistic Emperor an opportunity to rebuild Rome nearer to his heart's desire." Miriam T. Griffin, *Nero: The End of a Dynasty* (New Haven, Connecticut: Yale University Press, 1985), 129.

Regarding the letter Seneca gives Nero. The letter, *De Clementia,* or "Of Mercy," can be found in *Seneca: Moral Essays,* Vol. 1, translated by John W. Basore (Cambridge: Harvard University Press, 1928). The two quotes can be found on pages 365 and 371.

Regarding the persecution of Christians in Rome. Seeking to make a quick end to the rumors about his involvement with the fire, Nero acted decisively. Tacitus writes:

"First, then, those who confessed themselves Christians were arrested; next, on their disclosures, a vast multitude were convicted, not so much on the charge of arson as for hatred of the human race. And their death was made a matter of public sport: they were covered in wild beasts' skins and torn to pieces by dogs; or were fastened to crosses and set on fire in order to serve as torches by night when daylight failed. Nero had offered his gardens for the spectacle and gave an exhibition in his circus, mingling with the crowd in the guise of a charioteer or mounted on his chariot. Hence, in spite of a guilt which had earned the most exemplary punishment, there arose a feeling of pity, because it was felt that they were being sacrificed not for the common good but to gratify the savagery of one man." Tacitus, *Annals* XV, 44.

Regarding Nero's opulent home. "This Domus Aurea, the Golden House, was to take in a very large area in Rome. For it included not only the Domus Transitoria and the mansions and gardens it had bridged but also the valley behind the linking building, where the Colosseum stands today, as well as a sizable region beyond—perhaps extending right up the Viminal hill as far as the present railway station. . . .

"Whatever the exact size of the palace grounds may have been, it is clear that never before or since, in the whole course of European history, has a monarch carved out for his own residence such an enormous area in the very heart of the capital.

"Suetonius further describes Nero's estate: 'An enormous pool, more like a sea than a pool, was surrounded by buildings made to resemble cities, and by a landscape garden consisting of ploughed fields, vineyards, pastures and woodlands—where every variety of domestic and wild animals roamed about.' . . .

"The Golden House was full of technical novelties, mechanical wonders, and curious gadgets. The baths were served by a flow of both salt and sulphurous water. The music room contained the largest and most powerful hydraulic organ that had ever been built. There were dining rooms with ceilings of fretted ivory, containing moving panels which showered down flowers on the diners, and squirted them with scent from hidden pipes.

"The main banqueting-hall of the Golden House, which has not survived, is described by Suetonius as 'circular, and constantly revolving, day and night, like the heavens.'" Michael Grant, *Nero: Emperor in Revolt* (New York: American Heritage Press, 1970), 164, 165, 170, 174, 175, *passim.*

Nero's *domus,* or house, was buried after his death in AD 68. The next emperor of Rome built upon its ruins, and it was not until the end of the fifteenth century that Nero's home on the Oppian Hill was unearthed. Excavations did not begin until the eighteenth century. Restoration of the site is chronicled extensively in *Domus Aurea* by Irene Iacopi (Milan: Electa, 2001).

Tours of what remains of Nero's palatial home can be arranged by appointment. See also, Miriam T. Griffin, *Nero: The End of a Dynasty* (New Haven: Yale University Press, 1985), 134–42.

When in Rome several years ago, I took a tour of the excavated site of Nero's *Domus Aurea.* It is not a site that is on most of the public tours because it does not accommodate large groups, but it is worth the effort to make arrangements to see it.

Regarding Nero's dress. "The public image of the Emperor, as projected in his designation and dress, was a constant reminder to himself and his subjects of the military role he was expected to fulfill. . . . The most tangible indication of the way the Emperor and his subjects regarded his role was his dress. . . . This military emphasis was more in evidence when the Princeps attended festivals, for, like a few of the greatest generals in the past—Aemilius Paullus, Pompey and Caesar—he enjoyed the privilege of appearing then in the gold-embroidered purple toga of the *triumphator* (the *toga picta*). He might also wear it for the reception of foreign princes, as did Nero for the visit of Tiridates.

"As no triumphs were now granted to those outside the imperial house, the costume of the *vir triumphalis* soon became the characteristic imperial dress for high occasions." Miriam T. Griffin, *Nero: The End of a Dynasty* (New Haven: Yale University Press, 1985), 222–23.

Regarding the food at Roman feasts. For extensive discussion on everything from tableware to entertainment to food and wine that was served, see Alexander Adam, *Adam's Roman Antiquities* (Philadelphia: J. B. Lippincott & Co., 1872), 302–27.

Regarding the skeleton in Nero's dining room. "A skeleton was sometimes introduced at feasts in the time of drinking, or the representation of one, in imitation of the Egyptians, upon which the master of the feast looking at it used to say, 'Let us live while it is allowed us to enjoy life; drink and be merry, for thus shalt thou be after death.'" Alexander Adam, *Adam's Roman Antiquities* (Philadelphia: J. B. Lippincott & Co., 1872), 326.

Regarding coinage with Nero's image. Photographs of coinage at the time of Nero, along with discussion on numismatic innovations, can be found in Miriam T. Griffin, *Nero: The End of a Dynasty* (New Haven: Yale University Press, 1985), 120–29, 238–39.

Regarding the practice of using foreigners for military service. In his essay "The Roman Army and the Disintegration of the Roman Empire," Edward T. Salmon argues that the weakening of the Roman army by foreign recruits led to the demise of the Empire. "In its heyday throughout the first and second centuries AD that army was manifestly a magnificent instrument of power. It met all the basic requirements for a first-class fighting force: an organization careful to the point of elaboration, a singularly efficient system of administration, and a standard of training that enabled it to be victorious in the field. Yet gradually the personnel composing this incomparable force ceased to be respectable elements of the Empire's population. As time went on the army became so barbarized that by the fifth century and even earlier, the defense of the Empire was quite literally in the hands of Germans; this progressive and accelerating barbarization has long been recognized as an important factor in the so-called 'decline and fall.'" The essay is part of a compilation, titled *The Fall of Rome: Can It Be Explained?* ed. Mortimer Chambers (New York: Holt, Rinehart, and Winston, 1963), 37–38.

Regarding the martyrdom of Christians on a frozen pond. The inspiration for the last scene in the book came from the story of the forty martyrs of Sebaste, first told by St. Basil in a Homily on March 10, 320, the day commemorating their martyrdom. Later, other church fathers also spoke of the martyrdom, including St. Gregory of Nyssa, St. Ephrem, St. Gaudentius, and St. Chrysostom. The following account is a compilation of these sources by the Reverend Alban Butler.

These holy martyrs suffered at Sebaste, in the Lesser Armenia, under emperor Licinius, in 320. They were of different countries, but enrolled in the same troop; all in the flower of their age, comely, brave, and robust, and were become considerable for their services. St. Gregory of Nyssa and Procopius say, they were of the thundering legion, so famous under Marcus Aurelius for the miraculous rain and victory, obtained by their prayers. This was the twelfth legion, and then quartered in Armenia. Lysias was duke or general of the forces, and Agricola, the governor of the province. The latter having signified to the army the orders of the emperor Licinius, for all to sacrifice, these forty went boldly up to him, and said they were Christians, and that no torments should make them abandon their holy religion. The judge first endeavored to gain them by mild usage; as by representing them the dishonor that would attend their refusal to do what was required, and by making them large promises of preferment and high favour with the emperor in case of compliance. Finding these methods of gentleness ineffectual, he had recourse to their threats, and these the most terrifying, if they continued disobedient to the emperor's order, but all in vain. To his promises they answered, that he could give them nothing equal to what he would deprive them of: and to his threats, that his power only extended over their bodies, which they had learned to despise when their souls were at stake. The governor, finding them all resolute, caused them to be torn with whips, and their sides to be rent with iron hooks. After which they were loaded with chains, and committed to jail.

After some days, Lysias, their general, coming from Caesarea to Sebaste, they were re-examined, and no less generously rejected the large promises made them than they despised the torments they were threatened with. The governor, highly offended at their courage, and that liberty of speech with which they accosted him, devised an extraordinary kind of death; which being slow and severe, he hoped would shake their constancy. The cold in Armenia is very sharp, especially in March, and towards the end of winter, when the wind is north, as it then was; it being also at that time a severe frost. Under the walls of the town stood a pond which was frozen so hard that it would bear walking upon with safety. The judge ordered the saints to be exposed quite naked on the ice. And in order to tempt them the more powerfully to renounce their faith, a warm bath was prepared at a small distance from the frozen pond, for any of this company to go to, who were disposed to purchase their temporal ease and safety on that condition. The martyrs on hearing their sentence, ran joyfully to the place, and without waiting to be stripped, undressed themselves, encouraging one another in the same manner as is usual among soldiers in military expeditions attended with hardships and dangers, saying that one bad night would purchase them a happy eternity. They also made this their joint prayer: "Lord, we are forty who are engaged in this combat; grant that we may be forty crowned, and that not one be wanting to this sacred number." The guards in the meantime ceased not to persuade them to sacrifice, that by so doing they might be allowed to pass to the warm bath. But though it is not easy to form a just idea of the bitter pain they must have undergone, of the whole number only one had the misfortune to be overcome; who losing courage went off from the pond to seek the relief in readiness for such as were disposed to renounce their faith: but as the devil usually deceives his adorers, the apostate no sooner entered the warm water but he expired. This misfortune afflicted the martyrs; but they were quickly comforted by seeing his place and their number miraculously filled up. A sentinel was warming himself near the bath, having been posted there to observe if any of the martyrs were inclined to submit. While he was attending, he had a vision of blessed spirits descending from heaven on the martyrs, and distributing, as from their king, rich presents, and precious garments, St. Ephrem adds crowns, to all these generous soldiers, one only excepted, who was their faint-hearted companion, already mentioned. The guard being struck with the celestial vision and the apostate's desertion, was converted upon it; and by a particular motion of the Holy Spirit, threw off his clothes, and placed himself in his stead among the thirty-nine martyrs. Thus God heard their request though in another manner than they imagined: "Which ought to make us adore the impenetrable secrets of his mercy and justice," says St. Ephrem, "in this instance, no less than in the reprobation of Judas, and the election of St. Matthias."

In the morning the judge ordered both those who were dead with the cold, and those that were still alive, to be laid on carriages, and cast into a fire. When the rest were thrown into a wagon to be carried to the pile, the youngest of them (whom the acts call Melito) was found alive; and the executioners hoping he would change his resolution when he came to himself, left him behind. His mother, a woman of mean condition and a widow, reproached the executioners; and when she came up to her son, whom she found quite frozen, not able to stir, and scarcely breathing, he looked on her with languishing eyes, and make a little sign with his weak hand to comfort her. She exhorted him to persevere to the end, and, fortified by the Holy Ghost, took him up, and put him with her own hands into the wagon with the rest of the martyrs, not only without shedding a tear, but with a countenance full of joy, saying courageously, "Go, go son, proceed to the end of this happy journey with thy companions, that though mayest not be the last of them that shall present themselves before God." . . . Their bodies were burned, and their ashes thrown into the river; but the Christians secretly carried off, or purchased part of them with money. Some of these precious relics were kept at Caesarea, and St. Basil says of them: "Like bulwarks they are our protection against the inroads of enemies." He adds, that every one implored their succor, and that they raised up those who had fallen, strengthened the weak, and invigorated the fervor of the saints." Reverend Alban Butler, *The Lives of the Fathers, Martyrs, and Other Principal Saints* in 12 volumes (Dublin: James Duffy, 1866), Vol. III, "March 10, SS. The Forty Martyrs of Sebaste."

For further study. For much of my research on ancient Rome, I kept coming back to an old book by Alexander Adam, *Adam's Roman Antiquities* (Philadelphia: J. B. Lippincott & Co., 1872). I happened upon it years ago while leisurely browsing the aisles of an old bookstore. It has long been out of print, but it is a trove of well-documented details from original sources about Roman life, especially the life of the soldier. Adam's book is encyclopedic; it is also academic. Because of that, it is not my first recommendation of books on the history of Rome. There are a number of other books that are more accessible and readily available to further your study about Rome, should you be interested, two in particular.

One is by Anthony Everitt, *The Rise of Rome:* "The Making of the World's Greatest Empire" (New York: Random House, 2013, reprint ed.), 512 pp.

The other is by Nigel Rodgers and Dr. Hagel Dodge, *Ancient Rome:* "A Complete History of the Rise and Fall of the Roman Empire, Chronicling the Story of the Most Important and Influential Civilization the World Has Ever Known" (Leicester, England: Southwater, a division of Anness Publishing Ltd., 2013, reprint ed.), 512 pp.

ACKNOWLEDGMENTS

Special thanks to the following people for their friendship,
their prayers, and for the many ways they have been an
encouragement in this project. Without them, I would
be less of a man; and this, less of a book.

Nancy Carlson
Ron and Paige Crosby
Alan and Mary Ellen Davenport
Tim and Anne Evans
Bryon and Tricia Gossett
Tommy and Lucia Howorth
Greg and Becky Johnson
Loma Linda Kiehn
Bob Krulish
Alan Levi
Jerry and Martha Dell Lewis
Todd and Susan Peterson
Robert Orr
Denise Tomlinson
Randy and Carol Wolff

SPECIAL THANKS
for

Pam Pugh
For her thoughtful interaction with
my story and its characters.
She labored over each and every sentence,
each word, and every punctuation mark,
both for style and for substance.
Her skill and sensitivity with words
and ideas made this a better book.
Well done!

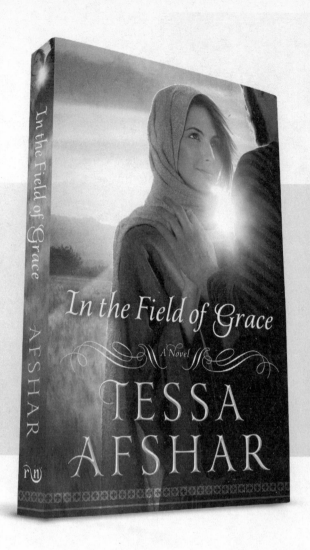

Romance.
Redemption.
Restoration.

TESSA AFSHAR was voted New Author of the Year by the Family Fiction–sponsored Reader's Choice Award 2011 for her novel *Pearl in the Sand*. She holds an MDiv from Yale University where she served as cochair of the Evangelical Fellowship at the Divinity School.

FICTION FROM MOODY PUBLISHERS

Fiction from
Roberta Kells Dorr

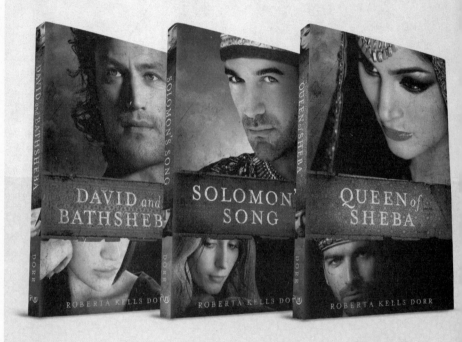

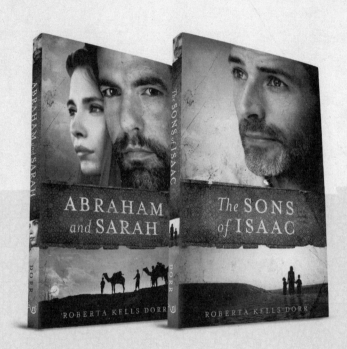

ABRAHAM and SARAH

ROBERTA KELLS DORR

The SONS of ISAAC

ROBERTA KELLS DORR

river north

FICTION FROM MOODY PUBLISHERS